FIST OF THE

A TALE OF MEDIEVAL AVIGNON

JOHN BENTLEY

D1338877

Copyright (C) 2019 John Bentley

Layout design and Copyright (C) 2019 by Next Chapter

Published 2019 by Legionary — A Next Chapter Imprint

Edited by Emily Fuggetta

Cover art by Cover Mint

This book is a work of fiction. Names, characters, places, and incidents are the product of the author's imagination or are used fictitiously. Any resemblance to actual events, locales, or persons, living or dead, is purely coincidental.

All rights reserved. No part of this book may be reproduced or transmitted in any form or by any means, electronic or mechanical, including photocopying, recording, or by any information storage and retrieval system, without the author's permission.

*dedicated to my school pals from Hanley High
School, 1961-1968*

Altiora etiam petamus

Special thanks go to my dear friend John Broughton for his moral, literary and technical assistance. Without him, 'Fist of the Faith' would not have been written.

CHAPTER ONE
CUENCA TOWN, KINGDOM OF
SPAIN — LA MANCHA, SPRING 1318

"What was that for?" wailed Albornoz, who by full title was Gil Álvarez Carrillo de Albornoz. His head was spinning from the vicious blow inflicted by his elder brother, Fernan.

"You cheated! I told you to count to twenty before opening your eyes, but you *must* have cheated to find us as quickly as you did," Fernan answered, rubbing his sore hand.

"I'm sorry, Fernan, but — "

"Right! And this time wait until you get to twenty. Understand?"

"I do."

Fernan and the other brother, Alvar,

scampered off through the trees. Hide and seek was their favourite game.

"One, two, three..." Albornoz counted. "I must do it correctly this time." The boy sniffled. Eight years old, but he already understood punishment, whether meted out by Fernan or his father. He was determined to improve his behaviour, to gain their praise, not retribution.

As far back as young Albornoz's memory reached, he only recalled his friends running faster, throwing farther and hitting harder than he could. They won races, skimmed stones way across the lake and held him down until he yielded in wrestling contests. He had become accustomed to second place, and it did not sit comfortably with his inner character.

Not until he uttered 'twenty' did he dare remove his hands from his eyes.

"Coming, ready or not!" he called out and began searching for Fernan and Alvar, but without success.

"I give up! Where are you?"

The brothers lowered themselves from a tree branch high enough for its foliage to conceal them.

"We've won again!" Fernan announced in a

mocking tone. "But at least you kept to the rule, so you're safe for today, my little brother."

"Thank goodness for that," Albornoz muttered, relieved at avoiding another cuff. "My turn to hide now," he announced.

Fernan and Alvar closed their eyes, and the latter counted, "one, two, three" while the youngest boy ran away.

The three brothers were not alone. For the young people of Cuenca, this place was their own to laugh, argue, cry and cheer to their hearts' content, and all this away from the meddlesome gaze of their parents in the town perched atop a rocky outcrop. The Júcar and Huécar rivers meandered sharply through a steep-sided, narrow gorge. A sumptuous, green valley contrasted with the arid Castilian Meseta to the north and south that enabled pines, junipers, elders and holm-oaks to grow side by side. Lining the rivers, bulrushes swayed gently in time with the flow of the waters and gnarled, old weeping willows afforded native creatures shade from the summer sun. This latter tree's graceful, elegant form, with its long, light green, pendulous boughs reflected in the current, created safe harbour for the beaver's lodge and the vole's hideaway. Both rivers flooded regularly to irrigate the thirsty greenery of the valley.

To a certain height up the limestone slopes of the gorge grew woods and shrubs. At a level where vegetation ceased, birds of prey made their homes in the nooks and fissures of the rock. Kestrels and kites hovered in ascending thermals, waiting patiently for an unsuspecting mouse or shrew to catch their eye and prompt a deadly dive. Fledgling chicks squawking from the nests anticipated their parents' return, a tasty meal in their claws.

A solitary, imperious golden eagle swooped into the ravine as if from nowhere, its mere presence sufficient to disperse the other birds amid terrified screams: they knew better than attempt to overrule this master of the heavens. It boasted golden-brown plumage and broad, long wings, its bill, dark at the tip, fading to a lighter horn colour. With talons, hooked and sharp, it possessed the power to snatch up hares, rabbits, marmots, even ground squirrels. In its majesty, it glided high above inferior birds and even Cuenca town, eclipsing the scene below. From its zenithal place in the sky, it surveyed the lands beneath it: silent, swift, supreme.

As light began to fade, it was time for the children to come together for the day's final amusement — a wrestling contest.

"Who is it today then?" came a call.

"I think it should be Albornoz's turn," came another.

"But he's only seven years old — "

"Eight!" corrected the children's choice. "And I'll take on anybody, see if I don't!"

One boy, who by his size and booming voice was evidently the leader, stepped into the middle of the crowd, waving his arms to silence the spectators.

"Back! Get back and make space!" The order was at once obeyed. He continued —

"So, who will fight Albornoz — and no girls, either, don't want him to go down too soon!"

At this mockery, they all erupted into guffaws and jeering.

"Hush! I'm the oldest, so I'll choose...ah... yes!" He pointed to someone who, although about the same age as Albornoz, stood tall against him, like a giant, with missing teeth and scars on his forehead.

"Yes, you! Come forward, Ramon."

A circle of expectant youngsters formed,

and in the centre the two combatants stood proudly upright, shoulders back. They exchanged opening blows but avoided any holds until they had each decided how to best tackle the other. Shortly, and to the encouraging yells from the onlookers, they came into a clinch to then fall to the ground. The stronger boy pinned down Albornoz and, as the shouting grew ever louder, rained punch after punch until the leader moved in to halt the one-sided contest

"Enough! I declare Luc the winner!"

Ramon raised his fists skyward in a triumphant salute, leaving Albornoz prostrate, his nose bleeding, mouth swollen and a cut over one eye.

The bell for Vespers in the cathedral rang out, and they all knew they had better make for home. A procession weaved its way up the steps cut into the rock that led to the town above. Despite the fight having finished, they continued ridiculing Albornoz, who walked unsteadily behind, struggling to keep up with his brothers.

"You didn't do much for the family name, did you?" Fernan barked, showing neither concern nor compassion for his sibling.

CHAPTER TWO
LIMOGES (LIMOUSIN), KINGDOM
OF ARLES, 1310

The same time, the same year, but in a kingdom far from Cuenca, Edmond Nerval married a local peasant girl, Jamette. Unlike Albornoz, Edmond came from a poor family for whom religion played little part. On the contrary, the boy's father set greater store by myths and fables, recounted by travellers and soothsayers in a language he understood, than by men dressed in long black robes, waving a shiny cross and mumbling that 'Father did this' or 'Father says the other.'

They lived in a one-room wooden cabin with a turf roof in a forest to the north of Limoges, down a winding track hardly wide enough to take a cart. Few people called on them, and Edmond preferred it that way. He was by nature a solitary soul and suspicious of strangers who might leap out from behind a tree and rob him of his money — not that he had any. He had been physically and emotionally abused when young by his own father and mother. And so, it was no surprise that he espoused the family gene. In his own life, he had no-one but Jamette to bully and blame for their wretched existences: but she accepted it with an indomitable fortitude. She knew no different and was relieved when he had eaten the evening meal she placed before him without deriding the food as being unfit for swine and had drunk sufficient hooch from the iron-hooped vat in the corner of the room to render him comatose for the night. Without money to buy wine or ale, he had turned to the common practice of distilling a potent liquor from potatoes.

He moved from one lowly paid job to another — swilling out pigsties, chopping wood and picking grapes on the estates in the region. If on a farm he was instructed to feed the pigs, he saw no wrong in helping himself to potatoes from their feeding trough. Equally, walking home through the fields, the farmers would never miss those he pulled up that went into his sack. An old gypsy woman had given him a recipe, and he set up the flasks, bottles, pans and muslin filters for distillation in an outhouse behind their cabin. The woman also told him how to make wine, but although the area abounded in vineyards, and he regularly worked on them, he drew a line at pilfering grapes. There were legendary tales of pickers in Limoges who took to stealing fruit off the vine. When caught, brought before the bench and found guilty, the punishment was often the public amputation of the offending hand. Few men dared ape this crime: the difference between right and wrong was unambiguous in the eyes of the judiciary for such a matter. Yet it was not as clear when the priesthood became embroiled in homosexual games or diverted well-intentioned donations from church to priest.

THE WEEKLY MARKET held along the length of Rue de la Tour, in the heart of Limoges, bustled with activity. All manner of produce and hardware was displayed on closely positioned stalls set up by the richer traders who paid a tax for the privilege of their pitch. Poorer dealers arranged their goods on the ground around them. Cries in the local patois or foreign tongues rent the air, inviting passers-by to draw near, inspect, touch, or taste whatever they had to sell. Vegetables, fruits, spices, wine, cloths, yarns, silks, cheeses, pots, pans and knives, all for sale or barter.

In another part, a pig speared through with an iron spit pole from head to tail rotated slowly, suspended over a white-hot charcoal fire with a toothless old man turning the handle of the mechanism. He basted the beast with its own melted fat, most of which he caught in a ladle as it dripped down, but sparks flew sizzling out of the fire when stray grease globules ignited. As the flesh cooked, a woman with a fork in one hand and long carving knife in the other sliced off pieces of meat to place it on chunks of bread and sell to hungry strollers attracted by the woman's cries and the aroma that wafted over the market. Those who had no appetite simply stopped to warm their hands by the fire.

For the citizens of Limoges and beyond, the market was a place of entertainment, a day of relief from their usual toil. Rich and poor people mingled, afforded a chance to watch each other and even converse — a rare coming together of opposite social classes.

In booths draped with colourful striped hangings, wizened old hags sat behind cloth-covered tables, their cards arranged, promising to foretell the fate of curious, credulous customers who would put a coin into their hands for the benefit. Weaving in and out of the crowd, stilt-walkers amazed men, women and children alike. Acrobats attempted to tumble faster or leap higher than their competitors; jugglers kept wooden clubs whirling and spinning in the air; sword-swallowers leaned backwards to open their throats and thrust a sword down their gullets. A band of minstrels, one playing a lute, another a fiddle, a third tapping out the rhythm on a tabor. Each sang, at times in harmony, occasionally in discord. A boy in a bright red tunic skipped along at the front, waving a basket at the audience to collect money for their efforts.

"Get here, right now!" a mother screamed, grabbing her young son by his arm and pulling him close. "I warned you not to wander off — there be bogey-men who will carry you off, never to be seen again!" With that, she clipped his ear so hard that tears rolled down his cheeks.

"Buy! Buy! Buy now! Not many left...buy now!" said a man as water in his barrel swirled with the violent contortions of live eels.

"Who will wager on the black one, then? See its fine red comb and sharp talons...it will dispatch that white cockerel, sure as I'm an honest man," called out the master of the cockfight. Within a fenced enclosure, the birds, held round the neck by two grinning assistants, scratched the straw-strewn ground, roused to a frenzy and straining to attack. The onlookers and punters had no idea that the black cockerel was blind, its eyes gauged out earlier, giving it no chance of victory. The cunning master raked in the money laid by his false exhortations on the sightless bird that lost — pure profit, easy takings.

HALF-CONCEALED in the shadows behind a fortune teller's booth, Edmond held a brace of pheasants upside down, tied together by a cord round their claws.

"Two deniers, the pair," the unkempt man

offered.

"Are you mad? They're worth twice that."

"Ha! ha! ha!" came the contemptuous guffaw.

"Hush! Keep your voice down...if I'm caught...there might be spies about, the Bishop has them everywhere."

"Worry not, Edmond, you lead a charmed life, we all know that. How many seasons have you been selling pheasants...how shall I put it...*on behalf* of Monsieur Dumas?"

"Maybe — alright, give me three deniers and they're yours."

"You drive a hard bargain, but it's a deal." They shook hands, and Edmond bit into the coins to test each one in case they were counterfeit. Satisfied they were not, he gave the man his trussed-up game. The customer clutched them to his body, pulled his cloak around to conceal them, and disappeared into the crowd of marketgoers.

EDMOND LEFT the market and took the track leading into the forest and his home. He had not gone far when a commotion caught his attention. Peering through the trees, he saw two boys fighting. One, a sturdy tall youth; the other, barely three-quarters as tall and decidedly weaker. The smaller lad was taking a beating. The blows were so ferocious that he dropped to the ground, curling his body up into a ball in an attempt to protect himself. Kick after kick was aimed at the torso and head of the whimpering, defenceless loser. Instinctively, Edmond rushed over, pulled the attacker off his victim and pushed him away, standing between the two.

"Let him be! I don't know the nature of your quarrel, but *you* — " he directed his words at the bully, "are twice his size! What's he done to merit such anger?"

"Sire, he's bad-mouthed my family and — "

"What? Is that all? Would you leave him bleeding thus, within an inch of his life for such a minor insult? All the families I know deserve to be bad-mouthed, and more! Be off, before I give you a good kicking!"

The thug scuttled off, muttering under his breath as Edmond lifted the unfortunate lad to his feet.

"You'll survive, my boy. Breathe in deeply… that's better now."

"I thank you, kind sire. I didn't say anything

about his family — don't even know them, and
— "

"Enough, it's finished, so go home. You'll find a way to gain your revenge, all in good time."

BACK IN HIS CABIN, he sat at the table saying nothing. His wife was glad to gauge his mood: whatever business he had done that day, it was good, and she would, at worst, receive the sharp end of his tongue, not the force of his fists. Silently, she filled a beaker and placed it in front of him, giving a half-hearted smile. Taking a deep draught of the liquor, he reminisced.

'That was not a pleasant morning. Sure, it was a decent enough sale...mouldy old birds, he'd better pluck them pretty quick and get them in the pot before they start to stink!'

It was the fighting earlier that day that brought old memories to mind, thoughts he tried to control and, whenever possible, to forget. He reluctantly recalled the incident when he was about the same age as the boys he had just sent off. In this same forest he, too, had stood over a bloodied, defeated rival he had beaten mercilessly. The picture in his head haunted him still, like the bogey-man the mother at the market had threatened her son with, a spectre that loomed behind the scenes, appearing only occasionally, and then fleetingly.

'Pierre Roger did deserve what he got, no doubt of that, yet I can't today even remember why we argued. But it was fair treatment, otherwise I wouldn't have thrashed the living daylights out of him, would I?'

In reality, it was *neither* fair *nor* deserved but delivered through a violent temper that regularly overcame his judgment. When he, Edmond, had beaten Pierre Roger, he could not have appreciated that the latter would rise to be crowned the omnipotent ruler of the greatest Church in the known world, the most Holy Catholic Pontiff, Clément VI.

'Pierre Roger, damn him! I did hear word that he had gone on to bigger and better things.'

THE NEXT MORNING, footsteps crunching the frosted grass outside heralded a knock at Edmond's door.

"Who's that at such an unearthly hour? Get

it, woman!" he ordered Jamette.

On the threshold stood a tall, thin man with a hunched back, dressed in a clerical black cassock that reached the ground. The crucifix hanging round his neck glistened in the weak autumn sunlight. A tight-lipped smile, aquiline nose and piercing dark eyes portrayed a ghostly apparition. Jamette breathed in sharply — a priest was the last person she had expected to come to their home. She was so taken aback that her jaw dropped and she failed to utter a single word of greeting. The priest broke the silence.

"Madame, you must forgive me this unannounced visit, and I sincerely hope it will not inconvenience you if — "

"Who is it?" Edmond bellowed from within.

The priest, who had taken a step forward as if to prevent her from shutting the door on him, was silhouetted dramatically in the doorframe.

"I am Father Caron. I minister from the Eglise Evangélique, Assemblée de Dieu, to give it its full title, Rue Marie in the town."

"What the devil do you want with *us?*" Edmond had gotten up from the table and squared up to the unwanted visitor. In a threatening tone, he asked again, "I said, what do you want — are you deaf? Church folk don't come around here — never have done — so don't tell me you were *just passing* because you weren't!"

"Monsieur Nerval, or may I call you Edmond, may I take a moment of your time?"

Starting, he answered, "How do you know my name? Has the sergeant sent you?"

"Calm! The sergeant has not sent me, so rest assured. I make it my business to know the names of as many of the Good Lord's flock as possible. My church, Eglise Evangélique, as I said, reaches out to all citizens of Limoges who reside, how shall I put it, outside the city confines."

"Do you mean in the forest? If so, what's the wrong in that?"

"No wrong whatsoever, Edmond. We value our parishioners equally, regardless of their wealth or abode."

A peace ensued, with both men exchanging only stares.

"You'd best come in, then." Edmond's initial antagonism subsided. "Please, sit. Will you take drink with me?"

"Purely to drive away the morning chill, of course, I will."

Jamette needed no telling. She filled two beakers with hooch from the vat and put them down before the two men. Her duty discharged, she melted away into the darkness of one corner of the room.

"I suppose you are wondering why I am here?"

Edmond all but choked on his drink. "You could say that, Father."

"I will explain. It has come to my notice that you have been intruding into Monsieur Dumas's estate and availing yourself of his precious eels with the intention of selling it on to our poor people at the market — people who have no idea of its origin. Do I make myself clear, Edmond?"

"Perfectly clear, Father, but you are ill-informed. I know nothing of such trade, and besides, only a fool would risk his right hand or, worse, his life if he were to be caught."

'How on earth has he found me out? Somebody's been shooting their mouth off!'

"You're right, my friend, only a fool." He took a gulp and continued, "And it is not the

Church's mission to tell the authorities of this or that crime, so do not worry on that score. What's more, I am sure the affair at the market is but a tale, bearing no truth."

'Then what does he want?'

"Have you heard of *confession?* I see you have not. Confession is the acknowledgment of one's sins or wrongs committed against God and neighbour. Through this avowal, a man is freed from his wicked acts, and, we believe, he is saved in the sight of the Lord. I am inviting you — your good wife, too — to attend confession in my church."

Edmond, although he had no plans to cease the lucrative sale of eels, saw the opportunity to silence wagging tongues. A penitent was an innocent man, or such was his naïve understanding of what the priest was saying.

"I see what you mean, Father. Perhaps I, or even we, will go to this confession thing…to give it a chance, as it were — not that I'm guilty of anything, of course, but it might be good for our souls. Ay, good for our souls."

"You have it right, my son."

He remembered his boyhood friend, Pierre Roger, who had urged him to read the Bible and repent. At the time, there had been no

Bible to hand, and more pertinently, he could not read.

"I once had a pal who attempted to convert me to that malarkey nonsense — "

"And he failed."

"He did so. However, now I'm a man, I see the advantages of confession. If I reveal my sin to a priest, it will go no further than the four walls of Eglise Evangélique. Is that correct, Father?"

"The Church hears your penance in absolute confidence. The matter concerns you, the priest and the Good Lord above, no one else."

"Then I agree. We will present ourselves at the church in the near future — at the present time I have gainful employment assisting the cooper at the Dumas vineyard, repairing barrels, don't you know — "

"Ah, the Dumas domain produces the most exquisite wine — "

"As I was saying, I'm currently rather busy, but I will keep to my word so those false accusations of heinous poaching can be laid to rest, with the Lord's intervention."

'I have a fair idea who has snitched on me. Wait til I lay hands on him!'

"Indeed. You are making a good choice, Edmond. I will now share a prayer with you both then depart. The Lord will show you the way." He took a small bible from the pocket of his cassock and, with great pomp, recited, "Dear Lord, we beseech Thee..."

Jamette remained invisible in her corner.

Alone with her, Edmond's temper erupted. He slammed his fist on the table, screaming insult after insult at the poor innocent woman. Red-faced, beads of sweat shining on his brow, he shouted,

"Ay! The Lord will show me the way!" — he mocked the priest — "but He doesn't give us bread to eat or ale to drink! Damn the cleric; I'll go to confession only to see I won't be revealed to Dumas. If I ever have a son, I'll teach him the tricks of my trade, for sure. He'll not survive for long if he relies on the scriptures to feed and clothe him. A poacher, like his father, that's how it will be. And if he doesn't get caught, it's an honourable profession."

FIFTEEN YEARS HENCE, and in a different town, Jamette would give birth to his son, Marius.

CHAPTER THREE
LIMOGES (LIMOUSIN), KINGDOM OF ARLES, 1310

Edmond Nerval panted heavily as he trudged along the path that rose from his cabin and through the forest to where the Dumas lands started. The breath he exhaled turned to a frozen white mist, indicating how cold the early morning was. He had reprimanded Jamette before he set out.

"Edmond, put on your cloak, you'll need it today."

"No, it will be warmer when the sun rises."

But he was glad she had insisted, pulling it tighter to his body. The narrow path was often blocked by an undergrowth of brambles and ferns — few people used it or even knew of its existence. Very fine twinkling gossamer threads floated in the air, mysteriously joining the tree branches on either side to form deadly webs, effortlessly ensnaring unsuspecting insects until hungry spiders arrived to satisfy their appetites.

After a half-hour, the trees thinned as the ground before him fell down to a grassy meadow. To his right, its banks concealed by overhanging willows, lay the object of his visit: a small still-water lake, its surface dreamlike, shimmering, dancing in the reflection of the faint pale-gold matinal sunlight. A stream at the far end flowing gently off the river Vienne caused a barely detectable current to pass through the lake — a pond by any other name — running off at its opposite side to re-join the main river. The shallow water, with quillwort and duckweed on its bed and broad-leafed lotus flowers sitting above, was the ideal spawning environment for the freshwater eel who, when sufficiently adult, would return to the sea to breed.

In the acute silence and beauty of the scene, Edmond found his line, weighted down in the water by iron discs with short rigs tied to lobworm-baited hooks. He undid the line, secured round a stone on the bank, and began to slowly pull it in. By its resistance to his effort, he recognised he had a good haul. One hook after the other bore a squirming, slimy nocturnal eel. With a skill honed over many years of angling, he twisted the fish's narrow head off the hook with a single turn of his wrist and soon had eight shiny, wriggling creatures placed side by side on the grass, their eyes bulging with fear. Hours earlier they had been safely hidden in their holes beneath the lake's surface.

Suddenly, the yapping of a dog broke the silence. Edmond froze. The noise meant only one thing, the arrival of the Dumas gamekeeper. The animal's bark alerted its master to an intruder into the estate, but the poacher was well hidden among the willows, and shortly the gamekeeper tugged his dog by its leash to heel and moved away. He took a deep breath, relieved that his illegal behaviour had not been discovered.

'That was close! I hadn't dreamt he would be out and about so early. But here's to you, Monsieur Dumas!' With that, he raised a single middle finger and stabbed the air in the direction of the departing gamekeeper.

He lowered each eel by the tail into his sack

and with the last one drew its string tight and slung it over his shoulder.

He was walking through the market before day had properly broken. The stallholders were already setting out their wares. The toothless old man was lighting kindling for the fire under his spit while his woman scored the pig's pink flesh with her long carving knife to help its thorough cooking and to allow its odorous juices to run out into her ladle for basting. The man looked up as Edmond approached.

"Good day, Mister Nerval. Splendid weather, hein?"

Edmond stopped but said nothing.

"I see by your sack that you'll do a decent business today."

The captive eels thrashed about, and any observer could see he had something live inside — fine for attracting potential customers but a giveaway should the sergeant or his men see it.

"Ay, and they're good 'uns, just out of the water, nice and fresh. I'll be back later."

With that, he continued past the stalls into

a narrow, cobbled street where his favourite tavern was doing a roaring trade, thanks to the traders who took ale for breakfast. He did not enter by the front door, instead going down a side passageway, leaving his sack in the rear courtyard where no one in authority would see it. He went into the hostelry through its back entrance.

Inside, the hullabaloo of men laughing, arguing, shouting, and cursing was in sharp contrast to the tranquillity of the courtyard.

"Hey, Edmond! Your usual?" the landlord asked him.

"Ay." A tankard of ale was set down on the counter.

"Before you touch that drink, I'll take payment! No tab for you today, not after the last time. 'I'll settle with you as soon as I've done in the market,' you said, and how long was it before I got my money? Over a week! A man can't make a living like that."

Taking a money pouch out of his tunic pocket, he reluctantly handed the landlord a coin. Glancing round the room, he saw several men he knew at a corner table, and he was soon immersed in bawdy tales and gossip about the criminal underclass of Limoges. By the time he left the tavern, the streets outside thronged with men, women and children, all coming from or going to the market.

Edmond blinked to adjust his eyes to the daylight and a shiver of fear ran down his spine. He realised, half drunk, that he had forgotten his sack.

'Damn it! It'll be gone soon as nod if anyone sees it.'

He rushed back down the passageway where, thankfully, the sack was where he had left it, still full of his writhing, slimy eels.

At the market, he waited in the obscured space between two booths for his regular patrons to find him. It did not take long.

"How much today, Edmond?"

"Two deniers each."

"Two?"

"Two! They were swimming around happy just three hours ago. Best quality, and if you can find any better — "

"Alright. I'll take one."

Accepting the man's money, he reached inside the sack, pulling one out by the tail and lowering it head-first into the other man's bag. His morning's business was concluded, all the eels sold, before the sext bell rang and, with the money he had made safe in his pouch, he called back at the tavern to drink more ale. As he left, the worse for wear, a tap on his shoulder caused him to spin round, fist raised.

"Edmond! No need for that, I am not going to rob you!" It was Father Caron.

"Ah...I see...so what do *you* want?" came the slurred question.

"Are you on your way to market with your sack?" He sharply held it behind his back, but too late.

"I...I am to buy vegetables that my wife requires for our humble stew-pot."

"Indeed, she is a fine woman."

"I can't disagree with that, Father, I'm blessed to — "

"Now then! Do not take the Lord's mercies for granted."

"What do you mean?"

"You are most certainly *not* blessed! You have not yet taken confession, as we discussed when I visited your house, so you cannot claim to have seen the errors of your ways before you bare your soul to God."

Edmond swayed unsteadily and was prepared to agree to whatever the priest said to be rid of him.

"I suggest we make a firm arrangement for you to attend my church. Let us say tomorrow? I shall be on confessionary duty between the terce and sext bells, so meet me in my vestry and I will tell you what to expect. When you are sober you might like to consider your many sins."

"I agree, Father." And with that the men carried on their separate ways.

AS HER HUSBAND staggered into the cabin, Jamette instinctively moved out of his way, fearing what abuse lay ahead. She knew his drinking would continue and subserviently filled his beaker, placed another log on the fire, and began sweeping the floor. He remained silent for some time at the table before speaking in a surprisingly soft tone,

"He wants me to go to confession tomorrow.'

"Father Caron?"

"Who else, woman! It's only *me* he wants, so I reckon he thinks my soul is more in need of salvation than yours."

She wasn't sure if he was making a joke or a statement, so she said nothing, discretion being the best choice. He took a draught of ale and continued,

"All this saving souls nonsense...beats me what I've done that's wrong...a man's got to survive, hasn't he? That's what I say."

THE NEXT MORNING, as arranged, Edmond presented himself at the church and knocked on the vestry door.

"Enter!" called a voice from within. The tall, thin cleric sat at the table, poring over an open bible. He nodded a greeting. A single candle flickered, emphasising Caron's imposing presence.

"Sit beside me, my son. Before I guide you through your first confession, it is incumbent upon me to ensure you fully appreciate the significance of the procedure."

Edmond sat down as instructed.

'I don't feel right about this — got to be better things to do than —'

"When you go into the church proper, you will see the confessional to the left of the nave. You will kneel inside and wait until you hear me speak. Is that clear?"

"It is, Father," Edmond uttered for the first time.

"Good. I will be on the other side of the grill, although you will not be able to see me. The curtain drawn across the front conceals my identity from anyone about the place." He closed the bible and fixed Edmond with a stern gaze from piercing dark eyes, gaining the man's complete attention.

"Where was I...ah, the significance of confession. Adam and Eve in the Garden of Eden chose to disobey God, so they were expelled to live in a harsh, inhospitable world. We mortals share in their guilt that we now call original sin. Our only hope of forgiveness comes through the mass, the sermon, and the confession. In your case, Edmond, we will grant you dispensation to undergo only the latter. When a soul is troubled, like yours, we need to make...*exceptions*." He pronounced this word in a contemptuous tone.

"Our Christian belief describes seven cardinal sins: pride, envy, anger, avarice, sloth, gluttony, and lust. It is for you to decide from which you seek repentance, and Canon Law prescribes pilgrimage, fasting and the donation of alms. I do not see you meeting any of these! Not to worry, though. May we proceed?"

Edmond had done his best to follow the priest's interpretation, and although much of it was beyond his comprehension, he nodded.

"The sooner we do this, the better. I will ready myself in the holy box and wait for your words, 'Father, I have sinned.' Then we will begin."

'WHAT SHOULD I TELL HIM? I frequent the town's inns that are full of ruffians and villains, and I suppose I should not seek their company. Then... envy...well, I wish I had Dumas's money, can't deny that...'

"Father, I have sinned," he recited, pressing his mouth to the grill. He was quite taken aback when a voice from the other side answered at once,

"May the Lord be in your heart and help you to confess your sins with true sorrow."

Accordingly, Edmond recounted the several wrong acts he had committed, surprised by how readily they came to mind, and Caron soon concluded affairs.

"God, the Father of mercies, through the

death and resurrection of His Son, has reconciled the world to himself and sent the Holy Spirit among us for the forgiveness of sins. Through the ministry of the Church, may God give you pardon and solace. Thus, I absolve you from your wrongs in the name of the Father, and of the Son, and of the Holy Spirit. Depart in peace."

EDMOND ROSE and left the church in silence. He hoped that his penance would satisfy Father Caron sufficiently that he would not denounce him to Monsieur Dumas.

CHAPTER FOUR
CUENCA TOWN, KINGDOM OF SPAIN, SPRING 1318

After playing their games down by the river, Fernan, Alvar, Albornoz and their friends who lived in the town returned home. These boys had homes that were warm, dry and comfortable, and tables laid daily with wholesome meals. The youngsters who did not climb the stone steps with them went in the opposite direction, upstream, to smallholdings and fields farmed by their tenant parents whose grace-and-favour cottages depended on the grain, produce and livestock sold on behalf of and taxed by their landlord, the Bishop of Cuenca.

Recent times had not dealt these people a

fair hand — war and political and social unrest had afflicted the province of Castile. Epidemics and famine were commonplace, and crop failure a constant worry. Wattle and daub walls rendered their places too hot in summer, bitterly cold in winter in spite of the open log fires, and the thatched roofs regularly let in rain. Small windows rendered them dark and dismal. Goats and cattle tethered overnight inside the dwellings ensured safety from robber bands but passed on animal diseases to the inhabitants who, if smitten, lacked the means to pay for a healer. Less serious but still most unpleasant was the foul odour emitted by the creatures.

These simple people knew better than to complain — the Church had power of eviction, and life elsewhere was certainly worse than that in Cuenca. However, this year they had harvested a good barrelage of wheat, and their beasts had fetched a decent price at market. Thankfully, they earned enough to clothe and provide for their children, but luxuries enjoyed by the 'people up in the town' — as they were known —were way beyond their means.

· · ·

JUANICO AND HIS BROTHER, Pero, trudged reluctantly the length of their field towards the byre at the far end where three cows and a horse fed from a wooden hay rack. To the family's relief, the spring weather meant that the beasts could live there rather than indoors with them. The ground was dusted with a white hoar frost, but as the day warmed, it would melt and in turn loosen the earth and assist scarifying. The two brothers were ten and eleven years old, but they were already experienced in the work on the land — without the children's labour, farms could not survive.

"You put on his bit, and mind he don't snap at you. Yesterday, you were lucky he didn't have your fingers off!"

"I'll be careful," the younger Pero replied, proud he was entrusted to carry out such an important task.

Juanico threw more hay into the rack for the cattle, then took down two long leather reins from a peg, uncoiling them to remove any knots. He led the scrawny draft horse outside and threaded one rein through its bit, Pero repeating the procedure for the other side. Next, the harrow was tied to its breast collar.

"Good job," Juanico pronounced, "let's get to work. You take his head today." Pero reached up, gripped the rope bit and pulled the horse into a familiar motion, drawing the harrow over the ground. Juanico walked behind, both reins in his left hand, a long stick in the other, tapping the horse whenever it strayed from a straight line. They would work all day, pausing only for bread and cheese at midday, until it was too dark to see.

ON THE ADJOINING FARM, a young girl, Francisca, not yet into her teens, stood in a fenced enclosure with a wooden pail over one arm. She took handfuls of seed and scattered it all around her. Twenty or more hens clucked excitedly, heads bobbing up and down, pecking away at their feed. Raising a flap in a crudely built hen house, she carefully picked out the newly laid eggs from the nest boxes and placed them in a basket. To complete her morning chore, she filled a trough with fresh water then returned home.

Down by the Huécar river, Gavriel and his father were busy on the bank of a stream that fed off the main current. Father steadily pulled out a free-running ledger rig, weighted to lie on the bed, its six attached lines baited with worms from the day before. They had to leave it all overnight because the eels they fished were nocturnal in their feeding.

"I'm 'appy with that, boy. See!" he exclaimed. "I 'ad a feeling yesterday that we'd get lucky — four out of six's not bad, not bad at all."

One by one, he expertly removed the hooks from the eels' snapping jaws and let them slither into the wicker basket held close by his son.

"Should fetch a good price at market, them beauties...they be alive an' twisting, that's 'ow they likes 'em. Mind 'e, the wife'll grab one of 'em for the pot, I'll wager!"

GIL ALBORNOZ'S mother stood aghast when he walked into the house, his lip cut and bleeding and one eye swollen and almost closed.

"What on earth has happened? A pretty

sight if ever I saw one! Come, come here...let me look at you."

"It's nothing, Mother. I fell from a branch, that's all," Albornoz blurted, a consummate liar at only eight years of age.

"This didn't come from a fall!" Teresa turned to Fernan and Alvar.

"Haven't I told you to always take care of your little brother? You can't be trusted, can you!" The older boys hung their heads, regretting they hadn't prevented the uneven wrestling contest earlier.

Teresa had been born into the important Aragon family of Luna. Her grandmother's effigy was etched on a slate block in the Albornoz chapel with veiled head and gloved hands carved in alabaster. Teresa expected her offspring to live up to the good Luna name.

"Both of you, up to your rooms and get cleaned for supper! I'll have to decide whether to tell your father, and if I do, you'd best pray he's in a good humour!" So, they made a swift exit.

As a mother, she found it difficult to relate to her two elder sons: their bravado and occasional rudeness offended her puritan upbringing — and their behaviour she attributed to her husband's malign influence. In contrast, Albornoz could do no wrong in her eyes. She was a short, plump woman whose comely countenance belied a sharp tongue that she regularly unleashed on her long-suffering housemaid while dictating the day's duties. Her time involved gossiping among a clutch of well-born acolytes whose intellectual stimulation rarely exceeded embroidery. Even indoors, she wore a lace bonnet and crisp white ruff and would never take the air without a rich purple velvet stole.

She filled a bowl with water from a pail and placed it on the table in front of the boy. Taking a strip of clean linen from the cupboard, she sat next to him. Although his face was contorted and bloodied, he was still a handsome young lad: blond curly locks and an impudent smile endeared him to his doting mother. She wetted the cloth and tenderly bathed his wounds.

"Ouch!"

"I'm sorry...but...that's better now. Can't have my little warrior succumb to his battle wounds, can we? You *are* a brave boy — "

"Albornoz!" boomed a voice from the doorway. "What's all this?" The master of the house, Garcia Alvarez, approached the table and leaned menacingly over the youngster, raising his fist even before an answer was provided.

"No! Garcia! He's not to blame — he fell… an accident…"

"Ah, that's better! If he'd been in a fight, he wouldn't have lost, isn't that right, boy?" He squinted expectantly at Albornoz.

"Of course, sir, I would never give you reason to be ashamed of me."

"That's well said…yes, a good answer!" The corpulent, thick-set man lowered his arm and slapped Albornoz on the back with approval.

"Maid! Damn you! Are you idling again? You'll have to go…we can't…anyway, bring me ale, and be quick about it."

At the bellowed command, a mouse-like wench dressed in a servant's brown tabard shuffled into the room, placed a pewter tankard on the table and bowed respectfully.

"Will the master sup presently?"

"Confound your insolence! Do we not always *sup presently*?"

"With pleasure, master."

The housemaid brought in a plate of cooked meat, a cheese platter and a bread basket. A bowl filled with fruit completed their evening fare. She poured ale for all the family except Albornoz, who received a cup of water.

Teresa, with her youngest beside her, sat on the bench to one side of the table; Fernan and Alvar took the other. Garcia's chair, heavy arm rests, carved leather back and cushion embroidered with the family crest by his wife, stood proudly at the far end. Father rose and, with great pomp and ceremony, cleared his throat. The family fell silent, in anticipation of a well-rehearsed routine. He began —

"Benedic nos Domine et haec Tua dona quae de Tua largitate sumus sumpturi.

Per Christum Dominum nostrum. Amen."

"Bless us, O Lord, and these Thy gifts, which we are about to receive from Thy bounty, through Christ our Lord. Amen."

"Amen," came the interjection.

During the meal, only Garcia and Teresa spoke, but in hushed tones. The children made not a sound. The master's rules were scrupulously and deferentially followed. Satisfied sufficient food was consumed, he nodded to each child in turn, the permission for them to leave the table and proceed to their rooms to sleep.

.   .   .

FROM HIS SMALL bedroom high in the eaves of the house, Albornoz stared out of the skylight, over Cuenca town, across the gorge and river to the country beyond. The moon was nearly full, so its brightness captured his attention and imagination.

'I wonder, what lies behind the stars? One day, I'll find the answer, of that I'm certain. I shouldn't have endured that beating today, but they will be the losers in the end, not me! And what of my brothers...they will go off to become soldiers, to fight for the king — they see that as their duty. Duty? They are welcome to it, but I am better than that. I'd rather follow a dream than die for an unknown cause in a foreign land.'

NEXT MORNING, the first thing Albornoz heard was the breakfast bell sounding. He leapt from his bed and hastily splashed his face with water from a bowl on the dresser. It was so early that day had barely entered the skylight, and it felt more like night. But the bell never lied, and anyone in the house partaking of a meal was expected to be at table promptly. One or other of the three brothers might arrive behind time when Garcia delivered a box on the ear or banished the guilty boy to go hungry and sulk in his room.

In a matter of minutes, Albornoz had pulled on his tunic, clambered down the ladder then stumbled down the stairs to the ground floor. He was late, but he breathed a sigh of relief entering the room: next to his father sat a man he did not recognise. They were both so engrossed, poring over a parchment sheet, pointing a finger to this part and that, that his tardy arrival went unnoticed.

"Here...sit by me," Mother hissed, the words coming through tight-closed lips. "Father must not be disturbed when about his business at any cost, or we'll all pay."

The mouse-like housemaid came over to fill the boy's beaker with milk. He took a chunk of bread from the basket, then cheese from a platter.

"Where are Fernan and Alvar?" he whispered.

"Shush, keep your voice down. They have already eaten and gone to the manor house past the big river. There's a sergeant there today, and Father has arranged fencing practice for them…"

Garcia Alvarez de Albornoz belonged to an important Castilian family who served the kings of Castile and Aragon throughout the century at a time of tension between the two kingdoms who remained separate until 1469. The master of the house was a man 'of landed assets' — the family coat of arms sculpted in stone above their front door attested to their standing. His income was the revenue from tithed farmers in the region, so he had a vested interest in their seasonal productivity. He knew, beyond reason but with unease, that he belonged to the wealthy fighting class, even if he had never raised a sword in anger. This insecurity about his societal ranking manifested itself, bizarrely, in frustration with his verbally and physically bullying his wife, children and servants.

ALBORNOZ LEFT THE HOUSE, a three-storey stone-built residence that sat in a prominent position next the town's cathedral in the Plaza Mayor, in which was to be found the family chapel. Day was dawning and the narrow streets were coming alive in the half-light to the sound of shopkeepers opening their shop fronts. There was not yet a customer in sight, but they could not help but advertise their wares with singsong voices. A boy pushed a barrow laden with melons, oranges and apples, its steel-rimmed wheels clattering on the street's cobblestones. At one corner sat a blind beggar, his eyes bound, dressed in a ragged tunic and rattling a coin in a pewter bowl on the ground between his legs to alert passers-by of his presence.

Our young boy had just walked over the Plaza Merced when a friend hailed him —

"Hey! Albornoz! What brings you out at this hour?"

"Hello, Samuel. I've got a lesson with Father Gelmiro."

"A lesson! I didn't know you did that sort of thing."

"What do you mean, stupid? My parents pay whatever for it, and they say you'll only be successful in life if you can read and write, so there! And, unlike most of you, I'm clever — I learn the Latin that they speak in church."

"Sure, you do. Anyway, how's that black eye

you got yesterday? Luc gave you a good hiding, didn't he?"

Albornoz grabbed Samuel's arm and pulled him close, their noses touching. Through clenched teeth he retorted,

"You're wrong, my friend, I *let* him win the wrestling. And why? Because I know there's been the scurvy in their house — they bring their beasts indoors at night — so I was being kind to him. I wasn't going to take advantage of a boy weakened by the scurvy, was I?" Eight years old, and Albornoz was ignorant that the effect of scurvy was not debilitation, but he showed the guile and duplicity of a wise adult.

"Ah, I understand now," the friend concluded.

The two boys stepped back from each other, the moment of aggression passed.

"See you by the river this afternoon?"

"Yeah."

YOUNG ALBORNOZ'S MIND STRAYED, and he recalled stories he had heard about the town's history.

'I can't imagine my town without — before — its people, although I know there was nothing here

until the Romans came. That must have been a long, long time ago. I can picture their legions, strong and disciplined, marching here and recognising an ideal location to build their base that would grow into a town. The gorge down at the rivers formed a natural defence, and no enemy would dare scale the cliff-face. Those Romans were skillful builders, as well as fierce warriors. But I wonder how they built the walls...how on earth did they pile one stone block on top of the other? It's thanks to my lessons that I know history — better than the grown-ups, I'll wager!'

After a few more minutes,

'...after the Romans, it was...err...yes, the Moors, and they weren't thrown out until 1147, by good King Alfonso. He called Cuenca "Noble and most loyal," and I suppose he's right. Father Gelmiro tells me that we live in a town in perfect harmony between nature and its architecture. Anyway, enough daydreaming, I'd better get on, or I'll be late for my lesson.'

ALBORNOZ CONTINUED WALKING through the town, to the Plaza de Mangana, then down the Calle de Zapaterías, where a Jewish enclave flourished. Next, he went to the Plaza del

Salvador that housed the town's bakery. After
a short time, he arrived at the Plaza los Carros
in Cuenca's southern quarter, where Father
Gelmiro's house stood just within the
fortifications on the bank of the Huécar river.

By now, the sun had risen, bathing the
colourful fronts of the houses in a mellow
golden warmth. Stone archways led to interior
courtyards; women leaned over the balcony
balustrades, exchanging gossip with their
neighbours; children, armed with brooms
twice their height, swept the frontages to their
houses — no play for them in the mornings,
only chores or lessons for the privileged few.

The young student reached up to pull on a
cord and a bell rang within. The heavy door
opened.

"Ah, good morning, Albornoz. Come in,
do," Father Gelmiro bid his pupil. He wore a
long black cassock of full-length sleeves that
touched the ground. A priestly tonsure
covered the crown of his head, and grey tufts
of hair formed the surrounding circle. A
simple silver crucifix hanging around his neck
completed the austere clerical attire. He
smiled, kind and mild-mannered, sharp blue
eyes twinkling, and indicated the bench at the

table in the middle of the room. Neither spoke. The ensuing atmosphere was calm and reverential as the man knelt at a prie-dieu, opened a weighty bible and mumbled inaudible words. The prayers concluded, he closed the book, rose to his feet and turned to Albornoz.

"It's well you arrive in good time today. I have many duties to perform after the lesson," he pronounced absentmindedly.

"I understand, Father." Of course, he did not understand, but he knew, instinctively, the correct tone to adopt when faced with authority.

Gelmiro's house comprised a single ground-floor room with stairs leading to the bedroom. A single shuttered window was the sole source of natural light. The only furniture was a washstand bearing a bowl and pitcher and shelves running along one whole wall, groaning under piles of dusty yellowed parchment scrolls — testament to his erudition.

"Yes..." he continued, "a marriage to bless followed this afternoon by funeral rites for a burial and, to complete the day, a child to baptise. They arrive in this world and depart the same, but all in the Good Lord's bountiful presence. Hatched and dispatched...we are all equal." He chuckled at the sound of his rhyming words, although any humour therein reflected sincerity and humility.

A short, stout figure filled the black robe; his square-cut chin portrayed the determination and passion of a man who had known trials and tribulations but endured them, triumphant, to rise through the ranks of the clergy and become the bishop's favoured priest.

The narrow, bright rays of sunlight illuminated a shiny bald pate with tufts of grey hair to either side.

He was an avuncular, considerate person. His house belonged to the Church, and his honourable work ensured it came tax-free. Ample meals were taken courtesy of the parishioners or, betimes, in the refectory at the convent, his girth witness to the amount he consumed. Yet, the poorer people who struggled to put food on their tables resented this prerogative. The priesthood, over the ages, considered themselves closer to God than their sinful flocks, while all too often they were the ones to fall from grace. Financial advantage and sexual promiscuity were frequent and usually overlooked by Church superiors. Gelmiro was innocent of the former but succumbed to the latter. The ecclesiastical elders, perversely, fined their priests for an incorrectly shaven tonsure but turned a blind eye to inappropriate, permissive behaviour.

"So, let us begin." Many priests taught privately — the unique source of education for the young — but their teaching was all too often meagre and basic, reserved for selected wealthy students with reading and writing in Latin, religious studies, philosophy and rhetoric being the common curriculum.

"I will test you now on the ten words I told you to learn." Albornoz straightened his back and gripped the edge of the table as if to assist his concentration.

"What is 'door'?"

"Ianua, Father."

"Correct. Now, 'window.'"

"Fenestrum."

"Correct."

"'Table.'"

"Mensa."

The boy answered all ten words on the list, perfectly learned.

"This is well done, young man. And so, to our reading. Take the sheet before you and let me hear you read."

Taking a deep breath, he began.

"Ave Maria, gratia plena, Dominus fecum. Benedicta tu in mulieribus, et benedictus fructus ventris tui, Jesus..."

'Hail Mary, full of grace, the Lord is with Thee, Blessed art Thou amongst women and blessed is the fruit of Thy womb, Jesus...'

"These holy words you have read with respect and without error, boy. Now, let us consider the gravity of the words, for there is always wisdom and instruction in the Good Lord."

The lesson continued, and the sensibility and intelligence of Albornoz's questions took Gelmiro by surprise. He had not expected such maturity and interest displayed by one so young.

After a half-hour, however, their study was interrupted by the doorbell tinkling. Gelmiro went to open the door. On the threshold stood a well-turned, plump lady of a certain age. She greeted the priest with a broad smile and took one step inside. On seeing Albornoz, she blushed and, bowing her head as if to prevent the boy hearing, whispered —

"Oh, I'm sorry, Gelmiro, I didn't know you had company...should I return later?"

"Off with you, woman! You should choose your visits here with greater circumspection. Don't you know I have a reputation to consider?"

CHAPTER FIVE
CUENCA, KINGDOM OF SPAIN,
SPRING 1318

Albornoz turned and waved a cheery farewell to his mother standing on the threshold of their house. She returned the gesture, resplendent in her customary lace bonnet and crisp white ruff.

'I must make haste. Mother says that Father Gelmiro has a busy day ahead with his many duties to perform. I wager he'll be meeting important people of the town in order to...'

The boy's thoughts were incomplete. Gelmiro had told him of but a few activities associated with his position, but he yearned to know more. *'What must it be like...in the cathedral, before the people of my town...'*

The youngster walked through the streets

at a brisk pace. Cuenca was just awakening, and he enjoyed privacy afforded by the dawn. In the Plaza del Salvador he passed the open front of the baker's premises and the glorious aroma of bread wafting from the fiery orange haze of the oven filled his senses. He was savouring the wonderful smell when the baker, a massively rotund, jovial man, his apron white with flour, hailed him.

"'Ey, boy! Good morning to 'ee."

"The same to you, Erec. Any chance of a crust of your finest bread, fresh from the fire?"

"Damn cheek! Still…your mother's one of my best customers, and we can't be upsettin' 'er, can we!"

He picked out a loaf resting on a metal grill and broke off a chunk.

"There!" he said, handing Albornoz his treat, his forehead sparkling with rivulets of sweat.

"Thanks, Erec. Must get on now."

"Right. Be a good boy." The baker urged him thus every time their paths crossed.

"Of course, I will. Bye." And with that he promptly continued on his way.

I'm looking forward to my lesson this morning. I've learned the words Father set me, so

I'm sure I'll get them right when he tests me. I don't understand why my friends poke fun at me about learning Latin. In church, I know what most of the prayers mean, the hymns as well. They're jealous, that's what it is, and even my brothers taunt me, saying, 'Latin doesn't win battles' or 'How are you going to kill your enemy with fine words?' But for sure, I won't make my way in life by wielding a sword. There has to be a better way.'

ALBORNOZ WAS ABOUT to reach for the cord and ring the bell when the door opened and the same plump woman he had met a few days earlier faced him.

"Ah, it's young Albornoz, isn't it?"

"It is, ma'am."

"...err...yes...Father Gelmiro has told me all about you. He says you are a diligent student."

"I do my best," and with these words he lowered his head and feigned an innocent shyness, knowing that adults preferred to see their young folk behave in a respectful, servile manner.

"Just how it should be, too. Anyway, I will bid you good day. I only came to deliver Father some…err…business for his attention. I like to help him whenever I can, don't you know."

Gathering her long robe in one hand, she patted him gently on the head and left. Within, Gelmiro adjusted his belt, ran his fingers through his tufts of grey hair, and took a deep breath.

"Sit down, Albornoz, while I pray a time. Must thank the Good Lord for the gifts He bestows upon us."

"Yes, Father, of course."

"Here, take this sheet; the prayer is written there, so you may follow it as I speak. It is a psalm."

Albornoz sat at the table, the parchment unrolled before him. Gelmiro knelt at the priedieu and began to intone the verses, with subdued reverence, but loud enough for his pupil to hear. The reading concluded, the priest rose, bowed his head and crossed himself. Turning to Albornoz, he asked,

"Did you understand the psalm, my boy?"

"I think so, Father. It began *the rightest…*'

Gelmiro smiled and, in a kindly tone, corrected him.

"The *righteous* will inherit the earth and dwell in it for ever."

"That word at the start is, I admit, not known to me."

"Righteous. No, we do not hear it in our ordinary lives. It is, as we say, a *biblical* word."

"Is it important then?"

"Indeed, it is."

"Please tell me its meaning so I might better appreciate the whole psalm."

Gelmiro winced, taken aback by the maturity of the prodigious boy's language.

"If a man attends church three times a week, he is righteous. If he does not curse and treats his servants with an even hand, he is, again, righteous. And…if he pays his tithe at the prescribed time, he is, equally, righteous. Do you follow my explanation?"

"Yes, Father, I do, and I, too, will be righteous, I swear. But what becomes of those men who are not thus? And — "

'He is, verily, a rare precocious talent, and one who must be nurtured.'

"Slow now! Those who stray and are not righteous, well, they shall not enter the Kingdom of God but be consumed by the fires of Hell for all eternity."

Albornoz's gaze had not left the man's face as he swallowed every dramatic word. He breathed in sharply, visibly affected by this philosophy that would accompany him throughout his life.

"So, from your explanation, I understand there is right and wrong, like black and white, one set against the other."

"You have it, but that is sufficient consideration of the Good Word for today. Let us address the Latin words you have learned for me. Words that are not as holy as His, but, nevertheless, of value."

"I hope I will remember them without error."

Gelmiro tested Albornoz, one by one, and he made no mistakes.

"Let us now..." But the man was interrupted by the doorbell ringing. On the step stood a ragged boy who handed over a scroll.

"If 't please 'ee, Father, take this. It be from Bishop's office. Says t' be seen t'day."

"Thank you, boy."

The runner nodded but did not depart until he had a coin pushed into his hand.

"God bless 'ee, Father." And he made off without further ado.

The priest sat next to Albornoz, but he

remained silent while he ran a finger down the sheet, clicking his tongue with each line.

"Mmm...there are busy days ahead, that's for sure. Five...six...seven tithes to collect."

"Tithes? What are they, Father?"

"If it interests you, I will explain."

He took a pitcher from the dresser and filled a cup with wine.

"Well, a tithe is one tenth part of a farmer's income from livestock and crops, as assessed by the Church. This is then given to the Bishop who, out of that amount, pays his priests, the poor and the upkeep of the churches. The farmer lives in a cottage that belongs to His Grace, as does the land he works on. It is a fair arrangement for all concerned."

"And what if he can't pay the tithe?"

"In times of abundance, the crops flourish and the harvest is plenteous. But when the Lord Almighty turns the river to flood and the heavens to open with torrential rains, there is no wheat or barley to sell. It is but a few years ago that an awful drought rendered the fields barren, and every growing plant died.

"Then, I have seen the grievous murrain, a sickness, smite the oxen and sheep out to graze. What price at market for an infected beast? Marauding vultures hover overhead and plunge earthward to scavenge the flesh of carcasses. What will the butcher pay for putrid meat?"

"Father, I asked you what happens if he *can't* pay."

"I consider each man on his merits and circumstances beyond his control. However, if he cannot pay, the Church may, *in extremis*, excommunicate him."

Albornoz's face contorted with incomprehension.

"Forgive me, I should bear in mind how young you are. Excommunicate means that he will no longer receive the Sacrament and may be shunned by his family and peers, but again this would be *in extremis* — that is Latin, and it means...err...as a last resort, if that man has not made every effort to triumph over his situation. But let it be known, and I quote from the Scriptures, tithing *'must be done in conjunction with a deep concern for justice, mercy and faithfulness'* — Matthew 23:23."

"I see," came the reply in a soft tone. "Then better he not be found wanting."

"Just so." Gelmiro turned his attention once more to the list, then looked up.

"As you show such an interest in tithes, you may accompany me down the gorge to the farms this afternoon."

"Really? Yes, please, Father!"

MARCHING BY GELMIRO'S SIDE, his head held high and chest thrust forward, he was proud to be seen in the company of one of the most important men of the town. The priest, carrying the purple velvet bag he used for tithe money, seemed to acknowledge every person they passed as they followed the track down the rocky outcrop.

"My old legs cannot cope with the steps," he panted.

The spring sunshine, now less oppressive than its midday heat, softly warmed their faces as they walked alongside the river in the direction of the farmsteads.

"Rest a moment while I regain my breath."

They sat on a fallen tree trunk. The priest threw back his head and inhaled deeply.

"Such sweet fragrances, such delightful— " As he spoke, he saw that his young companion was gazing into the distance.

"Hey, boy! Do you hear me?"

"Sorry, Father, what did you say?"

"Are your senses not assailed by…" Confusion masked the boy's face. Gelmiro rephrased his question.

"Are you not aware of the resin from the pines, the blossom of the magnolia, the babble of the water? How it transports me back to my youth."

"Your youth, sire?"

"Ay. Many a time I have walked this same track with my pals. We would fish, chase, wrestle…"

"Just as I do, then. But you say, 'in your youth'…so were you born here?"

"I surely was, in a village further down where the Júcar joins the Huécar. My parents traded in fine woven cloth, cotton, even silk damask. They bought it from Arab barges then sold it on at a decent profit to the townsfolk and places hereabouts. When I was seven or eight, about your age, they had sufficient money to buy a house up in the town. My mother and father, like yours, ensured that I was instructed in Latin, as well as other less important subjects. Then — "

"Then you were a priest!" blurted Albornoz. Gelmiro smiled affectionately.

"It is not quite that simple, far from it. But, briefly, yes, I became a priest of Cuenca. To this day, I am the only priest in the town who is a local person; all the rest are born in other parts of the country. Mmm..." His thoughts strayed.

"...yes, they are foreigners, if you will. But that is the way. The Bishop selects the priests for his diocese, and he prefers to bring in *fresh blood,* although I am living proof that there are exceptions and it can be done...err...from within."

"It *can* be done," echoed Albornoz. The cleric absentmindedly repeated the boy's name,

"Albornoz...Albornoz...your family name has been part of this region for many years, did you know that?"

"No, Father."

"Down the valley, maybe five or six miles, there was a village whose name was Albornoz. It is no longer there, I know not why — plague, flood, whatever. Your ancestors took their title from that village, or did the village give...it matters not. The church there was dedicated to Saint Gil. You were born on the first day of September, the feast of the saint, hence your given name. Excuse me if that confuses you, but history is like that."

"I believe you, Father, and it's a great honour for my family." Silence. Albornoz studied the man, always inquisitive, wanting to learn.

"May I ask a question, and I hope it's not impertinent."

"Of course."

"Why is your head shaven?"

Gelmiro breathed in, relieved it did not concern religious complexities he might find hard to answer. By now he had realised the boy was mature beyond his years.

"When the chief apostle, Peter, was sent out in the teaching and preaching of the Lord, his head was shaved by those who did not believe his word, as if in mockery. Christ blessed his head and changed dishonour into honour, ridicule into praise. This was a crown made not out of precious stones, but one which shines brighter than gold and shimmers more than topaz. It is a crown of faith."

"Brighter than gold!" Albornoz repeated. "I have neither seen nor touched gold, but they say it's kept safe in the King of Aragon's strongbox."

"I dare say it is, young man. But, and remember this well, gold is not worth as much as faith."

"I will, Father." He fell silent, considering Gelmiro's advice.

"The monks, marching around the town in their long brown robes, they, too, have the tonsure, don't they?"

"Yes, they do. It is according with their Order, how to put it...they have no choice in the matter, in what they wear or how they look. Their Abbot dictates the rules. I have had the pleasure of many theological discussions in their company. They seek out any opportunity to spread the Good Word. Yet, they each have different explanations when it comes to the tonsure. Some say that Jesus's disciples wore it thus, so they are right to copy them. Others maintain that slaves across the sea, over time, had shaved heads, and monks, too, are slaves... of Christ. Old Father Gironimo, a dear friend of mine, believes that the tonsure represents the crown of thorns that the Roman soldiers placed on our Lord's head at his crucifixion... but who knows the real reason...?"

"Thank you, Father, I am satisfied to have learned so much."

"Not at all, Albornoz, except you should always be aware that it is our actions that eventually define us, not our appearance." Gelmiro's pupil said nothing more on the subject — the old man was by now accustomed to moments of contemplation from him. Then,

"Not all priests wear their hair thus. My mother says that if Father Guillen's locks get much longer, he will trip over them in the middle of the cathedral aisle!" This statement was met with a hearty guffaw.

"Your mother is right about Guillen! As mere priests, we can choose the tonsure or not, unlike the abbey's monks. You never know, one day we might see *you,* as a man, with a shaven head!" he joked.

'Who knows, indeed,' Albornoz mused.

THEY WALKED some short way until they reached the first cottage in the valley where farming began.

"Is this the one, Father?"

The old man unrolled the parchment to check.

"No, it is the fourth along the track. The first three have paid their tithes." Then,

"Here we are."

Although the hovel in front of them had a wooden front door — a luxury — its windows had no expensive glass, only dirty threadbare curtains to keep out the wind and rain. Daub flaked away from the wattle, and the thatch on the roof was, in parts, so thin that the slightest shower would penetrate the interior.

Gelmiro patted dust from the sleeves of his black cassock, placed the silver cross to sit on the centre of his chest, and knocked firmly on the door. This he repeated thrice.

"Maybe they're out?"

"They are *not* out, believe me. They do not relish visitors who are, usually, bailiffs, debtors, beggars — who do not know *they* have more in their purse than the householders - or clergy like me. Do you see? They always owe money; it is a way of life for them."

After a wait, the door half-opened, but Gelmiro could not distinguish the face within.

"Woman! Show yourself! I come from His Grace, the Bishop, so open!"

The door slowly swung back and Gelmiro entered, pushing the woman aside, followed by Albornoz. She cowered, afraid of what was to come. Beneath her apron she wore a shoddy tunic that reached her knees. Matted grey hair hung either side of a face blackened by soot after she had stoked the fire. She gave an embarrassed smile to reveal more gaps than teeth.

Albornoz squinted to adjust his eyes to the almost total darkness. A stove in the middle of the only room belched smoke that eventually spiralled out through a hole in the roof. On a straw mattress in one corner, he made out three squawking babes. At the table sat four urchins that Albornoz thought younger than himself, noisily playing a game with wooden discs — they frequently exchanged blows, screaming out in a patois that he didn't recognise. His gaze then fell on a mangy goat tethered to a ring set in the wall. A girl, older than the other children, on a three-legged stool, squeezed the animal's teats in a vain attempt to obtain more than a trickle of milk. The woman smoothed her grubby apron nervously, looped the lank hair behind her ears, and spoke first.

"Father Gelmiro, you are welcome to our humble abode. Will you take ale?"

"Most kind."

"And the boy?"

"Too young for ale! He is my...err... assistant." She nodded towards him, then filled a cup that Gelmiro quaffed, keen to get on with the day's business.

"Where is your husband?"

"Blas is out in the field."

He put down the empty cup and ushered Albornoz through an archway at the rear of the property to a small courtyard. Hens pecked the ground, geese in a wooden pen flapped their wings violently and honked, as if to warn off the two strangers. Through a gate Blas's field extended before them down to a stone-built byre that marked the far end. The tenant led two yoked horses hauling an iron scarrier, kept moving by a boy tapping their flanks with a stick. From one extremity of the field to the other, the tilled soil was displayed in long straight lines, a farmer's skill perfected over a lifetime.

"HEY, Blas! I would speak with you!" boomed the cleric.

The man either did not or chose not to hear. The call was repeated, and this time, Blas looked towards them, raising his hand in acknowledgment. He passed the reins to the boy and walked up to them at a slow pace.

"Hard work, Blas."

"That it be, Father."

The farmer wiped the sweat from his brow with his forearm and stood squarely before them, hands planted on hips.

"What brings you here today?"

"Your tithe, my son. You have not yet paid last year." This was met with a sardonic guffaw.

"Tithe? And how much do you say that is?"

"Twenty reales."

"Twenty reales! Listen to the man! As much chance as me being crowned King of Aragon!"

"This is the amount reckoned by the Bishop's office according to the size of your field and number of beasts, so it is correct."

"Correct my arse! Ay, sire, if my crops had done well and most of my cattle had not been lost to I know not what sickness. Twenty reales, the man says! I made just enough to buy vegetables for the pot — my family had neither meat nor fish to eat for a whole year. Let me tell you, even the river was cursed, and if I had time to go fishing, which I didn't, I'd be lucky to land even an old pike. Do you hear me,

Father? I do my best, I work hard, as does my wife, but we do not earn enough to clothe and feed the children...we live off next to nothing. Twenty reales!"

Albornoz watched this scene unfold, fascinated by the whole affair.

'This man must, surely, pay what is due. He owes that amount, so it is right to settle. I feel sorry for him, but the law is the law. We should each defer to the good Bishop's office.'

Gelmiro, clearly moved by the tenant's plight, scratched his tonsure and mumbled a few inaudible words to himself. He unrolled the parchment and examined the figures carefully before pronouncing in a soft tone,

"You are a Godly man, Blas. I have seen you and your kin in church, and I am unaware of any transgression that has met the Lord Stewart's attention. This year, the weather augurs well, and you should, if it pleases Him, fare better. Therefore, I am persuaded to defer the twenty reales. We will review your situation after the harvest. Tithing must be done in conjunction with a deep concern for justice, mercy and faithfulness — so said Matthew."

Albornoz remembered this quotation from the Bible that Gelmiro had read out.

Blas knelt before the priest, took his hand, and planted a kiss, lost for any adequate way to thank him for such kindness.

"Enough, Blas. We will leave you to your labours. God bless you and your family."

The priest and Albornoz walked back up the field and passed through the forlorn cottage to be met by screaming babes and raucous children. He smiled at the mother and marked a cross in the air in the direction of the others, and they left to regain the track towards the town.

After a time in silence, Albornoz spoke.

"Father, the farmer did not pay the tithe, so he is not righteous. You explained to me what it is to be righteous just earlier in the day, and so should he not be punished?" Gelmiro fixed his gaze on the boy, angry at his naivety, and reprimanded him sharply.

"Do you think God's wrath should visit such sad souls, as if to satisfy the lynch mob who bay for blood? No! There come times in our lives when the punishment does *not* fit the crime. You will learn this one day for yourself."

Albornoz took a step back, shocked by the man's agitation. He thought,

'Father Gelmiro is a kind man, indeed, that I can't deny. But a blessing does not pay the tithe, does it?' Then, in his turn, the priest thought,

'This boy will go far. He is intelligent and shows wit and determination. He quite reminds me of myself at his age...until I met the real world.'

CHAPTER SIX
CUENCA, KINGDOM OF SPAIN,
SUMMER 1318

A temperate spring was giving way to the Meseta summer across the Castilian region. Torrential rainstorms had provided, to the farmers' relief, the newly planted crops a chance to germinate. With pragmatic realism, this year they anticipated a healthy harvest. Albornoz and his friends congregated in the valley, as was their routine, but later in the afternoon when the sun's ferocious heat had subsided. Mid-day saw the streets deserted and the shops closed: its inhabitants, young and old, remained indoors; the wise stray cats and dogs sheltered in shady corners and under benches. Cuenca was undeniably an attractive town, a tranquil, comfortable place at ease with itself. Sitting pretty on the steep rocky headland, it all but sneered at the poorer people of the valley and beyond. The proliferation of churches — Saints Peter and Michael, Our Saviour, San Felipe Neri, Nuestra Señora de Luz and the rest — bore witness to the Christian omnipotence that governed the town's devotees. The only remaining evidence of the place's Muslim occupation was the castle, much of which King Alfonso VIII's forces razed to the ground two centuries earlier to put an end to Arab domination.

ALBORNOZ MISSED HIS OLDER BROTHERS, Fernan and Alvar, who were absent from home. Their father had made arrangements, drawing on his circle of noble influence, for them to undergo military training in the castle of the Duke of Sessa in Guadalajara, two days travel by carriage. The thought of their adventures excited him, and he hoped his turn would come in time.

The children played their games with gay abandon, far away from the surveillance of parents. Yet, a hierarchy of power evolved naturally within their ranks. Their leader was the tall, strong Ramon, who gave orders, when needed, to organise teams and combatants — usually to his own advantage. He came from one of the wealthier families living in the town, although, since his father's premature death through consumption, Mother found it hard to support him and his two young sisters without the assistance of the Almoner and charity in the form of donations from sympathetic townsfolk. It was known by the authorities that Ramon was a dexterous pickpocket, but the Magistrate had either failed to catch him *flagrante delicto* or instead dismissed his offences as too minor to prosecute and take up too much of his valuable time. The miscreant sold stolen items in the market, and the proceeds were given to his mother. He realised that what he did was against the law, but justified it on grounds of necessity: poverty had visited him and his family — he had not invited it in.

THE YOUNGSTERS ENJOYED ALL the customary games: hide and seek in and around the valley's greenery; tag and catch-me; hood man's blind — the most popular. Here, one person was chosen to be 'it' and was blindfolded with a hood. The player was spun round several times and had to stop his tormentors who pulled at his tunic, shoved him and even whipped him. Ramon took pleasure in selecting the 'it' child and revelled in the whipping and shoving. His reputation and actions frightened the others, and his violent beating of Albornoz some weeks before was fresh in their memory.

Given the heat, the children's favourite pastime was swimming in the cooling river. The leafy catkin canopies of the weeping willows afforded welcome shade afterwards. The Huécar constituted a paradise of freedom: swimming, splashing, laughing, crying, all in the gentle eddies or against the rapids and whirlpools of its deep blueish waters. Their fun, chaotic and rumbustious as it was, posed no danger. They swam with the elegance and speed of an eel weaving in and out of the bulrushes. Hard knocks worried them not one jot. After racing across the river, Albornoz sat on a grassy knoll to rest next to two friends, a boy and girl of his age.

"Phew! The water's cold today!" Albornoz observed.

"It's *always* cold, stupid!" retorted the boy.

"Nice, though," added the girl.

She ran her hands over her bare shoulders, arms and legs. Albornoz and the lad had already pulled on their tunics, and while the latter watched his pals cavorting in the river, Albornoz could not avert his gaze from her naked body. It was quite natural for the youngsters to swim in the nude — they had no concept of modesty and, anyway, were too young to appreciate the connection between a state of undress and sexuality. This was the first time he found himself in such proximity with an unclothed girl. She innocently rubbed her stomach, then her hips, before covering her body.

'*What is this strange feeling inside me?*' he wondered, uncomfortable and having to wrench his eyes away from this girlish creature who, unexpectedly, began to weep.

"Madelena, what ails you?" he asked, holding her hand.

"Have you hurt yourself?"

"No, it's not that."

"Then, tell me, do."

"We…my brother Servet here, my mother and father, Johan…must leave our home…the farm…"

Servet nodded in confirmation.

"Why so? Surely there is no reason for you to quit…" But he stopped, picturing the scene when he had recently accompanied Father Gelmiro to Blas's farm to collect the tithe owing. He also recalled the priest explaining how the Church could evict tenants for non-payment, but he saw fit to waive the tithe until better times arrived.

"Has your father paid the tithe?"

"No. Last year's harvest was ruined by months without rain. The cattle fell in the field, day after day, from a sickness. Even our hens stopped laying."

"I see," Albornoz said in a comforting tone and, letting go her hand, asked,

"The priest who came to collect the tithe, was he short and fat with grey tufts of hair around his tonsure?"

"I do not know what this *tonsure* is, but no, he was tall and thin with long black hair. Why do you ask this?"

"Do not be upset. Go back home with your

brother and tell your father that there may be a solution to this problem."

Madelena and Servet could not understand what Albornoz meant though, with intuitive faith in their friend, obeyed, left the river and took the track towards their cottage.

THE NEXT MORNING, Albornoz had a lesson, as normal. They shared a prayer then Gelmiro tested the Latin words.

"Ten out of ten, well done! We will discuss some verses from the Bible that I have chosen — " when Albornoz interrupted him.

"Father…"

"Yes, what is it?"

"Yesterday, I was at the river with my friends and they told me they faced eviction from their cottage and farm…because of the tithe…and it was another priest, not you, who visited them. He was tall, thin, and…"

"Ah, I recognise that description." He paused for a moment, his brow wrinkled in thought.

"I know the priest. He is a Godly man, as we all are, but he has a reputation for always punishing people who stray from the Path, those who are not righteous."

The boy was transported back to Gelmiro's explanation of what it meant to be righteous.

"Father, these folk live and work on the farm next to Blas's, the one we visited. You gave him a chance to pay later, did you not?"

"I did, and if it had been me, I *would* have meted out justice but with compassion for the man, knowing his particular circumstances and accepting that the debt was not incurred out of intent and malice. All problems are not the same for all men. To show mercy is to emulate our Lord, Jesus Christ." After a time, he pronounced,

"When you next meet them, say they are to pass a message on to the father."

"Sire, what message?"

"Say that there is a way round the situation, that his Grace the Bishop may be minded to look into their case."

'I am amazed by this boy's command of language and his maturity of spirit. Such confidence in one so very, very young. It is rare, indeed.'

"It will be done, Father."

Later that morning, Gelmiro sat outside the Bishop's office. The chaplain came out.

"His Grace will see you presently." This was never the case: his ploy was to lessen the vehemence of a visitor, to afford himself the psychological advantage by keeping him waiting.

After some twenty minutes, the door opened and the chaplain ushered Gelmiro into the room. He had met the Bishop here many times before, and he was familiar with the interior. Two walls covered by piles of parchments and rows of books on shelves creaked under their weight. At the far end stood a solid oak desk bearing a leather-bound bible and two brass candlesticks. Behind was a high-backed carved chair; in front, a simple bench. A small fireplace had logs ready to light during the cold winter months. The single stone mullion window, with its coloured stained glass, permitted beams of sunlight to penetrate the office, creating a serene, mysterious ambiance.

"Good day, Gelmiro. Approach us."

As instructed, the priest moved forward and stooped to kiss the extended ring finger.

Good day, Bishop," came the reverential reply.

"What has brought you here today? I trust you have not come to report bands of flagellants or heathens running amok!" He was renowned for his keen sense of humour, although no one doubted his capacity to be decisive and, on occasions, ruthless. Gelmiro tutted at his superior's quip and sat on the bench, waiting for the invitation to speak. A nod was the signal.

"Your Grace, a matter concerning one of our farmers has been brought to my attention."

"Continue, pray."

"The man, Johan, has received notice to quit, as the tithe has not been paid."

"This is, indeed, unfortunate, but the law has to be obeyed, Gelmiro. Without revenue from the tithe, our churches would fall into disrepair and you would be out of a job! Did *you* serve the notice?"

"I did not, Your Grace, it was Father Gaufroi."

"Ah, I see." The Bishop touched his chin, knowingly. "So, Father Gaufroi interpreted the tithe law to the letter?"

"He did, sire."

The two men entered a discussion about the principles of the farmer's defence and implementation of the regulations therein. Finally, the Bishop gestured to Gelmiro that he was ready to pronounce.

"The farmer, Johan, is to be relieved of last year's tithe, but we fully expect the current harvest to be profitable for our tenants, and all debts will be paid."

"Your Grace speaks with wisdom," Gelmiro replied in a satisfied tone.

The Bishop took his quill, dipped it into an inkwell, and wrote down his judgment on a parchment sheet.

"There, go to the farm and inform Johan that he does not have to quit."

GELMIRO AND ALBORNOZ gave Johan the good news. He was so overwhelmed, he broke down and wept. The boy observed, from a respectful distance, and thought,

'I am, indeed, pleased for this poor man. But I cannot reconcile his happiness with breaking the law. Which is right, I ask?'

. . .

SOME DAYS LATER, Albornoz sat on the same grassy knoll on the riverbank with Servet and Madelena, to dry and regain breath following their boisterous games in the Huécar. The girl, with childish freedom, displayed a soft naked body before pulling on her tunic. Albornoz, as before, felt a physical reaction course through his veins: he realised that it meant something but was uncertain what it was.

Servet, usually the quieter of the three, spoke first.

"Our family is truly grateful to you and Father Gelmiro for your help. My father and I — we, who should never appear weak, as men — are overcome and have shed tears, yes, tears of happiness. How can we repay you?"

"Repay! You choose the wrong word considering the nature of your problem!"

Servet realised the irony and smiled.

"No need to thank me. Who knows, one day I might be a priest myself."

The three friends passed the rest of the afternoon chatting, joking, daring, nudging, laughing — amusements that children have enjoyed since time immemorial.

"Let's go for another swim before we have to go home," suggested Madelena.

"Good idea," agreed Servet, so they removed their tunics, running down to the river and diving into its cool refreshing water with splashes and squeals. It was a common game to duck someone below the surface until they waved submission and were allowed to bob up gasping for air. No-one ever came to harm — they all knew how far to take the game.

Their gang numbered six or seven that day, all joining in with great merriment and high spirits. Without warning, and by chance, Albornoz found his hands on the shoulders of a boy he had not crossed since the occasion, several weeks ago, when he had been subjected to a severe beating, by this very same person, Ramon. Time froze as their eyes met. Albornoz held the bully firmly. Such was the difference between their physiques that Albornoz should have been effortlessly cast aside by the stronger Ramon, but he felt an inner strength. Apprehension spread on his adversary's scarred face, and his jaw dropped to reveal missing teeth. Before he could say or shout anything, Albornoz plunged him below the water with shameful memories of their wrestling match running through his mind.

'I lied to mother when she asked what had happened. I did not admit the truth to protect her admiration of a favourite son. So, what do you think about it now? It is not pleasant to receive punishment for a change, is it?'

Ramon squirmed, fighting to break the surface of the river, but Albornoz's grip was too strong, his fingers digging deep into the brute's flesh. After a time — he was unaware of the duration — he released Ramon, who floated up slowly, his body limp and lifeless. Albornoz fell away, arms outstretched as if in supplication, a gesture entreating help. He let out a fearsome scream: had he taken this unreal situation too far?

Spotting the danger, a nearby lad swam between them, holding Ramon's head with one hand and slapping his face with the other. This had the desired effect and Ramon spluttered and coughed out mouthfuls of water in an attempt to breathe again. No words were said. Albornoz turned and calmly swam back to the bank.

Madelena squeezed his hand.

"That was wonderful! You sure showed him a lesson! He won't trouble you anymore."

"No, he won't." His words were spoken in a deliberate, measured tone. Then,

"We should get dressed now."

'Ramon did wrong; he is not righteous, so he deserves just retribution. Perhaps I held him under the water for too long, but I'm not sorry. People like him will learn to respect the rules. He should not have humiliated me so.'

CHAPTER SEVEN
CUENCA, KINGDOM OF SPAIN,
AUTUMN 1318

Albornoz and his parents were eating breakfast, but at their table, two chairs were empty: those of the brothers, Alvar and Fernan, still away at the Duke of Mendoza's castle in Guadalajara, experiencing military training for the first time. The family did not speak at meals until Garcia had said grace, after which, upon his nod, food could be taken and conversation begun. The mousy wench in her brown tabard put down a pitcher of milk to accompany the bread and fruit, took one step backwards, bowed her head politely and left the room.

Garcia emptied his beaker, wiped his mouth on a white linen napkin and placed his hands, palms down, on the table — a sign he was about to speak.

"The boys will be back home in time for dinner tonight. I have received outstanding reports concerning their swordsmanship and archery skills. I am reliably informed they are two of the most gifted young trainee soldiers ever to pass through the good Duke's gates." He paused, his gaze passing from his wife to Albornoz to satisfy himself that they were paying attention. He continued,

"I would expect nothing less, though…it does not surprise me in the slightest. Take after their father, I am sure."

"Has it crossed your mind, husband, that they might have plans other than becoming soldiers?"

Garcia's jaw dropped, shocked. He was not accustomed to hearing his judgment questioned.

"What! You dare — " But he controlled his anger, believing only fools took a woman's opinion seriously.

"So, woman, you are now an expert on the future career of our children. Well, there is a thing! Listen to me! The boys demonstrate the potential to become soldiers worthy of King

Alfonso's army, and Lord knows there are enough battles and campaigns presently to keep his forces busy. Do you have a better suggestion? Might they become *priests*? Tell me that!" Teresa shook her head, blushing.

"That is settled then. We will be entertained with their accounts at dinner this evening." Then, after a while, "As for *you...*" The man spoke with disdain and a sneer in his voice, a hostility with which Albornoz had become familiar. "As for you, we will see what the future brings. However," his tone softened, "I have spoken with Father Gelmiro."

"Is he not satisfied with my work?"

"On the contrary, he praises you and tells me that you show an intelligent interest in the Church, is that so?"

"I ask questions, I admit, but I see no wrong in that. In fact, the priest encourages me to learn, to be, what is the word he uses…ah, yes, inquisitive."

"I see." And without further ado, he folded his napkin, placed it precisely on the table and departed for a day's falconry.

"Mother," Albornoz began, a worried expression on his face, "will I have to attend the Duke's castle, too?"

"Calm, my boy, you are far too young to think about such things, and the way I see it, *you* have the brains in this house, and I expect you to uphold the good family name — my family — of Luna. That will not be done by fighting, drinking and, for all I know, *whoring!*" She stopped short, regretting having said that word before her son. "No, you must concentrate on your lessons with Father Gelmiro." Albornoz did not really appreciate what she had said but recognised the difference between praise and censure.

THE DAILY LESSONS WENT WELL, with him scoring full marks on the Latin words, reading the selected verses from the Bible with perfect intonation and interrogating his tutor in an incisive, bookish manner. Gelmiro enjoyed the intellectual demands made of him — the humdrum duties of a diocesan priest far from satisfied his need for academic stimulation.

Albornoz had rolled up his parchment sheets and was about to leave when the man touched him on the shoulder, inviting him to sit down.

"A moment, my boy. You have expressed

such interest in the Bible, the Church and my responsibilities, and I have been, I *am*, quite prepared to nurture the same, but, drat it, excuse my rambling! I would make you a proposition."

"A proposition, Father? I do not know that word."

"A plan, an appointment for you."

"I still do not follow, I am sorry."

"Let me explain. I propose that you become an altar boy, my assistant."

"Sire?"

"You will help me at the cathedral services. The Bishop, in his wisdom, chooses the boys on my behalf, but they are invariably boys of limited intelligence who prefer to giggle and chatter rather than behave properly, with due deference. To tell you the truth, they are more hindrance than help. So, Albornoz is my altar boy. Does that appeal to you?"

"Why, yes! It would be an honour."

"It is decided then. I will inform the Bishop and speak with your father. Tomorrow, instead of our lesson, meet me in front of the cathedral. There is no ceremony scheduled, so I will take you for a tour around God's magnificent building and explain your duties."

Albornoz walked back through the town towards his house with a boyish excitement and anticipation. It was unusual for children to be admitted to the cathedral, let alone its inner confines. He could hardly believe that he had been chosen, thus, above others for — in his eyes — such an important role. His reverie was broken by a man in front of him.

"Albornoz, good day." He looked up. It was Johan, the tenant farmer he and Father Gelmiro had seen in a state of such distress back in the spring when he could not pay his tithe.

"Good day to you, sire," Albornoz blurted, wondering what the man wanted.

"I have come from the Bishop's office."

"Sire?"

"The harvest this year has fetched a more than fair price, and I have delivered eight...no, nine fine beasts to the abattoir, each healthy and well grown."

"Why do you tell me this, mister Johan?"

"Why, indeed! Because had it not been for Father Gelmiro's intervention, ably assisted by your good self, I faced eviction, losing my livelihood. As I'm sure they say, I had a stay of execution, so with the proceeds of this year's crops and the slaughter of my beasts, I have paid off my debt. And there was enough left to buy Servet and Madelena good shoes and a new tunic for my wife." He paused, a proud smile lighting up his face.

"I am lost for words; I do not know what to say. Around these parts, Father Gelmiro's name is saluted."

MOTHER WAS ENGAGED in conversation with two women on their doorstep. As Albornoz approached them, she stopped her gossiping and beamed at him, patting his head. With a blush, he nodded to the ladies and entered the house.

"How went your lesson today? Remember, you *will* make your way in life by using your brain. Studying is very important."

"It went well, Mother, and..." He was uncertain whether she would approve of his news.

"What is it?"

"Father Gelmiro has asked me to become his assistant, an *altar boy,* as he puts it."

She took him in her arms and embraced him.

"Albornoz! This is splendid! My own son, in the cathedral, and…oh, I am *so* pleased for you."

"That is a relief. I was afraid you might not approve, for some strange reason."

"On the contrary, my darling boy."

LATER, by the river, Albornoz could not refrain from telling his good friends Servet and Madelena about his cathedral appointment.

"Really? Will you still speak to us — we who are not worthy to be in the company of an altar boy?"

Gazing at Servet, for a moment he thought his friend was being serious, but a guffaw told him it was said in jest. He, in turn, laughed.

"Of course, I will! I suppose I will mix with the dignitaries of Cuenca, but you are both my dearest friends, and may it always be thus."

"Well said!" Madelena chirped, on this occasion fully clothed, unlike their previous meeting. Albornoz smiled, a provocative expression on his face.

. . .

THE NEXT DAY, he waited, as arranged, at the foot of the dozen or so steps leading up to the Norman arches that framed the massive iron-studded oak doors of the cathedral.

'*Where is Father?*' he thought, impatiently. Then, on cue, the priest appeared at the far side of the Plaza Mayor, shuffling towards him, his long black cassock almost tripping him up in his haste.

"Phew! I was delayed by…by a woman who came to my house with official Church business on behalf of the Bishop."

"I understand, Father." In his naivety, he did not understand at all that the well-turned plump lady of a certain age was his visitor.

Regaining his breath, the priest began, "Come, let us enter."

Within, a mystical darkness enveloped Albornoz as his eyes adjusted from the midday sunshine outside. Slowly, a wondrous deep space extended before him; a void; to his innocent senses, an infinity of treasures, as yet unexplained. He turned around, and Gelmiro was not there.

"Father," he hissed, instinctively keeping his voice low. Then he spotted him to the right of the entrance, beckoning him over to a stone vessel sitting on a circular base.

"*Always,* when you come into this godly place, come to the stoup and cross yourself with holy water, like this— " He dipped two fingers of his right hand in the water, touched his forehead, down to the centre of his chest, then from left to right shoulder. Albornoz copied him.

"Now, I will show you around. Pay attention, but refrain from asking questions — the quieter and more peaceful the cathedral, the closer is our communion with the Lord. I will speak to you in a whisper, as best practice demands." Albornoz nodded, filled with awe.

"Good King Alfonso the Noble defeated the pagan Moors and began building this church here, where the Muslim mosque once was. That was more than one hundred and twenty years ago. As you should know, we dedicate it to the Mother Mary and to Saint Julian. Come, follow me."

The two stood side by side at the north end of the nave, looking towards the altar under the apse in the far distance, so vast was the space of the building. In a bemused state, the boy found it hard to comprehend.

High above the side arcades, on each side, stained-glass windows set into the clerestories permitted sharp rays of coloured light to penetrate the interior: straight, concentrated beams like arrows fired from the heavens.

"See, above us, the beautiful painted panels on the vaulted ceiling, each depicting a Biblical scene..."

Albornoz heard the start of the description, but nothing more, lost in a maelstrom of emotion, amazement and distraction.

"To the right, see the pulpit, carved and... now raise your eyes to the apse, seven-sided..."

But the boy was staring at a strange wooden stall with open seats on either side of a central curtained section.

"Father, what is —

"I said you were *not* to ask questions, for fear of disturbing the holy peace, although maybe I should explain its purpose, as it is at the heart of what we believe. It is called a confessional. There are four, two to each side of the nave." His voice descended to a barely audible sound. "There are seven Sacraments of our Church, of which one is the Sacrament of Penance and Reconciliation. The faithful may obtain absolution of their sins committed against God and neighbours. How do they do that? By confessing their sins, their transgressions of the Ten Commandments, and this, at least twice a year. The priest hearing the penitent's confession remains unknown, hidden behind the curtain. Yet, the confession itself is there for the world to hear." Albornoz was open-mouthed.

"And now, do you see the two doors over there, under the arcade? They will be important for the discharge of your duties." He opened the first door and led Albornoz inside.

"This is the vestry, or robing room, where the priest dresses before a ceremony in his alb — a long white robe — and his chasuble, an embroidered stole. He wears both over his black cassock. Do you follow?"

"I do, Father."

"I am pleased. All the vestments hang on pegs, you see, but some lazy brothers leave them crumpled on the benches. It will be your task to gather them up and ensure everything in the vestry is neat and tidy. So, on to the next room."

Albornoz nodded, confident he would be able to fulfil this role.

"This is the sacristy where we keep the

bibles, prayer parchments, candles, and so on." He picked up a shiny goblet — or that was what the lad assumed it to be. "This is one of our *ciboria* — that is the plural form of *ciborium* — the chalice with its hinged top that holds the Holy Wine and, yes..." He pointed to the table, "this is the plate from which we serve the host, the bread, during Communion. You will bring the necessary items and arrange them correctly on the altar for the priest to conduct the service. Do not worry!" he said, noticing the boy's confused reaction. "I will show you precisely how to do all this later."

TO CONCLUDE the tour of the Catedral de Santa María y San Julián, he showed Albornoz the altar and the Bishop's carved, upholstered chair.

"Well, my boy, for today that is sufficient for anyone to take in. You will be at my side tomorrow. We have a funeral ceremony for you to observe. For now, take this plate and chalice back to the sacristy, then you may go home."

"Of course, Father, and thank you."

· · ·

ALBORNOZ WAS CARRYING the things to the sacristy as instructed when, passing the vestry, he heard noises inside. There had been nobody there when he was with Gelmiro, and curiosity persuaded him to stop and peek in through the door that was slightly ajar. He held his breath, refraining from making the least sound that would betray his presence. On the bench sat two priests, embracing. One, definitely the older, corpulent and ruddy; the other, younger, slim and pale-faced. Both had their black cassocks hoisted to their waists, showing bare legs and nether regions.

He scarcely believed this scene. The men kissed with a passion that was unknown to him. They groaned, cooed, and murmured softly then loudly, their hands caressing each other's private parts. He felt his breath give in and he had to gulp, creating a click in his throat, enough to warn the two men they were being watched. Before they had time to react, Albornoz scurried off to the sacristy, although the fat priest was swift enough to catch sight of him.

The altar boy left the cathedral baffled, scared, excited — he knew not which emotion reigned — and he spent a sleepless night trying to make sense of what he had witnessed.

THE NEXT MORNING, reluctant to reveal the events to his parents, he had breakfast and left forthwith for his lesson.

The road was in early morning shadow, the side streets obscure, the alleys in almost total darkness. Without warning, a hand gripped his neck, and he was pulled violently into a niche between two houses. The hand thrust into his throat, forcing his head back against the wall, so he could scarcely breathe.

The fat red-faced priest put his face to Albornoz's and, eyes wide open, staring, hissed,

"Hush! Not a sound! Listen, and listen well. Yesterday, you saw nothing in the vestry because there was nothing to see. You must have a very vivid imagination, my little lamb, if you think otherwise."

Albornoz squirmed, short of breath and trying to free himself, but the man would not release his grip. Instead, he pushed the boy's chin upwards, ramming his head against the wall once more.

"Should I *ever* hear that you have spoken of our secret, to anybody, Gelmiro will not let you sweep the floor, never mind be his altar boy! Understood?"

He gestured that he did, and the hand round his throat at last eased.

The fat priest left as swiftly as he had arrived, leaving Albornoz on the ground, sobbing uncontrolledly.

After a short time, he came around and continued on his way to Father Gelmiro's house. He sat trembling at the table and, despite his tutor's entreaties, said nothing.

"What is the matter, Albornoz? Why do you shiver so? Are you cold? It is too early in the season to be lighting the fire. The money the Bishop pays me has to go a long way, and the woodcutter who supplies my logs has to make a living, too —

"Sire, it is a simple sickness I have caught from my friends, nothing more. Pray, let us to my lesson."

"As you say."

'I AM SO proud to be Father Gelmiro's altar boy, and I will do nothing to put that in jeopardy.'

CHAPTER EIGHT
CUENCA, KINGDOM OF SPAIN,
LATE 1318

The incident with the vicious priest weighed heavily on Albornoz's mind, and this was not helped by his having no one to tell. Above all, he was determined to become an altar boy, so he could not confide in his parents, Gelmiro or his friends lest the priest learned of his disclosure concerning the event he had witnessed in the vestry.

He was distracted in his lessons and, previously unknown, he achieved only six or seven out of ten when Gelmiro tested his Latin words. Gentle and understanding as his tutor was, he put the boy's poor performance down to the inherent laziness he saw in all his pupils.

This was not so, but it was a logical conclusion.

"Albornoz, this is not good enough! You had been making such good progress that I related my pleasure to your father. Then, I am rewarded by your lapsing and turning in scores a dullard would be ashamed of! You are not a boy who is satisfied with anything short of the best, I am sure of that, so I cannot explain it. Can you?"

"I cannot, sire. I learn the words every night, and I ask Mother or Father to check that I know them. I do not know what has changed." He knew full well what had changed.

The behaviour of those two priests in the vestry was wrong; he recognised it instinctively, and this was only reinforced by the attack in the street. If he told Father Gelmiro, he would not be believed. Priests watched out for each other, and in any case, who would take his word against two respected clerics? *Little Albornoz, a fanciful, even vindictive boy, who should not have been spying anyway. He should know his place!* That would be the people's point of view. Perhaps he had not seen the transgression as it was — maybe it was all inside his head, and he had imagined it. Uncertainty and isolation gnawed away at his childish inner self. He was in emotional turmoil.

OVER THE COMING DAYS, however, Albornoz did not cross paths with either of the priests while walking to his lesson or down by the river. Were they avoiding him, he wondered? This had a positive effect on him, and he did better work for Gelmiro, his concentration and memory restored. He decided to relegate the affair to history, and his confidence was further aided when the old man gave him the news he had been waiting for.

"I think it is the right time to expose you to the services we conduct in our churches and cathedral. The day after tomorrow, you will observe the funeral of Don Anrique. He was a worthy man, God-fearing and honest. His family raised arms against the marauding pagan Muslims and united with King Alfonso XI of Castile to drive them out of Cuenca once and for all. Yes…his was landed nobility, but one who donated regularly and in no small amount to our church coffers. The old gentleman saw three score and ten winters and left precise instructions for his requiem ceremony, which will, naturally, be followed.

"I have not attended a funeral in my life, sire."

"Worry not. Our brother Nicolás will be in charge of the proceedings. You and I will sit and watch from a side pew where I can whisper an explanation but where we will not disturb the event. You have not met Father Nicolás, although you might have noticed him here and there. He is a red-faced fat man who — "

Albornoz started and sat bolt upright. He needed no further description — this had to be the same priest he had caught in the vestry, the one who had all but strangled him in the street.

'So, his name is Nicolás. It's not before time that I discovered him, and he will surely not anticipate me watching him perform his duties. Don Anrique's funeral can't come soon enough!' Gelmiro prodded him to attract his attention.

"Albornoz! Do you hear me?"

"Sorry, Father, my thoughts were elsewhere."

"That may be so, but to learn, you need to listen — it is a prerequisite for any successful academic. I trust I have taught you that, if nothing else!"

"That is true. You were saying?"

Gelmiro sensed a peculiar arrogance in the boy's manner, a self-assured, superior attitude that he recognised in himself as a nine-year-old youngster. He returned to the present,

"I said that Father Nicolás will lead the requiem."

"I see, and you are right, I have not yet had the pleasure of meeting Father Nicolás."

"He is a good priest and nearer my own age than the other novices of the town. We share similar likes and dislikes."

"I am sure you do," Albornoz said, averting his gaze, fearing any sarcasm in his voice might reveal his actual thoughts.

"We will not have a lesson tomorrow, as I have an appointment elsewhere, but meet me the day after in front of the cathedral at the terce bell, and I will escort you inside before the mourners start to arrive."

"Thank you, Father. I am certain it will be not only a solemn occasion but also an education for me."

. . .

THE MORNING HAD BEEN SO eventful that he almost forgot today was his birthday — nine years of age, with the mind and interests of one twice as old.

His brothers now spent long periods training to be soldiers at the Duke of Mendoza's estate, so they were often away from home. He missed them, although it meant his mother had more time to spoil him. He appeared world-weary in conversation, but at heart he was his mother's little boy.

Garcia and Teresa were talking in a lively manner as he entered the house.

'I'll wager it's about me! I just hope they haven't made plans to send me away, too, like my brothers.'

"Ah, Albornoz," greeted Teresa, "run along and wash before lunch."

He obeyed, sensing there might be a surprise awaiting him. The housemaid brought bread, cooked meats and fruit, laying a pewter plate in front of each of the three people present. She filled beakers with ale, and milk for the boy. Garcia rose, bowed his head, and recited grace.

"Have you spent your morning profitably, my son?"

"Father, I always do, and — " He was about

to relate details of the forthcoming church service, but his father interrupted him,

"That is how it should be. But today, is it in any way different?"

Albornoz looked at the man with a quizzical expression.

"I do not know…"

"You did not think we could forget your birthday, did you? Happy birthday." He reached across the table and formally shook Albornoz's hand. "Now, give your mother a kiss."

He could never decide why *he* always kissed his mother on *his* birthday.

"Maid!" Garcia called out. The maid immediately appeared carrying, with great care, a model boat — some two feet long and half a foot wide at its beam — that she put down before the unsuspecting boy. His jaw dropped in amazement. He had seen nothing like it in his life. The maid bowed and left the family alone.

"What do you think?' asked Garcia, momentarily fearing he had made a wrong choice.

"Is it for *me*?"

"Of course, it is, boy! Again, a happy

birthday to you. That is from your mother and me." He had considered the present carefully, hoping that, as well as being a simple gift, it might stimulate his son to follow a career in the military as with his other offspring, although he was conscious of the Church's growing attraction for him. He continued,

"It is, without doubt, an object of extreme beauty. Let me explain its story to you..." It was unusual for Garcia to address his son thus, but he realised it was time to establish a relationship with his youngest child. He felt a sense of guilt for the distance he had created between them in the past.

"It is made by a certain craftsman who lives in an isolated cabin in the forest away to the north of our town. His fame has spread abroad for his breathtaking skill. Do you not agree, son?"

Staring at the gift, he answered, vaguely,

"I do, father."

"While this man, it is clear to see, has the ability to construct whatsoever model he chooses, he only makes boats. Strange, that. It has brought him no small wealth, yet he leads a pauper's existence. Do you know, he has made models on commission for the dukes and kings of our provinces, and beyond?"

Teresa nodded, dutifully, then called,

"Maid! More ale for the master!"

He waited to quench his thirst before continuing his spellbinding account.

"We call it a *cog boat,* a vessel that has carried goods and passengers on the Huécar river since ancient times. Without its cargoes of silks, wools, yarns and the like, Cuenca would not have become the prosperous, thriving place it is today. My ancestors amassed their lands and fortunes from its trade in textiles. Just as important, they sailed by the dozen to transport King Alfonso's troops to the rocky side of our town, near to where you play with your friends. Why? To surprise the Moors. They slaughtered the marauding pagan hoards so that Cuenca is, today, a holy Christian place." He paused to take a draught of ale, then continued, in a wistful tone,

"I had a boat like yours, and it was a birthday present, but nothing as grand as yours." Garcia Alvarez de Albornoz was a man of few words, and his wife could not recall the last time he had spoken thus, for anything other than a curt admonishment or instruction. She had, from the start, found herself in a loveless marriage and suspected that he had married into her Luna family name for his own profit. She gave her son a sharp nudge.

"Pay attention to your father and sit up straight. He explains all this for your benefit, so you are aware of your history and may be truly thankful."

"Of course, mother."

"As I was saying, and back to the boat. With a fair wind, the mainsail and jib were hoisted. See their fine cotton and the royal cypher, AR, emblazoned for the world to see and fear the king's fighting men on board. When not required, the sails were bound, unfurled, on the brace — see?"

Albornoz hung on his father's every word.

"On the planked deck, the hatch covers can be raised, then you peer into the holds and the crew's quarters. Do I hear you ask me how the boat sailed when becalmed? Well," and he pointed, "here are the benches, to port and starboard, where the rowers sat, six on each side. The craftsman has even made the oars... see them lashed together and..." his voice rose to an excited climax, "there are the rowlocks that supported the oars! Such faithful detail! A lantern hung from the quarter deck in front of the wheelhouse, and I could go on, but enough. You are now the captain of your very own river boat! Let us eat lunch."

AFTER THEIR MEAL, Albornoz was instructed to take the model to his room. He picked it up, carefully cradled it in his arms, and left the room, followed by the mousy maid. They climbed the stairs to the first floor.

"Here, take my boat, but do not drop it — that would be more than your job, no, your *life* is worth."

He went halfway up the ladder to his attic bedroom, then turned around and ordered her,

"Pass it to me."

The unexpected gift was set down on the dresser next to his wash basin.

THE AFTERNOON WAS NOW his own, so he set off through the town and descended the steps to the river. The ambient temperature had fallen of late, but that did not deter the band of friends from frolicking in the water — at their age, children do not feel the cold.

"Come on, Albornoz, I'll race you to the other side and back!" Madelena challenged him.

"You're on!"

They quickly wriggled out of their tunics and ran down to the river's edge.

"After three — ready?"

"Ready."

"One, two, three — go!"

They returned, gasping to get their wind back, then collapsed with Albornoz on top of the girl. Neither spoke, and she did not try to push him off her. On the contrary, she put her arms around him, pulling him close, and he reciprocated by pressing his body into hers. The sensation of naked flesh on flesh was completely unknown to them — he only nine, she eleven years of age. Still in their growing amorous clinch, he placed a lingering kiss on her lips.

After what seemed an eternity to the children but was, in reality, a few seconds, Albornoz rolled away from the girl. Neither spoke. Madelena pulled her knees up to her chest, realising he was gazing at her nascent breasts. Embarrassed, they both began to talk at the same time, but only nonsenses and quips, then burst out laughing and relieved the drama of the moment. They donned their tunics, feeling rather silly and distinctly awkward about this, their first sexual experience.

She reached into the wicker basket she always brought.

"This is for you," she said, sheepishly. "It's your birthday, isn't it?"

"Why, yes, it is, but how — "

"I remember you told me the date last year." She handed him a corn dolly.

"What is it?"

"Farming folk call it a corn dolly. I made it especially for you. When we have had a profitable harvest, we take some yellow stubble left in the field after the crop's been collected and weave it into figures like this. See, it has a head, body, legs...don't worry, though, I didn't try to make it look like you — that would have been impossible." She lowered her eyes with a genuinely coy innocence. Then she resumed.

"We give them to people, to our friends, to

bring them good luck, and we make certain to bury one in the soil to ensure another fine crop the following year. It doesn't always work, as you know too well. Anyway, keep this little corn dolly in a safe place, and health and fortune will be with you forever."

"It's so very thoughtful of you, Madelena," he said, leaning over, gently kissing her.

THAT SAME EVENING, Albornoz sat on the edge of his bed, his mind spinning. Moonlight shone in fragile rays through the skylight of his room and enveloped his model boat, picking out every tiny feature, casting dancing shadows through the sail rigging, landing on the decks below. As he watched, fascinated, engrossed, hypnotised, the boat began to raise its prow then subsided, rolling like a real ship negotiating a choppy sea. It pitched, side-to-side, perhaps in a raging storm. He heard the captain's furious commands to his crew to furl the mainsail and batten down the hatches. Even time-served matelots feared capsize of their vessel and prayed that Neptune or Poseidon — it mattered not which god — would save them from a watery grave.

Albornoz's thoughts, of a sudden, moved from the chaos on the high seas to the relative peace of his present condition: his gaze looked out of the window in the roof to the Huécar and the gorge beyond.

'What is the boat telling me — of travel to distant shores or even as a soldier? I cannot ignore the calling I feel for the Church, so will I forge a career as a priest?'

Staring in the direction of the willow trees on the riverbank, he thought, still confused,

'Madelena is a dear friend to me, and I now have the corn dolly to help me make the right decision.'

HE LAY DOWN and soon fell asleep. Tomorrow, he had to attend Don Anrique's funeral in the cathedral and scrutinise the person of his loathing, Father Nicolás.

CHAPTER NINE
CUENCA, KINGDOM OF SPAIN,
LATE 1318

Albornoz was awoken by the insistent crowing of the cockerel on the farm behind his house. He rinsed his face with water in the bowl on his washstand and cleaned his teeth with a linen cloth dipped into a white powder that their maid mixed up from sage leaves ground into salt crystals. When he had donned his tunic and pulled on his boots, he sat on the edge of the bed, his gaze fixed on the model ship Father had given him as a surprise birthday present. Propped up against its prow was the corn dolly from Madelena. Both gifts held a special meaning for him: the ship, in his imagination, represented future life journeys; the corn dolly, as his girlfriend had explained, would bring him good luck.

GARCIA AND TERESA had finished breakfast and, in earnest conversation, leaned over a parchment sheet, evidently columns of figures concerning the family finances. Albornoz sat at the table and wished them good morning.

"And the same to you, Albornoz," Mother greeted him. Garcia looked up and merely nodded.

"Are you prepared for your lesson?" she asked.

"No need, Mother. I am to meet Father Gelmiro at the cathedral today. There is a funeral service that he wants me to observe. The deceased is a gentleman by the name of…" For a moment, he forgot who it was.

"Ah, yes, Don Anrique — "

"I knew him well," Garcia interrupted, "a fine upstanding gentleman if ever there was. He supported King Alfonso in ridding Cuenca of the cursed Muslims. Your mother and I will both attend to pay our last respects, will we not, Teresa?"

She lowered her head in acknowledgement.

. . .

FATHER GELMIRO MET the boy as arranged: his prodigy, who showed a talent that, even at such tender years, presaged great things.

On entering the cathedral through its solid oak doors, Albornoz walked, without prompting, over to the stoup, crossing himself with holy water.

"That is well done, my lad, you have remembered what to do," the priest said in a soft voice. He, too, paid his respect at the stoup. "Now, follow me."

They were alone in the immense church, and as they made their way slowly down the nave towards the altar, their footsteps echoed around the high vaulted ceiling then faded to drift heavenward. A still darkness surrounded them, and Albornoz shivered, nervous, afraid that some monster or devil might leap out of the black side arcades to whisk them away. Gelmiro sensed the boy's agitation and said, to reassure him,

"Do not worry. If ever there existed a safe place, it is here. Can you feel the Lord's presence?"

"Father, how would I know? If you say so, I

will have to agree, though. There is certainly a very special atmosphere." Gelmiro raised his eyebrows, both surprised and impressed by such a mature utterance.

Halfway down the nave, the priest gestured a halt. In front of them an elegant wooden coffin with four shiny brass handles rested on two trestles. It had no lid. At its head and foot flickered two tall wax candles in heavy iron holders, their yellow light casting eerie shadows over the casket. Not until they got close could they properly see its contents. The boy gasped sharply, stopping short: never in his life had he seen or been near to a corpse. He froze with shock and amazement that seared through his whole body. He gasped a second time, and still he remained motionless. Gelmiro approached the coffin, touched its side, then bowed his head, mumbling a solemn prayer. Turning to Albornoz, he nodded for him to do the same. Moving forward, his legs quaked and his hand trembled as he gently stroked the receptacle that contained the body of Don Anrique. Crossing himself, he took two paces back, happy to move away from the righteous old man — rich and fine he might have been, but it mattered little to Albornoz, who was by now in a state of panic.

"There's nothing to be afraid of," Gelmiro reassured him. "Man has the capacity to be more harmful in life than death, but not Anrique. His wealth was accrued from the several farms he owned, and he treated his workers as his family, as well as making generous donations to the Church. Remember, my boy, avarice is one of the Cardinal Sins, so through his benevolence, he ensured he would not have to confess it. The better we are in this life, the greater will be the glory of our resurrection in God's kingdom, that is if we are granted entry." Albornoz tried hard to follow the priest's meandering speech.

"Yes, I saw him regularly at mass, listening attentively to the sermon, and of course, he confessed his sins, as we all must, with honesty and humility, baring his soul to God."

Curiosity overcame trepidation, and the young lad leaned over the body.

"He appears so peaceful, so still."

"Indeed — but you would not expect him to jump up and dance, would you?" The joke broke the tense atmosphere. "The pagan will never know salvation, but the good Christian embraces both life and death as the only true way to the Lord. His widow will have washed her husband's body then wound it with a winding sheet of the best quality. Note his eyes are closed. He has done with affairs of the earth and will open them again only when he arrives at the gates of Heaven. The dead man has resided here, in God's house, for the last two days."

"What is the reason for that?"

"We call it the *viewing period*. People are entitled to know that the man has definitely passed, as a legal matter. Upon such certainty depend affairs like endowments and rights of title. The donations he made during his lifetime have ensured that our priests have said prayers for him, by the coffin, at every bell from leuds to compline. Funerals for the poor are far less elaborate, as you might assume."

"Why are there no visitors now, to view the body?"

"By now, everyone will be in their homes, the men putting on their best tunics, the women their finest dresses. They will arrive soon. Let me show you now to the side pew from where we will observe proceedings." He then explained that he had a little business to attend to.

"I will not be long. Stay seated here until I return."

From the assigned pew, Albornoz had a perfect sight of the entrance to his left, the grand altar to his right, and the shadowy coffin in front. Realising he was the only living person within the cathedral's four walls — or, at least, as far as he could see — he felt at once isolated, vulnerable, insignificant, and worthless. These emotions were so complex that he did not possess a vocabulary adequate to name them, but they were real. The mystical power of a religion still unexplored by him cast its authority over his being.

'Here I am, a mere boy, in the presence of Don Anrique's spirit and the Lord's benevolent omnipotence. I am not worthy.'

His gaze focused in the half-light on the deceased man, the winding sheet covering his body to the neck, his face serene, facing the illuminated panels telling of God's saints and Jesus's life painted on the vaulted ceiling above. For one moment, he thought he saw a hand rise up from inside the box, waving, beckoning him to come forth. Blinking twice, he rebuked himself for being so foolish, although he could not deny that he now felt protected by his divine surroundings, even if he was within touching distance of a cold, ghostly cadaver. Comforted, he waited for Gelmiro's return.

'This is a truly wondrous place. I feel it inside me...a numbness, an authority I have not known... as if the angels on the ceiling speak to me, telling me I must serve them in order to find the state of righteousness that Gelmiro told me all men should make their goal in life.'

His daydreaming came to an abrupt end as noises from the direction of the doors hailed the arrival of the funeral guests. Men, women and children filed slowly down the nave, stern expressions on their faces and, by the quality of their clothes, people of wealth. Reaching the coffin, the adults solemnly placed a hand on the body, lifting the little ones so they could peer inside. The pews to the front were soon filled with mourners, smartly dressed in garments only worn for special occasions. As the bell fell silent, an attendant priest appeared, swinging a thurible to cense smoky grey swirls of sweet-smelling incense around the dead man, stopping at each side to utter a barely audible prayer. In addition to the censer, the old man's money had paid for the candles, wooden coffin and a boy chorister in a spotless white cassock who, standing in front of the altar, intoned a monotonous funeral dirge. The children in the assembly were becoming increasingly fractious.

His business concluded, Gelmiro returned, sat down beside Albornoz and bowed his head.

"Won't be long now before things begin. Do you wish to ask me anything?"

"What is that smoke? It has a wonderful smell."

Smiling at the boy's innocence, he replied,

"It is burning incense — a form of candle mixed with oils — and, in accordance with the rite of our Church, the thurible, the container, if you like, is always swung in groups of three. This represents the Three Persons of the Holy Trinity, God the Father, God the Son Jesus Christ, and God the Holy Spirit. In Psalms there is a verse,

'Let my prayer be directed as incense in Thy sight, the lifting up of my hands, as evening sacrifice.'

"Don Anrique must have been a righteous man."

"A righteous man, indeed." He paused, again bowing his head in respectful contemplation. "I have now told you about the body and the incense. You can see the two candles at either end. They symbolise light in the darkness of life and light in the next world. Christ is the light."

'Why can I not avert my eyes from the flickering flames of the candles?' Albornoz thought. *'It is as if I do not have control of —*

"Do you understand that?"

"I...I think so."

At that moment, the chorister stopped the dirge, and a fat red-faced priest in a white robe appeared on the steps in front of the altar.

"See now, that is Father Nicolás," Gelmiro said softly. "He's waiting for silence."

Before starting proceedings, Nicolás turned directly to where Albornoz and Gelmiro sat. His cold, dark stare fixed on the boy who had the power to ruin his reputation if the Church and town learned of his promiscuous liaison with a fellow priest. The message it gave to Albornoz was as clear and loud as screams from a drunken tavern brawl.

'He is afraid of me! He has beaten my body, but

he cannot destroy my spirit! He has done wrong, and eventually, he will pay for it.'

"Merciful Father," Nicolás began, "hear our prayers and comfort us; renew out trust in Your Son, whom you raised from the dead; strengthen our faith that Thy servant, Don Anrique, and all who have died in the love of Christ, will share in his resurrection; Christ who lives and reigns with You, now and forever. Amen."

"Amen," came the reply from the congregation.

At this juncture, Nicolás again looked up at the reason for his fear. Gelmiro took it as a religious sign and crossed the air in the direction of the officiant, as an acknowledgment.

THE SERVICE CONTINUED, Nicolás reading a series of prayers, each one supported by the amen of the people. Moving forward, he sprinkled holy water from a brass aspersorium at the four sides of the casket. The chorister started singing a final dirge.

"Brothers and sisters in Christ, we will now exit for burial in the graveyard, as was Don

Anrique's wish." At these words, four young men emerged from the mourners, and each gripped a brass handle to lift the box off the trestles and carry it out of the cathedral, Nicolás leading the way, the people behind. At the newly dug grave, the four bearers tied a cord to each handle and lowered it slowly into the ground. Don Anrique's family and friends gathered round while his widow and two daughters scattered handfuls of earth symbolically onto their beloved father. Nicolás took a bible from his cassock pocket to read the closing prayer.

"O God, by whose mercy the faithful departed find rest, send Your holy angel to watch over this grave, through Christ our Lord. Amen."

"Amen," came the sad, tearful response as they turned to make their way back.

ON THE CATHEDRAL STEPS, Nicolás bid farewell to the mourners, shaking hands, offering condolences in a respectful tone. Gelmiro went up to him.

"Father Nicolás, you conducted a most dignified ceremony."

"Thank you, Gelmiro." But his countenance darkened when he saw Albornoz by his side.

"May I introduce you to my outstanding young student, Master Albornoz, for whom I predict great things."

The boy held out his hand, but Nicolás merely nodded. The evident hostility between the two was immediately noted by the other priest, who made no further comment.

'There is something amiss there, that's for sure. I will ask the boy what goes on that they do not even shake hands,' he thought.

Father Gelmiro was not the sort of man to sleep and forget such matters.

CHAPTER TEN
LIMOGES (LIMOUSIN), KINGDOM OF ARLES, 1324

"Father, I have sinned." There was no reply from the other side of the confessional box.

'It had better be Caron...I don't want anyone else knowing my business.'

He repeated, in a slightly louder tone,

"Father, I have sinned."

"God bless you, my son. Which sins do you repent?'

"Ah, it's you, Father Caron," he hissed, then, gathering himself,

"I confess anger. My wife made comments in our conversation that I thought to be... um...disrespectful, and I raised a hand to her.

Although she deserved it, I realise that I behaved badly, so I confess my anger. Any husband would have done the same — "

"Quiet, my son. I do not ask for any explanation, nor does the Good Lord, who hears and forgives us sinners without judgment. What further sins do you repent?"

EDMOND NERVAL HAD ATTENDED confession occasionally since the priest first convinced him of the appropriateness of that particular religious ceremony. There had been no conversion to the Faith, far from it, but it was in his interest to ensure that Caron did not inform Monsieur Dumas of his poaching on the estate. Donations of eels ensured the priest maintained his silence. Where Edmond saw no wrong in stealing, Caron saw none, either, in receiving: such polarised attitudes pertained then and prevailed thence. The confession continued.

"And for what else do you feel shame?"

With several such meetings behind him, the wily man knew to come prepared, and he responded without hesitation,

"Gluttony, Father. Ay, gluttony."

"How come?"

"Last week, we were fortunate in that my wife's sister called on us. She lives with her husband and five children a fair way from here. He's a farmer and a successful man if I say so, and all within the law, if Father follows."

"I follow."

"She pulled up her pony and trap outside our humble home — I don't know many folk wealthy enough to get around like that — "

"Do move on. What is your sin? Explain it."

"Excuse me for rambling, Father. On the back of the trap there's a sack of potatoes, carrots, turnips, onions and other vegetables... from the farm, you see...a gift, no less. Don't get many gifts, you see. And, to round it off, she gave us a cured ham!" He paused for breath, then concluded,

"After she left, and for I don't know how many days, we ate like royalty, but not accustomed to eating well, I fell sick...pains in the belly, and I think they call that gluttony."

"Indeed, it is. I impose five Pater Nosters and ten Ave Marias. Now, go in peace."

"I will do just that, and...will Father accept

two freshly caught eels? I will be at the market tomorrow morning."

"Most kind, Edmond, most kind."

DURING THE YEARS from the first auspicious meeting between Edmond and the priest, the former's life in his secluded cabin had not greatly changed: the taverns of Limoges were as rowdy and bawdy; the market as lively; his poaching still a major contribution to his household. From the old gypsy's recipe for distilling liquor from potatoes, he learned to use the wheat and barley readily available from the surrounding fields as the base for a potent spirit that he sold by the flagon around Limoges. He regularly drank to excess, and a fiery temper caused many a brawl in the town, while at home, Jamette was all too often, with beatings, a victim of his intoxication: she knew no different. She was a sad, childless woman. Motherhood eluded her, and advancing years, with her husband's lack of concern for the carnal side of their marriage, only served to deepen her sadness.

. . .

A CHANCE ENCOUNTER with Father Caron in the street was to give Edmond reason for optimism. He was prepared to consider any work to make money — sloth was not one of his sins. He eyed the priest with suspicion and asked, in a soft tone,

"Good morning, Father. What do you want with me today? It's not long since I last did the confession thing, and I've got no eels, they're not taking the bait lately — "

"I do not want anything from you, Edmond. On the contrary, I have heard about an opportunity that might be of interest to you."

Still suspicious, the man replied,

"And what would that be? A man like me doesn't get *opportunities*, as you put it. That's the province of the well-to-do."

"Listen to what I have to say. You should not assume that the whole world is against you. For any man who has turned to the Lord, as you have, through confession, there can always be good fortune around the corner — "

"Father, I have to get on, so what exactly have you heard?"

The cleric resumed.

"An acquaintance of mine, namely a monk from Saint Martial Abbey, tells me that men are required for the building of the new cathedral, which is to be named Saint Etienne, after the venerated saint. I take it you are a good worker?"

"I am that."

"Good. Present yourself to the bishop's foreman and say I have recommended you."

"Well, I thank you, Father. I did not expect such news when you approached me — not much good news nowadays. I will pay the foreman a visit."

The two men nodded respectfully and turned to continue on their opposite ways.

THE CATHEDRAL'S construction was in its extremely early stages and, largely through lack of funds, would not be completed for another six hundred years. Edmond walked up the hill leading to the building he had often seen, but from a distance. He entered the space that would become the richly carved stonework framing the grand north portal but was presently unclad blocks. Inside, the nave, set with rectangular granite slabs, extended to meet the semi-circular ambulatory choir — the oldest part of the cathedral and the only section to boast a roof in the form of vaulted panels, fifty feet high. To either side of the nave, the pillars to support pointed arches were already erected, but the exterior flying buttresses announced their existence by little more than sandstone piers, spaced regularly just above ground level.

Edmond sat down on a low trolley used to move heavy blocks around the site. His gaze surveyed the scene and the sheer enormity of the cathedral — even in its far-from-finished state — overwhelmed and seduced him. To imagine the cavernous ceiling adorned with magnificent paintings flowing from centre rose bosses, hundreds of feet above the congregation was beyond his capabilities.

Each arcade column was scarcely visible, enveloped in wooden scaffolds and ladders to afford an army of masons safe access to carry out their work. On the floor, men pushed and pulled carts laden with stones, some plain and square, others ornate and shaped by master craftsmen into frightening gargoyles, faces and angels. Their work would remain largely anonymous despite the skill and elegance of their creations. Around an enormous barrel, three men with paddles stirred a mixture of lime, sand and water to provide the stone layers with a steady supply of mortar. The correct consistency achieved, other men filled buckets that were fastened with ropes and hoisted by pulleys up to the working platforms.

A tap on the shoulder jolted Edmond out of his idle reverie.

"Hey! What are you doing here? You're not a regular, that's for sure."

Turning around, he was confronted by a giant of a man, stripped to the waist, muscles bulging, the sun reflecting off his bald head.

"Point me to the bishop's foreman."

"Over there, see that hut?"

"Ay, I thank you."

The modest cabin stood, protected from the elements, under the choir. By its side, a table formed from three long planks supported on trestle legs displayed parchment sheet after sheet. Each was weighted down with a stone: these were the architects' plans for the construction of the cathedral.

Edmond knocked on the door and a faint voice from within answered,

"Enter."

Inside, it was not at all as grand as might have been expected for an office that oversaw every activity on that complex building site. As his eyes adjusted to the dimness within, the first thing he saw was a huge chest, bound with iron straps, and two brass escutcheons mounted around two keyholes. *'Must be gold inside...never seen a box as big...'* Along one wall ran a single shelf groaning under a load of small books, each spine bearing a letter of the alphabet. Deep in the hut, Edmond then made out in the light of a flickering candle a sloped-top writing desk. Almost concealed behind a thick leather-bound ledger, a diminutive man, one eyebrow squeezed to hold a wire-rimmed monocle, looked up at Edmond's presence in the doorway.

"I said *enter,* didn't I? Come close, let me see you."

Approaching the desk, Edmond waited for the other man to speak.

"Your name?"

"Nerval, monsieur, Edmond Nerval. I have

to say I have come here on the recommendation of Father Caron — ”

“Caron? Ah, yes, the priest from the Eglise Evangélique, Rue Marie — a decent enough man.”

Removing his monocle, he pursed his lips into an inquisitive, mischievous expression.

“Are *you* a decent enough man…who is it… ah, Nerval?”

“I suppose I am, monsieur.”

“And are you reliable?”

“For certain.”

“Then, going on Caron’s word, I will take you on. It’s an eight-hour day and two deniers a shift. Agreed?”

“Agreed, monsieur, and I will not let you down.”

“Better not! Report to the stonemason — he’s out there working in one of the chapels… the one wielding a cat o’ nine tails! Only joking!”

‘The money’s not good, but while the eels aren’t biting, needs must, got no choice.’

. . .

EDMOND PICKED out the stonemason easily from the other workers by the parchment in his hand.

"Excuse me, I've just seen the Bishop's Foreman, and — "

"And it's your first time here. Welcome to the most important part of the cathedral — at least, one day it *will* be the cathedral."

This overseer spoke in a gentle tone that Edmond had not been expecting. In his experience, any person in a position of authority was harsh and uncaring.

"I will explain everything to you — ah, your name?"

"Edmond Nerval."

"So, Edmond, our stone comes by cart from a quarry a day's travel from here, but it's in rough lumps. The carter unloads it, then the masons and their men cut and dress it into smoothed blocks — you came past them at the entrance. It's your job to bring those blocks to use up here, on the flat trolley. They'll show you how to use the hoists and so on. Then I give the carver a design to copy — could be a bird, flower, face, whatever. Our finished work is then laid on mortar, in place according to how the architects have shown. Is that clear?"

"I think so," answered Edmond, who was not clear at all.

"Once again, welcome to the construction of Saint Etienne's cathedral, a building that will be the equal of anything in the whole of Christendom! I don't say I agree with *everything* the Church people say, but that doesn't matter; my job on earth is to leave pictures in stone for them who comes after to enjoy. You can start today. The stores will give you an apron."

EDMOND COULD NOT HAVE KNOWN that his own son would be doing work identical to his, albeit in a different place and time.

DURING THE COMING MONTHS, the poacher-cum-cathedral worker turned up when required, carried out his tasks with diligence, and was paid a wage. However, he did not put much money by - his usual tavern was situated on his route home from the site. The more he earned, the more he drank.

ONE AFTERNOON, he sat at his favourite table in the tavern. The day had been rewarding — a sack of eels soon sold at market, and his money pouch was full of coin. That same week, he had also worked four shifts moving blocks of stone around. His world was a pleasant place.

"Edmond, do you mind if I join you? A fellow shouldn't drink alone."

"Acelin, you old devil! Of course, sit down. Landlord, more ale!"

Acelin was a rogue who Edmond met occasionally, a poacher, but from another estate south of the river Vienne.

"So, how's business? And your good lady wife, Jamette? A fine woman, for sure, and it's time there was the patter of tiny feet, is it not?"

"Business goes well, and concerning *tiny feet,* that's none of your concern!"

"Hey, I didn't mean to be snoopy, it's just a while since we talked."

"Ay, it is that."

Their conversation soon turned to each other's poaching escapades.

"Still doing eels?"

"I am, but —

"But you can't catch enough."

"How do you know that?"

"I've not known an eel man yet who makes a living from them alone."

"You're right. Today, I had one on every hook, but yesterday nothing at all on the entire line. What are *you* doing nowadays?" Edmond asked, leaning across the table, his voice becoming a whisper.

"Boar, wild boar, *that's* where there's money to be made. There must be a few herds on Dumas's estate, what with the forest being so close, too…ideal for boar, I'd say."

"Yes, there are."

Edmond swallowed a draught of ale, his curiosity increasing. Acelin continued,

"I could show you how to trap 'em — *secrets of the trade*, if you will."

"Even if I agreed, why would you do *me* a favour?" Edmond asked, his gaze scanning the adjacent tables to ensure they were not overheard.

"It wouldn't be free; I never does favours for nothing.'

"That doesn't surprise me!"

"No, I'm prepared to show you how to

catch boar for a share in the profit — nothing could be fairer than that, and afterwards, I'll leave you to act on your own. Everybody ends up smiling — except old Monsieur Dumas! Seriously, though, I wouldn't trespass on another man's patch, would I? But hark, the boar is a fearsome animal, especially when it's cornered or trapped or in pain. I've seen it trample a man into a mess of flesh, blood and bone! If it gores you with its tusks, you'll not survive, I guarantee that... It will toss you higher than the trees..."

"I'm always open to new ideas, Acelin, so tell me why boars are worth risking your life for? The Duke doesn't take kindly to poachers, and I've come close to getting caught. He likes to hunt them with his wealthy friends for sport."

"Then you don't get caught, you oaf! Anyway, the thing about the boar is 'most every part of it has a price, 'most nothing is wasted."

"Go on, I'm listening."

"I use snares or nets, depending on the lie of the forest and the beasts' runs. I finish 'em off with my dagger then drag 'em back to my cabin — takes no special skill, just luck. Even *you* could do it!" he joked, in a sneering tone.

"Back home, I take off its head and feet with an axe, and it's ready for the pot. I boils it slow in my cauldron for five or six hours then — and this is how you can make real money —
"

Edmond's attention had not left the other man, so enthralled was he by the explanation.

"— out of the pot and onto my bench. With my sharpest knife, I slice into its hide and try to get it off in one piece. I scrape off all the flesh and fat, and believe me, any tanner will pay you handsomely! They sell it on to saddlers, cordwainers, girdlers, whoever, and it makes fine leather goods for them that can afford it. But don't forget the *bristles*! I clip 'em off and tie 'em in bundles. There's a man I know who makes brushes and sells 'em to maidservants who care for their mistresses' hair, do you understand?"

"Yes. Carry on, pray."

"What's left is the meat. With a serrated blade, I cut it up into joints, rub in a pinch of salt, wrap 'em in muslin, and it's ready for my customers, for a good price. So, how's that for a pretty affair? Hide, bristles, meat...are you interested, Edmond? It would be better than slimy eels, but you can do both..."

The men drank up their ale, Edmond mulling over what Acelin had proposed.

'One of the sins Caron banged on about was avarice, but wanting to improve your lot in life isn't greed, is it? I shouldn't feel guilty. What's more, Dumas will never miss a few rotten old boars. If they roam in the forest, I could claim I had a right to hunt them on...um...common land, that's what I'm trying to say.'

"Ale, landlord! Is our money not good enough?"

"Coming, Edmond," a barman called from behind the counter.

There followed a pause, neither men guessing how the other would respond. Edmond spoke first,

"I accept your offer, my friend. I will need to purchase a suitable cauldron, but the smith has all sorts of pots and pans displayed outside his forge, so it won't be a problem."

"Good. We're at the start of the rutting season when the males will all be out and about, searching for sows. I will sell you a net and trap for a small consideration. Next Monday, then? We will set everything out, you can put me up overnight, and the next day we'll see what we've got for our trouble."

"Agreed." The men shook hands on the arrangement. Acelin rose from the table, tottered towards the door, then departed.

"Is Jamette cooking a stew to feed an army? Yon cauldron's big enough for that. Don't sell many that size." The enormous toothless smith wiped his hands on a blackened overall. "Anyway, that will be two deniers, Edmond."

"There's three to cart it up the track to my cabin."

"My boy will see to it tomorrow."

"Just one thing, smith, nobody needs know what I've bought from you because — "

"Edmond, your affairs are your affairs, nothing to do with me. Not long ago, I had an order to make up a scold's bridle. Most terrible thing I ever had to do. It goes around the head like a Viking helmet, a bit at the front that goes into the mouth over the tongue and a bolt in the back to make certain it couldn't be taken off by the poor woman. The customer was sick of his wife's gossiping, and he thought it was the best way to silence her! The entire town saw her for what she was...but, as I say, it doesn't concern me. One man's money is the same as another's."

"I wish you good day."

"And you, Edmond."

Back in his cabin, he told Jamette nothing of his and Acelin's plan. The less people knew, the better.

CHAPTER ELEVEN
LIMOGES (LIMOUSIN), KINGDOM OF ARLES, 1324

The next day, as promised, the smith's boy pulled up his horse and cart outside Edmond's home.

"Hey, there! Got a delivery for Monsieur Nerval!" the boy shouted to herald his arrival. Jamette came out to meet him, drawing her shawl tight around her shoulders against the morning chill. She knew nothing of the enormous cauldron on the cart. Her husband rarely shared household decisions with her.

"What have you for us?"

"A large cooking pot, see." He tapped it with his stick, causing a resonating ring.

"Biggest one I ever seen! You could fit an ox

in there, and it's too heavy for me to shift alone. Need another man to help."

"Monsieur Nerval is away, though he should be back soon. Will you come inside and take a drink to pass the time?"

"Thank 'ee kindly, missus," he accepted, doffing his cap and following her into the cabin.

"Sit, pray." Without further delay she filled a beaker with liquor from the wooden barrel and placed it in front of her unexpected guest. Sparks leaped in the fireplace as she raked the embers and threw on more logs. The fire was the only illumination in the room — Edmond forbade careless use of expensive candles in daytime. The boy drank in silence. Jamette busied herself wringing out clothes in the washtub. Shortly, the door opened and Edmond appeared, dropped his sack with its wriggling contents and went over to the fireplace to warm his hands. He smacked his lips, drinking from the tankard his wife offered him.

"Ah, that's better. I suppose you would like me to help you unload the cart?" he asked, acknowledging the boy's presence for the first time.

"Too heavy for one man to move, mister."

"Come, then, and once we've done that you can give me a ride into town. I need to be at the market this morning."

"With pleasure, mister."

Together, they lifted the iron cauldron off the cart and hauled it to the rear of the property.

"In here," Edmond ordered, nodding towards an open-fronted shed where he had placed two stones, apart, to support the pot over a pile of kindling. He took a step back and admired his new acquisition.

'I'm looking forward to boiling up an old boar inside that!'

He then returned to the cabin to collect his sack of freshly caught eels, giving Jamette no idea why her husband had purchased a second pot. *'The one they used day after day was perfectly adequate,'* she thought to herself.

"I will be back at midday. Make sure the house is swept and tidy; we are taking in a guest who will spend the night with us." Although it was most unusual to have anyone stay, she had learned over the years to not question him; he could readily perceive it as disrespect, with dire consequences.

He threw the sack onto the cart then climbed up and sat next to the boy, who cracked his whip across the horse's flanks to set it off down the track. A taciturn man, today Edmond had plenty on his mind that left him unwilling to entertain conversation with the smith's assistant. After some twenty minutes of the cart trundling along, jolting from side to side on the rough surface, the trees thinned, and the sight of buildings indicated that the town lay ahead.

Edmond jumped down, seized his sack, and, without a word of thanks to the boy, walked up the main street to where the market was already bustling. The six writhing eels were soon sold, and the tavern called to him. To the landlord's surprise, Edmond drank only one ale, wished him good day, and departed.

"Hey, Edmond, so soon— " an acquaintance shouted, but too late.

AT THE HOME, Acelin was undoing the leather straps from the shafts of his cart as Edmond arrived.

"Hello, my friend." He looked up.

"Ah, you're here then. I trust you've had a profitable morning?"

"I certainly have — sold six eels in as many minutes —

"They're so slippery, I bet you couldn't keep hold of them," his friend said in a jeering tone, "and, don't forget, that's not where the *real* money is. Anyway, unstrap the other side, and we'll feed and water the horse."

"I've already thought about that. Over there, there's a bucket of water and a pile of hay — you can tie him up to the tree."

"Excellent. Look after your horse, and he'll look after you — I learned that many years ago." He led the animal and tethered it securely.

You'll be fine there until the morning, old boy." Acelin spoke softly, giving it a gentle slap on its haunches. Then, he turned to Edmond, who had observed the last few moments in respectful silence.

"And now, to the reason for me being here. Come, come." He ushered Edmond over to the cart and removed an old cloth that covered an iron trap and a heap of netting.

"They're yours. We can agree on a price

later — I told you the other day I don't do favours for nothing."

"I understand, but first, you'll take food and ale with me — can't go a-hunting on an empty stomach."

"That's true," Acelin agreed, and they went inside the cabin where Jamette had prepared the table with bread, cheese and two beakers as soon as the neighing of a horse told her the guest, who her husband had alluded to earlier, had arrived.

"Greetings to you, Jamette. It's many a long day since we last met. How are you?"

"I'm well, thank you," she answered, "but I did not expect you were his *guest*." Her gaze fixed firmly on the visitor's face, and she continued, with a critical edge to her voice, "So, your calling on us is not unintended…it must concern poaching, am I right?"

"If Edmond has not explained our plan to you, it is not my place to —

At that moment, the husband came in, slapped Acelin on the shoulder, and invited him to sit down at the table.

"Eat and drink, then we have work to attend to."

Her wifely service performed, Jamette

retreated discretely to the rear of the room, leaving the menfolk to their business.

"Time we got going," Acelin concluded. "You carry the net, and I'll take the trap. Now, follow me."

They walked along the forest path, both panting and sweating with their heavy loads. The canopy overhead thickened as they progressed, and their surroundings dimmed. Suddenly, Acelin, in front, stopped short.

"Hush! Not a word!" He put down the trap and cupped a hand to his ear, straining to listen.

"Do you hear that?" he hissed.

"What?"

"Over there." He pointed to their left. "There's boars — now, they've gone. Let's rest while I explain." They sat on a fallen tree trunk. Edmond removed the stopper from a leather bottle tied round his waist and passed it over.

"That tastes good."

"Ay, all my own work, too."

"Now, I know we're near to where they run

because I heard them scatter. They're not cowards, but they're easily frightened if they can't see you. It's when they *do* see you that you've got problems." He listened again. "Come on, but move slowly and keep calm. I don't think they'll bother us until dusk when they hunt down the sows, and we'll have left by then."

The two poachers forged a way through the dense undergrowth until Acelin once more brought them to a halt.

"Here it is — this is their run. See where they've snapped off ferns and trampled the grass?"

"Yes, I see, there's a real trail, isn't there?"

"Sure is. What's strange is they'll use the same run, time after time, sow chased by boar then boar doing its business. Let's get started. The net first. Some men have either a net or a trap, but I like to use both, just in case, as it were — double your chances. See, it's made from best nettle-hemp, knotted to make the mesh. Then, this thicker cord is threaded through one edge. You take one end of the cord and tie it onto yon tree branch, over there, about waist high...that's it...I'll do the other end here."

When the cord was securely fastened, the net hung down across the run like a curtain across a window.

"Good — do you see? A stampeding boar will hurtle straight into it, and the more it struggles to get free, the more entangled it becomes! And now for the trap — bring it down here." The men moved some fifty yards away from the net.

"Watch carefully — next time you won't have me to show you. Mind, there's no skill in it. It's called a leghold trap, for obvious reasons."

The closed jaws had sharp teeth, notched like a saw. He knelt on the snare to prise it open, grunting with the effort required. Once fully apart, he slipped a catch that had a broad pad over the spring, moved his hands away and rose, wiping his brow with his forearm.

"Phew! It's set now."

"It reminds me of when my father once took me to the docks. I saw a boat manned by dark-skinned sailors. On its deck lay the longest shining blue fish I'd ever seen. They sliced it into pieces and sold it to folk on the quayside. Its mouth frightened me out of my wits, rows of pointed white teeth, gaping, wide open. The sailors didn't speak our language, but as they hacked off chunks of meat, they kept calling out the word *shark*! Your leghold trap is a shark's mouth!"

Acelin listened to his friend's tale with interest.

"I don't know about such a fish, but when a boar treads on the pad, it lets off the spring and the jaws snap shut, through to the bone. A real little monster, she is! The beast will probably bleed to death before we get to it, but either way, it's captured."

"It all sounds like easy money to me."

"Spot on, Edmond! We'll come back tomorrow for our spoils."

Dusk descended on the forest as the two of them made their way back down the path to the cabin, smugly satisfied with their work.

CHAPTER TWELVE
LIMOGES (LIMOUSIN), KINGDOM OF ARLES, 1324

"That was truly fine, Jamette," Acelin said in between belches, "my compliments."

"You are most welcome. We receive visitors so rarely, it makes a pleasant change."

She had prepared a vegetable stew and baked fresh bread in the stone oven beside the fireplace. Edmond did not notice, but she had brushed her long auburn hair to a sheen and put on her best embroidered smock. An uneducated woman, she took an avid interest in the world around her, such as it was. With a twinkle of curiosity in her eyes and even white teeth, she was an attractive wife, undervalued by her husband. She often wondered what life would be like away from their rustic cabin, in the company of folk who laughed and sang with abandon and worked hard for a prosperous future. But for Jamette, these were, and would remain, mere dreams.

"Fetch us more drink, my dear," Edmond requested in a kind tone for the benefit of their guest, without its usual harsh edge. Jamette took their beakers to the barrel and refilled them as instructed. Setting them down on the table, she retired to a rocking chair in the corner of the room to pass the evening sewing in silence.

"...AND do you remember the time we put our bets on that mangy old cockerel? They looked at us as if we'd taken leave of our senses, and we got real good odds, didn't we!"

"Ay," Acelin answered wistfully, "but we knew the other had been fed an evil draught that stopped him even seeing straight, let alone putting up a fight! We took our winnings and made off before anyone suspected malpractice. Good times.

"Indeed, and I predict you will have them back again once you've mastered the art of boar hunting."

"I hope so, Acelin, I could certainly use some decent money."

The two men reminisced and drank into the night.

"We'd best get some rest, my friend. There's a busy day ahead tomorrow," Edmond slurred.

NEXT MORNING, they woke with sore heads after the excesses of the previous night and were gratefully revived with fresh water Jamette had drawn from their well. She had also laid out their breakfast of bread, cheese and a basket of wild forest fruits.

"Eat," she encouraged, "you'll need your strength today. I'm guessing you're off into the woods hunting?"

"You're right there, Jamette. And with luck, your Edmond may well have enough money to buy you a new dress!"

Edmond's countenance was sullen. A treat for his wife was not the first thing that he had thought of; raucous drinking sessions at the tavern appealed to him more.

"Sorry," Acelin continued, "I didn't mean to cause a marital dispute. Anyway, we'll bring the boar we've caught back here, and I'll show you what to do with it. After that, you can be off to market, to the delight of all those greedy customers of Limoges." He turned to Jamette,

"You can help, too, by filling yon new cauldron with water and lighting the fire under it, ready for our return."

"Of course, I'll see to that," she replied.

The men pulled heavy capes over their tunics and set off.

"We'll be back by midday, so have food ready for us," Edmond called over his shoulder.

THE EARLY MORNING was cold and crisp but without the slightest breeze, pleasant enough for their passage along the trail leading to the traps they had set the previous day.

Dawn had scarcely broken, the half-light casting shadows and creating imaginary figures between the trees flanking the path. White hoarfrost and frozen dew flew around as they brushed against overhanging shrubbery.

"Not far now."

"Correct. I feel quite excited," Edmond admitted.

"Yes, but don't build up your hopes; we might have caught nothing at all. Mind you, it's the right season for boar. They prefer to come out mating in cool weather, so our luck might be in."

"You should know, Acelin."

Another ten minutes and Acelin brought them to an abrupt halt.

"Down! Down! And quiet," he hissed, tugging his friend's tunic so they knelt below the tops of the surrounding bushes.

"I can hear them snorting and scratching over there. I think it's coming from where we stretched out the net." Then, "Damn it! Nothing!"

The net remained untouched, still perfectly barring the track.

"Never mind, the noise must be from further on by the leghold snare. Come on, but keep low behind me."

Edmond followed these instructions, in awe of the other man's knowledge. Suddenly, a rustling of the undergrowth, accompanied by squealing and scattering sounds, rent the air and seemed to surround them. Edmond instinctively knelt, as before, motionless through apprehension. Acelin parted the branches of a bush, peered through, then exclaimed triumphantly,

"Excellent! See!"

He looked over his companion's shoulder, and as they had hoped, a fat bristly boar lay on its side, whining, whimpering, distressed, its foreleg gripped between the sharp-toothed jaws of the leghold trap. They could not say how long the beast had been snared, but it had to be several hours, and its life was clearly ebbing away.

"Hey! A good morning's work, what say you, Edmond?"

Recovering his composure, he answered,

"Without a doubt. I've never seen the likes."

Acelin drew a dagger from his waistband, approached their catch, and ordered,

"Watch me and learn, boy!"

The victor strode forward with confidence and grasped the boar by a tusk. It did not require a great effort to hold the weakened animal still. With two sharp thrusts he exposed the veins in its neck for blood to seep out, streaming in a pool around it. After a few minutes, all movement ceased and he let go the tusk, replaced his dagger and strained to slowly prise open the jaws.

"Phew!" he said, grunting and rising to his feet. "There he is, one ill-gotten but profitable dead boar and — "

Of a sudden, their joy was destroyed by four burly men who rushed, swords drawn, from all sides.

"Stop! Do not move! We come in the name of Monsieur Dumas on whose land you trespass. We arrest you for the crime of poaching his livestock!" the leader of the men shouted.

In a flash, Acelin dodged between two of the men and was gone, leaving his friend to face the consequences of their hunting expedition.

"Get this one!" commanded the same leader. "Bind him tight."

Edmond's arms were jolted behind him and tied, rendering him defenceless, his legs starting to shake with fear. Another man spun him round, raised a hand and delivered a hard blow to the captive's face, sending him reeling to the ground.

"I do not know the name of your spiritless brother, although you're better off without him — he didn't stay around for long to help you, did he?" he laughed.

The leader resumed,

"So, Edmond Nerval, we're taking you into the safekeeping of Monsieur Dumas for the offence as stated when...oh, bother! We're taking you, that will do." The oaf struggled to string together anything but a simple sentence. Edmond failed to wonder how they knew his name: but tongues wag, especially when ale has loosened them. "It will be up to him to decide what to do with you, but he's a man who does not take kindly to this sort of thing." Aiming a casual kick into Edmond's ribs, he ordered,

"Get up, man! Up!"

Edmond struggled to his feet, his head still spinning, to be marched off, two of his captors prodding him from behind, the other two leading the way ahead.

AT THE NERVAL CABIN, Jamette was surprised by a furious banging at the door.

"Jamette! Let me in!" came a frenzied call.

"I'm coming, I'm coming!"

Acelin faced her on the threshold, panting for breath, sweat running down his face. Without waiting for an invitation, he pushed past her and entered the home. He sat, exhausted, at the table, and while he regained himself, she filled a beaker from the barrel.

"There, drink that. What on earth has happened, and where is Edmond?"

"We were ambushed — didn't stand a chance. Dumas's men came out of nowhere — huge brutes, too! I managed to escape after a hand-to-hand fight with one of them — I tried my best," he lied, "but they got Edmond. I'd guess they've taken him to the Dumas chateau."

"And did they know he was poaching?"

"Of course, you stupid woman, they caught us red-handed! But there's nothing I can do to help him now, it's all part of the game — "

"Game! You call it a game? Get out! Out of my sight!" she screamed, feeling a need to stand up for her husband for the first time in their relationship. Acelin wanted no further bidding. He left the cabin, never to be seen again.

DUMAS'S MEN forced Edmond along the track leading to the chateau, ridiculing him, prodding him without mercy. Hands tied tightly behind his back, he stumbled every so often only for one or another of the men to give a kick to make him stand up and continue on his way. They went through the stout wooden gates and up the drive leading to the imposing ivy-clad house where the Dumas family had lived for generations. Although not of noble ancestry, they curried the favour of dukes and even kings by virtue of their wealth.

Before the main house, Edmond was pushed towards a row of low stone outbuildings. The leader of the gang untied his arms, then ordered,

"In there!" He steered him through an open door into a windowless cell. The door slammed shut, and he was pitched into complete darkness. He felt along the walls, and the only solid object he found was a bucket filled with water. In one corner was a pile of dirty straw, nothing more. Fatigued and in pain from his mistreatment, he drank then collapsed onto the straw bed, falling into a deep, uneasy slumber.

HE WOKE — hours or even days later, time was lost — by daylight flooding the place as the door opened. The figure of a man outlined in the doorway threw in a chunk of brown rye bread, calling,

"There's your dinner! Enjoy it, we don't know how many more you have left!"

With a cruel chuckle, he shut the door, and Edmond's prison was once again plunged into darkness. Cold and afraid of what his fate might be — for he was very aware of punishments that had been meted out to poachers he knew — he forced himself to eat some of the crude bread, drank some water and fell back onto the straw.

'What have I done to deserve this? Now, there's a question for the Lord above to answer! What use has going to Caron's damned confession achieved? And all that time, cooped up in his confounded little box, waiting for him to ask, "What sins do you confess before the Good Lord?" — all so that the priest wouldn't give my game away to Dumas. Ah, now I see it; it must be him who's told the old man where to find us. Yet, how could he have known...'

Edmond abandoned any hopes of discovering the truth and resumed sleep in the total obscurity of the cell, his very soul tormented and his spirit weak. All manner of punishment ran through his mind.

. . .

BACK AT THE CABIN, Jamette sat in front of the fire, watching the sparks leap and the embers glow. She sipped Edmond's liquor from a beaker — normally, she did not take alcohol, reasoning that her husband drank enough for the two of them. Despite the quarrelsome nature of their marriage, she respected their wedding vows and remained loyal and supportive to him.

'What can I do to rescue him? I've heard say that Dumas is a cruel man who beats his servants and dismisses his workers on a whim. So, what hope for Edmond?'

As her thoughts raced, seeking a solution and taking more drink, an idea flashed into her head.

'I have it! I will attend confession and explain our plight to Father Caron. He will help, and I know he has Dumas's ear. Yes, that's what I will do. Now, what day are we...ah, on Friday this week it's his day to take confession. I remember that Edmond does it before going on to market. I just hope he won't die of shock when he realises that I have, of a sudden, become a religious woman.'

Considering her terrible situation, she slept

well that night, confident that the power of the Church would influence Monsieur Dumas to show clemency with, at worst, a day in the stocks to alert the townsfolk of Limoges of his crime, not that they needed much alerting, such was his reputation. Friday soon arrived.

"WHAT SINS DO you wish to confess?" came a voice she instantly recognised from the grill dividing priest from confessor.

"Father, forgive me, for I have not always been the best wife to my husband."

"My child, that is not necessarily a sin. We are all prone to finding human relationships difficult, and the Good Lord gives us guidance — "

Jamette interrupted him.

"You do not understand, Father. Do you know who I am?"

"I think I do not, but I do not require names to absolve the soul."

"Please, listen to me. I am Jamette Nerval, and I plead for your help with a most serious ill that has befallen my husband, Edmond."

"Ah, I thought to have recognised your voice, Jamette, but you will see that this is most irregular. The confessional is not a fitting place for advice." He paused to consider her request.

"Father, are you still there?"

"Yes, of course I am, my child. I admit that over the last year I have been impressed by Edmond's attendance for confession — I did not think he would honour his word to me, but I was wrong." He paused once more.

"Present yourself at my office this afternoon, and we will discuss your problem in private."

"Father, I do not have the words to thank you — "

"I promise you nothing, Jamette, and the Lord will direct me. Until this afternoon."

JAMETTE LEFT the Eglise Evangélique and wandered up to the market to pass time until her appointment with the priest. Roaming around the stalls, she met many women that she knew, and those she had not seen for some time were, naturally, inquisitive concerning her affairs.

"Jamette! Now where have you been hiding away? How is Edmond?"

It seemed that the world was asking her how Edmond fared. She said simply,

"He's well, thank you. I will say you asked after him." Her voice feigned pleasure.

She could say no more and hoped the worry etched on her face did not betray a very different reality. It was with both relief and trepidation that she heard the sext bell ring — time for her to meet Caron and implore his assistance to have her husband released.

'What if he says he cannot help? What then?'

SHE ENTERED the church through a side door, reluctant to be seen by anyone. But there was no need to have worried; the dark interior was deserted. She found Caron's office without difficulty, its door bearing his name. She knocked gently and waited.

"Enter. Ah, it's you, Jamette, come in and sit down, please." He indicated a chair in front of his desk, laden with yellowing rolled parchment sheets and a heavy leather-bound bible.

"You said that Edmond has a problem."

"More than a *problem*, Father. He has been

caught poaching boar, and Monsieur Dumas's men have taken him away to — "

Overcome by the events of the last few days, she broke down, sobbing uncontrolledly.

"Now, now, compose yourself. Monsieur Dumas is an honourable God-fearing man, and from my dealings with him, I would say he is reasonable and open-minded. Leave the matter with me, Jamette, and I'll see what can be done." She was heartened that he so readily agreed to assist her.

"My sincerest thanks, Father Caron."

"Go now."

LATER THAT DAY, Caron and Dumas exchanged pleasantries and shared a bottle of the man's fine claret in front of a roaring fire.

"So, you see there's no gain in further punishing this wretched man. He is my parishioner and leads an honest life, doing his best to provide for his wife. They have nothing. Sometimes, days will pass without food on their table, so I would intercede, in my capacity as the Lord's representative here on earth, and ask your noble forgiveness. God favours those who show mercy, as is His wont. What say you, Dumas?"

"Mmm...more wine, Father? It's our best vintage."

"For medicinal purposes only, you understand." The priest drank Dumas's claret and resumed,

"What's more, if this case were brought before the Magistrate, he might well argue that the forest is not a part of your estate and, therefore, not under your jurisdiction. It would have an adverse effect on your good name. People might view you as some sort of tyrant who usurped his rights and subdued the common man." Caron leant back in his armchair and drank more wine, a smug expression on his countenance following his well-reasoned argument.

"IF YOU PUT it like that, Caron, I have to agree with you. If it got back to King Alfonso's court... We enjoy an enviable arrangement with His Majesty when it comes to paying our land taxes and customs duty on our wines, and that must be protected at all costs. So, I'll let the man go free. Satisfied, Caron?"

"Indeed. Monsieur will receive his rewards in heaven, I'm sure of that."

EDMOND BLINKED hard to adjust his view of the burly figure standing in the doorway to his cell, silhouetted in the bright morning sunshine.

"Get out!" barked the man. "And we'd better not see you around here again. Hope you learned your lesson. Out!"

Helped on his way by a hefty kick to his backside, he needed no further encouragement.

Edmond Nerval could not have known — nor would he have cared — that the intervention of Father Caron on his behalf had been replicated six years earlier many miles away in the town of Cuenca, situated in the Kingdom of Spain. On that occasion, a certain Father Gelmiro beseeched his bishop to show clemency for a poor farmer fallen on hard times who was thus faced with eviction and ruin. The bishop demonstrated compassion and continued the farmer's tenancy in perpetuity. Along with Caron's actions, the two instances were evidence of the Church's power to influence, intervene and boldly display a caring merciful attitude towards its flocks.

THE POACHER ENTERED his humble cabin and, to his wife's surprise, embraced her even before he spoke.

"We were checking the boar traps we had set, me and Acelin. Without warning, Monsieur Dumas's men seized us — or rather, seized *me*; Acelin got away. They took me to the chateau and threw me into a cell."

"I know this. Acelin came here and described everything."

"He didn't try to help, he just fled. But why was I freed? I can't explain that."

"Father Caron."

"What do you mean?"

"I do not know how or why, but he pleaded your case with Dumas and — "

"So, me going to his lousy confession turned out to be a wise move!"

She nodded, deciding to take no credit for her own part in Dumas's decision.

"I can see now. I have all too often been lacking as a husband, and I intend to make amends." Jamette said nothing but returned his embrace. She was overwhelmed by such kind words, the likes of which she had not known from him. She had other news, but it could wait until he was rested.

THE FOLLOWING DAY, Edmond ate breakfast. His wife sat next to him.

"Edmond, I have something to tell you."

"As long as it's good news —

"It is, or at least I hope you will think it so. I am with child."

"Repeat that."

"I am with child. Two months gone for certain. A woman knows these things."

He rose from the table, donned his cape, and made for the door.

"I am taking a walk. I need to consider the situation."

She all but swooned with emotion.

'The Lord help me if he is displeased. He will blame it on me, and just when I see a change in the man for the better...'

He returned some two hours later. Smiling and trying hard to control his happiness, he said,

"I hope for a son! But there is no future for us here in Limoges. In the new year we will move to Carpentras, where our son will be born."

"Carpentras, how so? We have nothing to do with that place."

"I have not mentioned it to you before because I did not consider it a serious prospect. Let me explain. Pour us both a drink; we have reason to celebrate." His manner was gentler and more protective than she had seen since their first days of courtship.

"I met a man in the tavern who was here on business, a merchant trading in fine cloths, if I recall correctly. In the course of our conversation, I confided that I had to resort to illegal activities for a living. *'My dear fellow, that's no life, is it? In my hometown of Carpentras — you will not be familiar with it — there's an inn that needs a tenant. The old landlord died just last month, and I could put in a good word for you with the duke who owns it. Upon my say, he'd give it to you, I'm sure. Let me know if you're interested.'* I thanked him for the proposition but declined. That was before our recent good fortune, and times are different now. I'll not be poaching anymore, and I'm about to become a father! It's high time I earned honest money, so we'll take the tenancy, I've decided, after Christmas, ready for the new arrival. What do you say?"

She was taken aback but readily agreed, yearning for a better existence away from Limoges and its painful memories.

Their son, Marius, was born in Carpentras, 1325.

CHAPTER THIRTEEN
CUENCA, KINGDOM OF SPAIN, SPRING 1319

Some months had passed since the old man's funeral in the cathedral, when Father Gelmiro had noticed the silent but obvious hostility between Father Nicolás and Albornoz. Seeing them within sight of each other, the gazes they exchanged were so intense and burning such as to melt ice into water in an instant. When he had reason, Albornoz at his side, to converse with Nicolás, the man and boy did not say a word, their countenances dour. His disquiet grew until he felt compelled to confront his pupil.

One day, their lesson concluded, Albornoz was about to leave the priest's house.

"Sit, my boy."

"Father?"

"Sit. There is a matter about which I must question you."

The boy sat at the table, wondering what the old man had to say.

"Father Nicolás is a good priest. He fulfils his parish duties as I direct, and who am I to doubt the intentions of a righteous man? He seeks neither promotion nor favour."

"So, why must you question *me*?"

Gelmiro paused before answering, aware of the need to choose words that would elicit a response concerning a serious subject from a mere child.

"Do you have cause to dislike Father Nicolás?"

The question was to the point, focused on his genuine worry.

"I do not understand."

"There is an atmosphere verging on hatred when you are in each other's company, and I would know why this is so. Do you have anything to tell me?"

Albornoz bowed his head and did not reply for an interminable time. Then,

"I saw Father Nicolás in the sacristy."

"And what of that?"

"He was not alone. Another priest — I do not know his name — sat beside him. They kissed and placed their hands under the other's habit. Their breathing was heavy, and they made strange noises."

"Ah, I see. And did Father Nicolás see you watching them?"

"Although the door was only ajar, he did see me, and he stopped at once, pulling his robe down and shuffling away from his colleague. I left as quickly as I could."

"Was that all?"

"No. He came across me in the town and beat me in an alley, ordering me to never reveal what I had seen to anyone. Do you remember, Father, when you explained to me the meaning of *righteous*?"

"Indeed, I do."

"You told me that in order to be righteous, a man should attend church, not curse, pay his tithe, treat his servants well, but...can a man perform such acts as did Father Nicolás and still be righteous? According to what you said, he shall not enter the Kingdom of God, but burn in the fires of Hell. That is what you taught me."

Gelmiro had already known about the

deviant relationship between Nicolás and the other priest, as had the clerical community of Cuenca. They all chose to turn a blind eye. How could he satisfy Albornoz's intellectual inquiring mind? Did he expect the boy to appreciate nuances, shades of meaning that permeated every verse of the Holy Book?

"Of course, I did not witness what you saw and — " He was interrupted.

"What does the Bible say on the matter?"

Gelmiro was taken aback by such an incisive question and could not immediately quote any relevant passages.

"What you ask is…is reasonable. So, let us see." He opened the leather-bound volume on the table and searched for suitable chapters.

"Here it is, Jude, chapter seven." Then he read,

'Sodom and Gomorrah and the surrounding cities, which likewise indulged in sexual immorality and pursued unnatural desires, serve as examples by undergoing a punishment of eternal fire.' He turned to another page.

'You shall not lie with a male as with a woman, it is an abomination.'

"That is Leviticus eighteen. Then we have Romans, where they talk of *'impure lusts,'* '*dishonourable passions*,' '*a debased mind*,' and '*all manner of unrighteousness*.' Now, Albornoz, as a child you should not, *must not*, concern yourself unduly about adult behaviour — "

"Adult behaviour!" The boy's tone rose from inquisitive to being aggressive, demanding, angry.

"Father, I do not need telling that what Nicolás and the other priest were doing in the sacristy is *wrong*. The verses from the Bible you have just read out say it is so. *It was wrong!*"

They both fell silent, the tension palpable, the expectation acute. Gelmiro closed the Bible, pushed it away, and took a deep breath.

"The Good Book is composed of many accounts of the events before, during and after our Lord Jesus's time on earth. They survive as a shining beacon for our guidance and enlightenment. However — "

"Yes, Father?" Albornoz cut in, sensing a qualifying statement.

"However, the Church, in its wisdom, interprets these articles of faith for our...for our understanding, as relevant to our own lives. Who knows, one day you may study theology yourself. Religious texts are not as exact or distinct as they might at first appear.

Their meanings can have *grey* areas, if you follow."

"I do follow, Father! Perhaps I am not familiar with some of your fancy words, but I understand your meaning. So, please tell me, is Father Nicolás a *righteous man*? The answer, in the light of what I observed, is yes or no, without your *grey areas*."

Gelmiro had not felt more uncomfortable in all his days as a priest. Never had he been asked to justify the behaviour of any cleric under his authority. He wiped his brow on his sleeve and wrung his hands together in agitation. He knew he could not denounce Nicolás.'*The Church must stand united in its beliefs, protective of its clergy.*'

"Albornoz, my dear boy, you must leave this matter with me. I undertake to examine the priest in question, and if he admits to carrying out *unnatural deeds*, he will fully repent his sins in confession."

In Albornoz's young eyes, Nicolás had done wrong and should receive a punishment far greater than mere penance. He rose from the table, gave Gelmiro a withering glare, and left the house without further comment. His intransigent perception of good and bad would become embedded in his missionary vision as he progressed his theological studies and rise to power in the Church.

Albornoz's lessons with Gelmiro continued, but the issue concerning Nicolás was not mentioned again. It came to the lad's notice that the errant priest and his friend were no longer to be seen in the town of Cuenca.

LATE SUMMER 1319

ALBORNOZ ENJOYED the routine of morning lessons with Father Gelmiro, accompanying him in the cathedral for weddings and funerals, then swimming and playing with his friends down by the river. Physical contact between him and Madelena grew, naturally, both of them at the age of puberty.

One afternoon as he returned home, he was surprised to see Gelmiro leaving the house, nodding politely, and going on his way.

Within, his father and mother sat side by side at their dining table.

"Albornoz, good, we were waiting for you — you have done nothing wrong, so do not worry. Go and wash, then we must talk with you," Garcia said in a brusque tone. Albornoz did as he was told then joined his parents, sitting opposite them.

"We have spoken with Father Gelmiro — "

"Yes, I saw him leaving — "

"Quite." His father's voice was softer. "Your mother and I have pondered your situation for a while. You are of an age to move on in your life." Albornoz's mouth opened, and a look of concern furrowed his brow. Garcia went on,

"Your mother's opinion is that your future lies in the Church — a priest, for all I know! Father Gelmiro estimates that he has taught you sufficiently — your questioning, your thirst for knowledge, in his words, challenge him. He calls you a *precocious talent* and reasons that it is time for a properly qualified mentor to assume his role. On the other hand, it is my contention that you should enter the military, as your brothers have. How do we reconcile these two different career pathways? Gelmiro has the answer."

"What is it, father?" he asked, his voice trembling.

"You will become a pupil at the Castle of Calatrava. You will not have heard of this place. It is a town three days' journey from here."

"When am I to leave?" He knew it was futile to fight the decision.

"Within the week. You will serve as an *intern* — a student who eats and sleeps there."

"I do not understand you. When will I return home?"

"Calatrava is to *be* your home for the coming year. We may visit you there, but we do not intend to interrupt your studies."

This unexpected announcement overwhelmed the boy, causing him to break down in tears, sobbing violently.

"Now, now, none of that. See to him, woman!"

Teresa moved to sit by her son. She put a comforting arm around his shoulders and pulled him to her ample bosom. His sobs gradually ceased.

"As I was saying, our decision is final, and you should be grateful for such an opportunity. None of your friends will ever have an experience like it. You are a privileged young man, and don't forget it! In his generosity, my Lord Bishop has met the cost of hiring a horse and cart. You see, it is useful to move within the circles of important people, although I will fund your tuition fees. Father Gelmiro will accompany you."

"Is it a school then, father?" he asked meekly.

"Of sorts. A long time ago, King Alfonso the Seventh needed to enlarge his army, there being many conflicts in his kingdom. In the castle resided a papal order of Cistercian brothers, with Abbot Raymond its superior. When the latter heard of the king's lack of troops, he offered his monks, who became known as *Soldiers of the Cross.* So, the lay friars trained as a militia, independent in temporal matters, but at the same time learning of spiritual affairs. You, Alvarez Carillo Gil de Albornoz, will grow as a proud Cistercian Soldier of the Cross, in the Order of Calatrava. In this, your mother and I are satisfied that your capabilities will be fully employed to ensure a rewarding, God-fearing future. What say you, Albornoz?"

Fear gripped him. He would have to leave

his parents and the home of his birth to become the young man he was, this auspicious day. He knew he would have to abandon his friends, Madelena in particular, and the duties he had so taken to in the cathedral.

The following afternoon, he met those friends and broke the news to them.

"You're a lucky lad! Wish it was me..."

"I'm glad it's not happening to me..."

Most reactions were polarised — either like or hatred for the idea — although some were ambivalent.

"That's life, Albornoz. Just the way it is..."

Happily, Madelena was there that day. He embraced her, and they kissed with a youthful lustiness. It would be their final meeting.

After dinner, he sat on his bed staring out at the starry void beyond Cuenca. Those stars comforted him and fired his determination to succeed in the next chapter of his life. As he drifted into sleep, through half-closed eyes, he looked at his beloved model cog boat and was so sad he could not have it with him in Calatrava.

CALATRAVA, KINGDOM OF SPAIN, AUTUMN 1319

THE POSTILION REINED the horse and cart to a halt outside Garcia's house, then leapt agilely from the front seat to the ground. He gave the animal a hearty slap to its flanks and tied it to an iron tethering ring set into the wall. Gelmiro was sitting under the cart's covered top, pleased to be sheltered from a rainstorm whipped up by icy blasts of air, common weather for this time of year. Day had not broken, the surrounding houses in darkness, the only light a flickering candle visible inside the Albornoz residence. The Bishop's post boy tapped on the front door, soon opened by the maid. He entered without speaking and a few moments later emerged carrying a small wooden trunk that he fixed securely to the rear of the cart. On the threshold, Albornoz's mother hugged her son, and Garcia shook his hand.

The cold, wet, miserable weather perfectly reflected the boy's mood: he was not prepared to the move away from his family and friends, and whereas his interest in religious matters grew apace, he failed to understand how things military would feature in or enhance his life. He turned around and gave his parents one last rueful wave. Pulling his cape tight on his shoulders, he hauled himself up to sit next to the priest.

"A very good morning to you."

"And to you, also, Father. But I do not think there's anything good about it."

"Take heart! It is for the best, believe me."

The postilion untied the horse's reins, took his place on the driver's bench and called to his passengers,

"All ready, gentlemen?" Receiving no reply, he repeated the question and the priest responded,

"Ay! We are ready."

The cart creaked as the horse took up the strain and the cart rumbled down the street and across the Plaza Mayor, its steel-rimmed wheels rattling on the cobblestones, singing an eerie duet with the horse's shoes. No one was about to appreciate their passing.

Through the Jewish quarter, they left the town's boundary by a gateway in the walls and headed down towards the Huécar river, a swirling, foaming mass of currents churned further upstream by seasonal rainstorms. The road shortly gave way to a narrow track following the riverbank. After some fifteen minutes, with the town well behind them, that track became rutted and in parts muddied through the now relentless rainfall. For a lesser horse, the effort of drawing a cart and two passengers in such conditions would have proven too much, but the Bishop, in his bounty and as an expression of the esteem in which he held his friend, Garcia, had provided one of his finest steeds for the journey. The boy, unlike the two sitting behind him, was unprotected from the elements and let out an almost incessant stream of oaths — some unfamiliar still to the ears of an enlightened man like Gelmiro.

The cart bumped along the track, the two passengers passing the time in conversation about all manner of subjects. The priest enjoyed his pupil's lively questioning mind, even when the issue was contentious or sensitive. For too many years, his intellectual aptitude had been starved by the predictable traditional dogma of the Church establishment.

"We learn that Mary was Jesus's mother, but who was his father?" Then,

"When we die, is that the end of everything?" And,

"Why were the people so insane as to choose Barabbas, a murderer, to go free, yet condemn the Lord Jesus to death?"

Gelmiro answered Albornoz's questions honestly, according to his beliefs and learning. However, he was taken aback by one enquiry.

"Why have I not seen Father Nicolás in the church or around the town for this last year? We have not mentioned his name since — "

"Indeed, my boy," he interrupted, "he has gone to serve another parish and...and it is far from Cuenca."

"Is that so, Father?" The tone of voice was definitely suspicious.

"Why, yes. The other priest in the...how to put it...in the affair has also moved on. No need to be concerned on that score anymore."

'He is lying. The Church will not admit that what they did was wrong.'

THE POOR WEATHER changed to sunshine with a gentle breeze, and they covered a good distance that first day. They reached their overnight stop, a small village inn, before nightfall. The landlord had been forewarned of their arrival, and as the horse snorted and whinnied, shaking its head from side to side with its exertion, a lad came out to greet them.

"Welcome. My father - the landlord — says for you to take your horse and cart to the stable just around the corner. There's hay and fresh water ready."

The postilion held the horse's bridle while the travellers climbed down and entered the tavern. A roaring log fire, spotlessly swept floor, and a rotund, jovial proprietor combined to make for a satisfactory ending to the first day of their journey.

"Greetings, gentlemen, greetings. The Bishop has advised me of your requirements, which we are honoured to fulfil. Sit, pray. Your meal will be served shortly." He ushered them to a table covered with a crisp white linen cloth by the fire. A woman, just as rotund and jovial as her husband, appeared at the counter with a foaming pitcher from which she filled pewter tankards, then placed them on the table.

"It is good to have you visit our humble

abode," she said, a toothless smile beaming from ear to ear. She clapped her hands, and the son who had met them outside emerged from the kitchen with two steaming bowls of pottage made from peas, carrots, beans and onions; a dark rye grain loaf, and the meal was complete. They both enjoyed a deep, restful sleep that night.

TWO MORE DAYS TRAVELLING, with a further night's accommodation at another inn, and their journey was nearing its end but not before Albornoz had asked his mentor what the Cistercians were about.

"They are known as *Whitemonks* because they wear a white *cuccula* — a choir robe over their habit. They are self-sufficient, growing and rearing all they need, and for this reason, manual labour in the fields is essential and expected of each monk. They often come from knightly families, and therein is the association between the Whitemonks and royalty. They believe in poverty, chastity and obedience, their three fundamental vows, with silence observed for three days a week. When not silent, they recite a number of Pater Noster prayers throughout the day. In short, Albornoz, their devotion to duty depends on a strong inner self."

"I wonder if I will live up to their expectations."

"Worry not; once you have settled in, you will be more than adequate."

"God willing," came the reply, full of doubt and apprehension.

THE TRACK PASSED through a heavily wooded area, then into clear pasture, widening as it approached Calatrava. The town had an ordinary appearance: tightly arranged houses along narrow streets, squares and alleys leading off — what one might expect, but to the west, atop a rocky outcrop stood the castle. Thick, crenelated outer walls, rising from a moat long since dry, showed small death holes through which defenders could fire a mortal barrage of arrows at attackers. From these walls it was evident the castle boasted two levels, testament to the wealth and importance of whichsoever lord kept his household there. Within the walls, barracks for the garrison, stables, workshops, storage buildings and residences — the military nature of its construction an aspect of former troubled times. Now, the clergy, in the guise of Cistercian monks, occupied the whole castle. All commoners lived outside the stronghold as was necessary to perpetrate the difference in status between Church and citizens.

The cart entered through the main gate, its iron portcullis permanently raised in a time of peace, into a courtyard, lined — strangely for a military edifice — on three sides with cloistered walkways. The postilion held the horse still while Gelmiro and Albornoz stepped down. A monk, dressed as the old priest had described in a brown habit covered around the shoulders with a white cuccula, approached the cart.

"Father Gelmiro and Albornoz. In the name of the Lord, I welcome you to the holy castle of Calatrava."

"Amen to that," came the instant reply from the priest.

"I hope your journey went well. Albornoz, follow me, please. I will show you to your dormitory."

Gelmiro gripped his pupil, hugging him close like a father to his son.

"Farewell, my dear boy. Work hard, listen and learn. This is a wonderful opportunity — your first step on a ladder that will surely take you on to great things. God bless you."

An assistant monk untied the wooden trunk, and the cart was turned around, ready to depart. A tear ran down the boy's cheek, so deep was his sadness to lose his teacher and friend, and words were unnecessary: he simply gave a wry smile and followed the Whitemonk into the cloisters to embrace the next chapter in his remarkable life. He could not have been aware that this was the last time he would see Father Gelmiro: four weeks after returning to Cuenca, he passed away peacefully in his sleep.

CHAPTER FOURTEEN
CALATRAVA, KINGDOM OF SPAIN,
LATE 1319

At the end of the cloisters, a flight of stone steps led to the first floor of a building that had other steps along its length. There sat the dormitories for novices and monks of lesser rank than those who performed designated functions within the monastery and resided in their own single-room accommodations.

The Whitemonk who had met Albornoz introduced himself.

"I am Brother Aldonso. Throughout your stay with us here, I will be your supervisor and, particularly during the time until you become established, you may direct any questions or concerns to me. I am here to help." Seeing the expression of fear and confusion in the boy's countenance, he was quick to reassure him.

"Do not be afraid, my boy. It is natural that you should be uncertain and overawed. This is a new world for you, but I am sure you will do well. You come highly recommended by the Lord Bishop of Cuenca. Come, follow me."

They climbed the steps and entered the first dormitory. The interior was gloomy and cold, the only daylight penetrating through one small window, and that at head height. Four candles in holders flickered in a draught that swirled around the place, producing strange, otherworldly shadows, and Albornoz blinked several times to adjust his sight. The room contained six mattresses on each side with coarse woollen blankets, neatly folded. On pegs set into the wall, nightshirts hung, the only sign of any clothing. At the foot of one bed, at the end of the row, was his small wooden trunk.

"This is where you will sleep," said Aldonso softly. It stood out from the others by a dark garment, again neatly folded next to the blanket, a leather belt and a pair of sandals.

"Undress, please, and put on this black robe — we call it a habit. All novices, for that is what we call newcomers, wear it to distinguish you from the brothers who have taken vows." He waited while Albornoz followed his instructions and pulled on the habit.

"There, you have now put your past behind you, and you can look to a dutiful, rewarding future, in prayer and devotion to the Lord Jesus Christ."

A bell sounded.

"Your previous life will not have been ordered by the ringing of a bell, Albornoz. Suffice it to say that the way we use our time reveals who we are. In our day, prayer comes first, and as the church is the focal point of the castle buildings, so prayer — in common and alone — is the focal point of our monastic day. You will become familiar with the different tolls. That is vespers, the call to evening prayer. I will show you to the church, and after the service you will join us for supper in the refectory."

"Refectory, sir?" Albornoz asked, disappointed at not understanding this new word.

"Call me *Brother*, if you will. The refectory

is the dining hall where we take our meals. Now, we must go to the church."

Tired after the journey to Calatrava and troubled by these unfamiliar surroundings and what lay ahead, it was with a heavy heart that he left the dormitory and walked by Aldonso's side to vespers. They crossed the courtyard and passed through an archway to the church: a long low building with a pitched roof, incongruous with a place of worship. *'More like a stable block,'* he mused. The supervisor noticed the boy's furrowed brow.

"Are you surprised that this is our church?"

"It is not like any I have seen."

"Remember, every building within the castle walls originally served a military purpose — guardroom, barrack, prison, stable, weapons store, whatever — but since the Cistercian Order came, it is a house of God. Lay brothers are responsible for the training of soldiers; it is a requirement demanded by the King for our continued residence and his support here. Some novices, like yourself, will undergo a soldier's education in addition to religious studies. But enough of that. Let us attend vespers."

. . .

THEY JOINED the line of Whitemonks filing into the church through a wooden door of simple construction. Aldonso leaned over Albornoz and whispered,

"Inside, apart from the Abbot leading the service and our replies at his invitation to respond, we observe total silence. Silence is, of course, an essential tenet of the Order: when you talk to others, you share earthly thoughts, but in silence you are talking to God. Everything will be clear, and it is my responsibility to help you in this respect. I have special dispensation from the Abbot to talk with you in places where in the future it will be prohibited."

Through the door stood a stone stoup filled with holy water for the supplicants to cross themselves with on entering. The benches to either side of the nave were taken, row after row, with tonsured monks in spotless white cucculas, heads bowed. A simple wooden altar bore two brass candlesticks and an open bible. To the left of the altar, four monks holding parchment sheets sang a low chant that floated gently up and around the unaffected, simple place, lending a feeling of mystery and reverence that Albornoz had never experienced. From oil lamps fixed at intervals along the walls glowed a soft orange, mellow, peaceful light. Placing his hand on the boy's shoulder, the supervisor guided his novice down the nave to the front benches, occupied to the left and right by figures who stood out from the rest of the assembly by their black habits — novices like himself.

"Sit here," whispered Aldonso, indicating a space on the bench. "After the service I will speak with you further."

Albornoz sat where told. The person next to him did not look up, sitting motionless. Head lowered. As a tall fresh-faced monk appeared in front of the altar, the singing stopped. The others wore no accessories save their cucculas — but this man's status was shown by a silver crucifix on a chain round his neck. He was Abbot Sabastian, head monk of the Cistercian Brothers of Calatrava.

Opening the book held ceremoniously in his hands, he began to recite a verse, or was it a prayer — Albornoz knew not which. Although the abbot's voice carried around the church, his words were mumbled, but it did not matter overly to the young novice.

'When I entered this monastery earlier today, I was filled with dread, afraid of the unknown, and convinced that I would not live up to the expectations of my parents, Father Gelmiro or the Bishop of Cuenca. But a strange sensation surrounds me, and a powerful spirit enters my very soul. I need fear nothing. Such relief! Such happiness!'

VESPERS CONTINUED, and Albornoz rose and sat down as the novice beside him did. Shuffling, but not a single spoken word, indicated the end of the service, and everyone began slowly walking down the nave to exit the church. Brother Aldonso was waiting outside.

"Did you enjoy your first vespers?" he whispered, although everyone knew he was not breaking the vow of silence in his mentor role.

"I did, Brother, and I am excited for whatever lies ahead, except I could not hear clearly a word that left the Abbot's mouth — "

"Ah, I am not surprised you say that. Abbot Sabastian, the youngest Cistercian to ever hold the office of Abbot and a most learned man, is not the best of speakers. I trust you will get used to him, and they say Julius Caesar spoke with a stammer, but he was reasonably successful as an orator."

Albornoz smiled and followed the man out of the courtyard towards another low building.

"This is the refectory."

Three heavy oak tables with benches on either side ran the length of the hall. The tables were laid with bowls, spoons, tankards, and baskets of bread. Chatter and laughter showed that the vow of silence, as the brother had said, did not apply in the refectory.

"Let us sit and take pleasure in the Good Lord's bounty."

Albornoz needed no further invitation; he had a huge appetite after the day's journey and reception at the castle.

Some monks wearing white aprons came through a side door and ladled a soup of vegetables and pork into the bowls, while others filled the tankards with ale from leather bottles. Albornoz ate with gusto, his well-being enhanced by the jovial atmosphere in the room. The meal eaten, Aldonso said,

"Now, come with me to my study. There is much to tell you."

. . .

ON ENTERING THE ROOM, Aldonso removed his cuccula, hung it on a peg, then beckoned his novice to sit in the chair in front of his desk. He paced across the room several times as if in thought, then he, too, sat. He started,

"There are many things to say about our community, but at the end of your first day, it is better to inform you of just a few important things you should know."

Albornoz saw intelligence in the man's sharp blue eyes and heard a softness in his voice.

"When a novice takes his vows upon one year's satisfactory completion of his training, he undertakes three oaths: poverty, chastity and obedience. You will come to appreciate these oaths fully as the days and months unfold. I always think that the last one, obedience, should be the first to consider. Do you believe that obedience is important, my boy?"

"With all my heart, Brother. I have seen things already in my short life, and by people who should know better, that convince me of it. Right is the direct, unquestionable opposite of wrong, and there should be no confusing or blurring the distinction between them — that is the word of God." The *people who should know better* were the two lascivious priests he had observed indulging their unhealthy desires in the sacristy.

"I could not agree more." The Brother was taken unawares by his novice's profound and passionate utterances, not at all usual for such a boy on his first day with them.

"To continue, we maintain silence in the church, the cloisters and the dormitories, after lights out. Elsewhere, conversation will always be kept to a respectful level. We live in solitude and silence, and we aspire to that interior quiet in which wisdom is born. We practice self-denial in order to follow Christ. Through humility and obedience, we struggle against pride and sin, and in simplicity and labour, we seek the humbleness that is promised to the poor."

'I cannot find anything to contest what he is saying. I can see how straightforward and singular it is to become righteous. It seems to me that he who strays from the path that the Lord shows us is a man who does not open his eyes and chooses

whatever retribution the Church dictates,' the novice decided. Aldonso resumed,

"The atmosphere of silence has long been counted among the principal monastic values of the Order. It opens the mind to the inspiration of the Holy Spirit and fosters attentiveness of the heart and solitary prayer to God. And yet, we do not adhere to total silence when, for example, in the far courtyard for military training. Then, we cultivate a field, outside the walls, where we converse pleasantly with the local folk passing by. One day every week, we have a stall in the market over in the town where we sell produce that we do not need for ourselves — the money goes straight into the Abbot's purse for safe keeping; the castle frequently requires maintenance. So, we could not sell anything to anyone *in silence,* could we?"

"Certainly not, Brother."

"But the oath of silence does not apply to those places, so we are breaking no rules. Is everything clear to you so far?"

"No, actually...there is one thing..."

"What is that?"

"You tell me that the Order's profit from the market is received by the Abbot. That cannot be right. The poor people of Calatrava are not concerned with maintaining the castle when they do not have the wherewithal to put food on their tables. We should give away what *we* do not need, so the Abbot would do well to read Isiah 55:1:

'Ho! Everyone who thirsts, come to the waters. And you who have no money, come, buy and eat. Come, buy wine and milk. Without money and without cost.'

Aldonso was amazed by the lad's knowledge of the Scriptures and his ability to select, seemingly at will, a verse to support his argument. Disconcerted, the monk moved on.

"THERE ARE two services in the church that you are obliged to attend each day: early morning before breakfast and in the evening before dinner. You see, we associate our praising the Lord with eating food." He paused, waiting for his weak attempt at humour to elicit a smile from Albornoz, which it eventually did.

"You are joining a community of monks. What is a monk?"

"A man who wears — "

"As I might expect! Clothes? Robes? Sandals? All things that envelop the body, sure enough, but not the soul! No, a monk is one who seeks God! In the depths of his heart he has heard the call of Christ! He is told this message: '*Go, leave your homeland, your family, your possessions and come, follow me.*' In faith he responds: '*Here I am. Speak, Lord, your servant is listening.*' We embark on this search in the monastery in company of brothers who have heard the call before us and in a life in which everything is directed towards bringing us, through the experience of a deep personal love, into close union with Christ. Only by holding nothing dearer to us than Christ will we be happy to persevere in a life which is ordinary, obscure and laborious." He took a deep breath then continued, gratified that the explanation he had given a hundred times was being carefully absorbed by this boy. Usually it elicited expressions of boredom, and yawning was not unknown.

"As I was saying, the church services for you are at the prime and vespers bells. Finally, I will explain how the novices' week is divided. Monday, Tuesday and Friday, you will study the Scriptures with other of your colleagues under the tutelage of the senior monks. Wednesday and Thursday, you will undergo military training from our lay brothers. Saturday and Sunday are the days for private contemplation — reading your Bible either in the cloisters or in the dormitory. I nearly forgot that on these last two days you will work in our field, as requested. Do you have any questions?" Albornoz breathed sharply and gulped.

"No, brother."

"Then you may return to your dormitory. You will have time to meet your fellow novices before lights out."

IN THE DORMITORY, the other eleven newcomers had returned earlier and were already in their nightshirts. Some lay covered under their blankets on their mattresses, others sat up and were idly chatting. Upon Albornoz's entrance they all froze, and a strange quiet reigned, but only for a few moments. Seeing his embarrassment, one of them approached him, smiling, and extended a warm hand of welcome.

"You must be Albornoz. We heard you

would be number twelve here. My name is Ineso. Allow me to introduce you to everyone." Albornoz shook hands with each of the boys in turn.

"Right, it will soon be lights out, so you had better get into your nightshirt. You will get to know us better tomorrow."

No sooner had Albornoz pulled his blanket over him than the compline bell rang. Ineso, clearly the principal novice, extinguished each of the four candles with a snuffer, and the dormitory was plunged into darkness.

"God bless you all," Ineso spoke out.

"God bless you, Ineso," the novices replied in near unison. The rule of silence after the compline bell was strictly obeyed.

ALBORNOZ THOUGHT he had barely slept for a few minutes when he was roused by the other boys yawning, stretching, and donning their black habits.

"Rise and shine," Ineso called to him. "This is the procedure every day: wake, dress, wash, prime service, then breakfast. Come on, else we will be late."

Young Albornoz quickly pulled on his robe,

fastened the leather belt and tied his sandals. They trooped out of the dormitory, down the steps and across the courtyard into a building he saw was the washroom. He watched his newly found friends douse their faces with water from an iron trough then dry themselves on the sleeves of their habits. He did the same, just in time before the prime bell resounded throughout the dark stillness of the Castle of Calatrava.

In the church, the novices took their places on the front benches. Unlike the previous night, no monks sang, and the prior — the Abbot's assistant — led the service. He, like the Abbot and all the other monks, wore the plain brown habit with a white cuccula and was tonsured, an obligatory condition of the Order. The only difference between those two men was that the prior's adornment was just a small brass crucifix — the Abbot's was larger and made of silver.

'As yet, I do not understand what the prior is preaching, nor the responses the monks are making, but I am sure this is the right place for me. It feels natural...even predestined. That night, when I sat on my bed at home, looking out at the stars over Cuenca, I had a sensation of the heavens saving a

place for me, in the name of the Lord. Good fortune sees me truly blessed.'

As they all filed out of the church, the crenelated tops of the castle walls rising above them in the half-light of dawn appeared like soldiers standing to attention. Ineso took Albornoz's sleeve and whispered,

"This way, time for breakfast."

The refectory tables bore only bread baskets and pitchers of milk: simple fare that reflected the humility of the Order. Although the hall was crowded, conversation was subdued with everyone considering his spiritual day ahead. Albornoz sat next to Ineso, who explained,

"It is Monday, so we have Bible study all day. Our classes will be taken by monks who are rightly proud of their teaching position, see, over there." He pointed to the other side of the refectory. "They are the most learned men in the community, and in addition to their teaching, one works in the library, another in the infirmary, then there is the castle garden, the wine cellar, and the scriptorium — where they copy biblical texts. Without them, the monastery would come to a halt. Oh, I nearly forgot the kitchen and the laundry, but those are run by outsiders from the town."

AFTER BREAKFAST, the novices assembled in a small meeting room. On the tables were laid out parchment sheets, each carefully copied in the scriptorium, containing — appropriately — the text from Genesis. The senior monk stood in front of them, cleared his throat, and began,

"God bless you all. As novices in our monastery, you are embarking on a wondrous journey, so it is right and proper that we commence our studies with the Word. Take your sheets and repeat after me,

"*In the beginning God created the heaven and the earth.*" They repeated the line.

"*And the earth was without form, and void,*
And darkness was upon the face of the deep..."

At the end of the chapter the monk sat, and a discussion of its meaning ensued.

'*I am unworthy of such company. Father Gelmiro did his best for me, but his lessons did not delve beneath the surface of the verses. This is so different, and I will value and enjoy every second I am here,*' Albornoz contemplated.

His day was rewarding and uplifting, but in the dormitory that night, just before lights out, a more sombre tone prevailed. One of their number, a slightly built boy, entered, tears running down his face.

"What happened?" Ineso asked.

"Twenty, with the belt, twenty lashes."

"You were talking in the cloisters, and you know the rule, do you not?"

"Yes, of course I do, but I do not know — "

"Enough of your excuses! It is the rule, and you should have respected it as such. Just as well you did not tell the Prior the name of the other boy, or there would be two of you crying. You break the rule and you take your punishment."

Albornoz looked on with a detached interest. Whether the punishment was harsh or not did not figure in his mind. He agreed entirely with Ineso's reasoning. Right and wrong, he thought, were inalienable concepts, and throughout his time in the Castle of Calatrava, that belief became increasingly resolute.

For certain, Albornoz realised he was an independent spirit, a boy with his own mind, and nobody could tell him what to think. In the church that morning, he had experienced a quasi-divine emotion that gave him real hope for the future. But after his albeit brief time in the monastery, he felt an acute misgiving, a strange anticipation that he would, by force of his determined, intransigent nature, and perhaps on many occasions still to come, rebel against routine and defy authority. He found that mundane and trivial matters annoyed him more than obscure biblical verses or a philosophical consideration of the afterlife did.

'Aldonso says they adhere to a vow of silence, yet in the same breath tells me when and where they do not follow it. How do I reconcile my conscience when faced with such ambiguity? Then, he gave me a list of things that I must do — two services each day; when to have breakfast and dinner; scripture study on this day, military training on that. I will be ordered when to work in the field and when to go to market. Well, I am not minded to sell my soul to appease Aldonso! But I will have no choice. I must follow their rules until I am in a position where it is I who decides them.'

WEDNESDAY WAS a complete contrast to the two preceding days: military training. A layman wearing a commoner's tunic and rough woollen shawl, to protect against the late autumn chill, was waiting outside the refectory after breakfast.

"Novices, follow me,' bellowed a corpulent man with blackened teeth and a squint in one eye. He led them through two courtyards to a large open space at the perimeter of the castle walls. Its ground was compacted sand. Albornoz decided it looked more like the arena of a Roman amphitheatre ready for the gladiator's parade than a religious place, but he accepted this soldiering side of his education.

"Line up! Today, preferably!"

Surrounding the training ground stood various outhouses and sheds in which staves, bows, javelins, shields, swords, clubs, batons, flails and hammers were stored — the accoutrements of medieval combat.

"Listen up!" the fat man boomed. "You will be with me and my colleagues here for two days every week. We will show you what it means to be a soldier in good King Alfonso's army — how to attack, how to defend. Some of you might never have even seen a sword, let alone wielded one in anger. Worry not, gentlemen! You will quickly learn."

Two lay brothers came out of an outhouse carrying bundles of long wooden staves. They moved along the line for each novice to select one.

"We will begin by learning how to employ the staff to either render the enemy unconscious or fend off an attacker's blow."

He demonstrated how to deliver different blows with the staff, then ordered the novices to form pairs and practice the skill.

"You never know," he said with a chuckle, "the King could enlist you tomorrow, so best be prepared."

The thought of imminent combat filled the debutants with dread, and they cracked staff against staff with gusto, anxious to become proficient. The pair of boys next to Albornoz were unequally matched — one short and slightly built, the other a foot taller, brawny and thickset. After exchanging a few strokes, as instructed, the stronger boy began to hit his partner intentionally on his arms and swirled his staff, narrowly missing his head and causing him to recoil with fear.

Albornoz could not fail to see the smaller boy's distress and reacted instinctively, striking the assailant hard on his knees, bringing him to the ground, writhing and whining in pain. Albornoz, like a victorious warrior prior to thrusting in his deadly sword, leaned over the bully.

"I am sorry, such carelessness! My skills will have to improve if I am to be of any use to King Alfonso!" A forgiving nature came with his free spirit, but he did not suffer fools gladly, nor would he stand by and watch a wrong unfold if he could prevent it. The smaller boy looked at Albornoz, gratitude in his eyes. With that, normal training continued.

They learned that and much more: the axe, to bludgeon and cut, held in one or two hands or on a pole; the dagger, its pointed two-edged blade for thrusting motions; the bow, made of yew or ash, its glue-soaked string capable of raining down arrows from two hundred yards; leather shields, reinforced with metal banding, showing the monarch's colours around a heavy central boss, combining to form a shield wall.

OVER THE WEEKS of his novitiate, Albornoz, after an uncertain start, came to appreciate the relevance of the monastery's insistence on martial arts alongside religious studies in order to yield a well-rounded Whitemonk, one who could preach the Gospel, defending the Church's stance on right and wrong and, when times called, could answer the call to arms to protect the King's authority. Although a nascent ecclesiastical thinker, he saw associations between weaponry, tactics, and the quest for wealth and power — all of which would be borne out in his later career as both ecumenical figure and military strategist.

AS A BOY GROWING up in Cuenca, Albornoz was physically equal to his peers — broad-shouldered, with strong thighs and powerful arms. The occasions when Ramon had given him a beating by the river, in front of his friends, and when Father Nicolás had attacked him in the street to persuade him to remain silent about what he had witnessed between him and the other priest in the sacristy, were rare. He was more than capable of defending himself. By the time he had left Cuenca for the monastery, he was a good six or seven inches taller than the other boys. Close-set eyes immediately fixed on you with a disarming calming effect. Their dark blue depth symbolised, to the people of that age, intelligence, truth and heaven — all elements of his personality. His nose was narrow, his cheeks high-boned. Tight lips revealed even white teeth upon a smile.

Through his fairly innocent liaison with Madelena and the attention of other girls in his circle, he had become aware of his good looks and attractive character. However, it remained for him to interpret and apply the Cistercian vow of chastity. Poverty and obedience were far easier concepts to accommodate in this young man's determination of the world.

ONE MONTH after his arrival in Calatrava, Albornoz received a message from his father. It read,

"My dearest son, your mother and I trust in the Lord to ensure you are in good health and benefitting from your time with the Whitemonks.

It is with heavy heart that I must inform you of the passing of Father Gelmiro. May his soul rest in peace. Your father."

Saddened as Alvarez Carillo Gil de Albornoz was by this news, it served only to consolidate his resolve, for the old priest's memory and for his own aggrandisement. He was now single-minded and determined to rise in the Church and to become an essential soldier and diplomat in the royal heritage.

CHAPTER FIFTEEN
LIMOGES, KINGDOM OF ARLES, 1325

Despite his wife, Jamette, being heavily pregnant, Edmond had decided now was the time to leave Limoges, although he had no idea where. His luck as a poacher had run out since Dumas's men had caught him hunting wild boar and he had been incarcerated in the dark cold cell at the chateau. He was a marked man and could not expect to escape with his life if similar events occurred in the future. No, after years of treating Jamette without consideration or respect, spending whole days drinking to excess with like-minded reprobates in the town's inns, he had to change. With a baby expected, they must come first.

His initial experiences of the confessional had been forced upon him: he agreed to participate so that Father Caron would not reveal his illegal hunting to Dumas and the authorities. But purging his soul in that little wooden box in the Eglise Evangélique took on a new meaning after his close call with the law. His freedom was due to Caron, and Caron was the Church. He realised that his good fortune was a gift from God, and his honest work on the new cathedral had been obtained through the priest's recommendation.

"Edmond, my son," Caron said softly one morning.

"Yes, father?"

"As you know, I have observed your situation and that of your good wife carefully — as I do for all my parishioners. You have had a hard life, that I know, and an opportunity has come to my attention that may be of interest to you."

"Father Caron, you have already shown great kindness to us. We ask nothing more — "

"Hear me out, Edmond," the priest interrupted. "Carpentras is a pleasant town with a worshipful bishop and virtuous clergy. It is situated some three days' ride from here.

The licence for a tavern there is to be renewed and, for whatever reason, no suitable applicant has come forward. While you have no experience in this trade, your good character over recent years — hard work at the new cathedral and regular attendance at my church for services and confession — all mark your eligibility for appointment as a landlord. What say you to that, Edmond?"

"This comes as a complete surprise, Father. A landlord, Edmond Nerval? It's a pretty sounding word if ever I heard one...landlord," he repeated, "but I have no money to put into any business."

"I have already looked into it. The Bishop and I have exchanged correspondence, and the tavern will be taken as a going concern. Accommodation is in the form of upstairs rooms, and the first three months' stock are on credit, courtesy of a local investor. So, you see, it is an ideal chance. I suggest it to you because the duties of a landlord are not restricted to selling ale — he has an eye on local issues and matters of concern for the town authorities. He can identify families who merit our largesse and support from Carpentras's benefactors. Last, but by no means least, he is a public figure whose opinions are respected, and therein rests the possibility for evangelism — spreading the good word. There will be poor, redeemable souls among your clientele, and through your own belief in the Lord, you would be able to help them find the Way." He paused.

"I am not sure — "

"They say that he who hesitates is lost. A decision is needed by the end of the month — three weeks hence."

"Father, it is surely divine intervention, for just before you met with me today, I had decided to leave this town. Jamette is with child, and the young one deserves a good start in life, away from the place of my past indiscretions. I did not know which direction to take, but you have provided the answer! I accept the honour that goes with the title of landlord and anticipate happy and rewarding times ahead."

"I am delighted for you. Leave the formalities to me, and you had better let Jamette into the arrangement! Prepare your household for its relocation!"

. . .

EDMOND HIRED a horse and cart and loaded their few possessions, and he and Jamette set off along the rough track leading eastward towards their destination, Carpentras. They overnighted in two wayside hostelries and made the town by dusk of the third day's travel, as Father Caron had estimated. Their luck was in, for they had escaped the attention of any highway bandits. As Edmond reined the horse to a halt in the Rue Mercière, a stone's throw from the Saint Siffrein cathedral, a man with a broad smile approached.

"Welcome! Welcome! You will be Edmond Nerval, the new landlord."

Edmond returned the smile.

"I am, and this is my wife, Jamette."

The stranger doffed his cap in her direction.

"Tether your horse here," he indicated a post, "then, I have the keys, so...come..." He unlocked the front door of the inn. Inside, a roaring fire greeted the travellers, and bread, cheese and ale were laid out on a table.

"You will be tired after your journey. Eat, have a look round, then sleep well! I will return tomorrow morning to provide you with what you should know to get started. The place has been closed for some two months, but it will not take long for the locals to hear it has a new occupant. Once again, Edmond and Jamette, welcome to Carpentras." With that, he turned and left the inn. The cart unloaded, the couple ate their supper, drank good ale and, as the man predicted, slept very well.

THE NEXT MORNING, Edmond and Jamette came downstairs from their quarters well rested. He stepped outside and threw open the shutters to let in gentle sunlight through the glass windowpanes.

'This is definitely an inn of some standing,' he thought, *'with glass rather than cloth behind the shutters.'*

Rue Mercière, to left and right, was deserted. In the Provençale lands around Carpentras, people started their day late, and it continued at a leisurely pace into the warm evenings, still pleasant after the midday heat.

"Ah!" Jamette pronounced, hands on hips. "There's been neither man nor beast inside here for a time, as the man said last night." Running a finger over a table top, she continued, with an air of distaste, "Dust! Dust everywhere! And the floor's filthy! There's some work to be done here before we can let in customers."

Edmond glanced around and immediately agreed.

"But first, let's finish off last night's supper for our breakfast. Then I will help you to clean. In your state, you must not exert yourself."

As they ate and drank what was left from the last night's meal, neither spoke, but the silence was not awkward — on the contrary, the smiles they exchanged said they were pleased that such a landmark in their lives had been achieved.

No sooner were they done eating than there came a knock at the door. Edmond rose from the table to answer it. On the threshold stood the same man with the broad smile who had greeted them the previous evening.

"Good morning to you, Edmond, and to you, madam."

"Good morning, er — "

"My name is Donard. I am an assistant to Bishop Otho, whose office is two streets away from our cathedral. As you will see, there is much building in progress, but it will not be finished in our lifetimes. His Grace the Bishop finds he is occupied supervising the work, and he delegates many clerical duties to me. Your inn comes under his jurisdiction. It is a complicated arrangement whereby a portion of your profits goes to his coffers. But do not worry, I will take care of everything."

He saw the puzzled expression on Edmond's face.

"It is a lot to take in, I understand that, but selling ale to folk in these parts is a simple affair even if you find keeping order when they consume too much is quite a different matter. Anyway, if it suits you, I will escort you around Carpentras for a while. It will give you an idea of our town."

"Most kind, Donard. Get your shawl, Jamette, our friend has much to do, I am sure."

ALTHOUGH FEW PEOPLE yet walked the streets, the cathedral site was a hive of industry: men calling orders, hammers striking stone, saws cutting timber.

"Beneath the grand altar, we have already buried a most sacred relic, a nail from the cross of Calvary. Come, follow me," Donard invited.

The three made their way along this and that road, their guide pointing out buildings of interest and introducing them to whosoever they met in the streets bathed in coolness and light. *A most pleasant town,* Edmond decided.

An hour or so later and their tour completed, Donard offered to show Edmond the cellar of the inn where the barrels of ale were stored. He agreed readily, the working of a tavern being quite unfamiliar to him. Jamette put on an apron and started to dust the tables and sweep the floor. Before leaving, Donard broke important news to Edmond:

"I have arranged for a dray to bring you six barrels this afternoon. They come from the best brewery in town. The drayman will help you unload and lower them down into the cellar — he's a good sort and will not take advantage of you, which is more than I can say for some." He twitched his nostrils and grumbled some unclear words, then,

"You will settle your brewery account with me at my office in the Bishop's house in due course. Finally, I have had notices posted around the town alerting our citizens that the inn will again be open for business, as from tomorrow. It's then up to you, Edmond, and I'm confident you will enjoy good trade and a happy residence here in Carpentras." He shook Edmond's hand and left the inn. Turning to his wife, Edmond took a deep breath and said softly,

"So, my dear, a new start for you, me and our child."

"Indeed," Jamette answered with a demure smile.

THE FIRST FEW days of his tenancy were spent getting to know the regular drinkers, asking politely how they were doing and how fared their families. The customers, in their turn, were weighing up the new landlord. It did not take long for Edmond to demonstrate his intention to maintain a peaceful establishment. A dispute between two men concerning, as far as he heard, a particular woman erupted into fisticuffs, a table overturned with ale splashing around. In an instant, Edmond rushed from behind the counter, stood between them and forced them apart.

"Out! Both of you! Settle your differences

elsewhere, but not on my premises." Although Edmond was no match physically for either man, they respected his forceful command and shuffled out of the inn, muttering insults, and parted in opposite directions.

But he began to see both good and bad in people, not to prejudge nor apportion blame. As the years went by, he would become a wise counsellor, drawing on his experiences and acquired kindness to advise or put in an influential word on behalf of a fellow man who had fallen afoul of the authorities.

Jamette and Edmond had been hosts of the tavern for only a week or so when their sleep was rudely disturbed by her shaking to wake him.

"Edmond! Edmond!"

"What is it, woman?" he asked in an annoyed tone.

"My waters have broken!"

He immediately gathered his senses and leapt from their bed.

"Keep calm," he urged, though the panic on her face told him his words were, at best, naïve. "I will return as soon as possible."

He rushed downstairs, threw his cape around his shoulders, and ran out of the inn, down two streets to a house he had been told he would need when his wife came to this stage of her labour: the midwife's residence.

"Madame! Please, come quickly," he shouted, banging on the door that promptly opened. A short, stout woman came out.

"Ah, Edmond, so it's her waters?"

"I think so —

"*Think?* You'll know if they have, my friend, that's for sure!"

"Of course...yes...a short time ago."

"Come then, let's be away."

EDMOND AND JAMETTE'S first and only child, Marius, was born on December 14, 1326. Edmond could not have envisaged the glorious sense of expectancy before the boy was born. Equally, when the babe arrived, his pride knew no bounds, and awed at the miracle of a new person in miniature, he prayed that his son would enjoy a long, healthy, happy life.

EDMOND'S PATRONS accepted his house rules, and by and large, he had little trouble. He greeted them with a smile and served the best ale from the best brewery in Carpentras. For some, he became a confidant, for others an introduction to the Church, the light it had brought into his own life never far from his thoughts. With the man branded a petty criminal, say, a pickpocket, he saw beyond the offence: there was a reason for such behaviour, he believed — often poverty or sheer human weakness, and when a few coins could be of help, Edmond obliged. On many an occasion, he took pity on a customer who could not afford to buy drink and provided it free of charge. But he encouraged that same man to consider putting food on his table before indulging his desire, avoiding his family responsibilities, hiding his problems in alcohol. His advice often fell on deaf ears, but it did not deter him from his mission.

He regarded certain punishments dispensed by the town's magistrate excessive, and his opinion carried clout in having them reduced. Edmond Nerval's enlightened thinking ensured him a place among Carpentras's higher echelons, and Marius, from childhood, was influenced by the life of his father.

. . .

ALTHOUGH SEMI-LITERATE, Edmond understood simple messages from the Bible through his duties as a church sides-man, his experience in the confessional and discussions with townsfolk better educated than himself. He was in no doubt about the value of learning and wished to provide such for his son, within his limited means. From a young age Marius attended lessons with a priest of his father's acquaintance, which would benefit him throughout his days.

TWENTY-TWO YEARS LATER, **Carpentras, Kingdom of Arles, late 1347**

MARIUS AND DOMINIQUE, she cradling her baby, Fabien, close to shield him from the icy wind, stood on the steps outside the church, acknowledging the words of condolence from the mourners as they left.

"He was a good man."

"Thank you for saying so," Marius answered in a rather mechanical tone.

When the last person had gone by, Marius took his wife's arm and led her down the street towards the inn. Dominique took Fabien upstairs to their bedroom and laid him gently in his wicker cot. In the deserted place they sat, each with a tankard of ale, neither knowing whether to speak first. Marius broke the silence,

"It is hard to believe what has happened to us. First, mother passed away, then, without warning, father was lowering a barrel into the cellar when his heart failed him." Dominique reached across the table, squeezing his hand to comfort him.

"Do you know what mother's last words to me were? She made me promise I would try to be as good and generous a man as father. While it will not be easy, I will respect that promise."

"I know you will," she said softly. He clenched his teeth in steely determination then drained his tankard, filling it again from the jug.

"It's as well that we will be leading a new life in Avignon because — " He hesitated.

"Yes, Marius?"

"I was not going to tell you this, but when father passed away, I had a visit by a man from the Bishop's office. He told me that father had run up debts, putting off paying the brewery. The man said we were to quit the inn as they wanted a new landlord in place, not me because I am too young and do not have the funds to clear the debts."

"It does not surprise me," Dominique said with a resigned tone. "He was a fool when it came to money. But surely you see that it is written in the stars — your mother and father are now gone, but you have secured work and accommodation in Avignon. It is meant to be! Lord knows you tried hard enough to find employment here."

MARIUS KNEW he would meet the Papacy in Avignon, but never in his dreams could he have foreseen the antithesis of the idyllic world he had imagined. He would not have knowingly exposed his wife and child to such danger, but he was no fortune teller, and a scourge would dominate and determine the next year of his life.

CHAPTER SIXTEEN
CALATRAVA, KINGDOM OF SPAIN, 1320

A Cistercian brother approached Albornoz in the cloisters one day and whispered, barely audibly,

"Albornoz, the abbot requests your presence in his study."

"Am I in trouble?"

The brother smiled and reassured him,

"Nothing of the kind, do not worry."

Albornoz knocked three times on the door beyond which Abbot Sabastian's hallowed inner sanctuary was rarely penetrated. There came no reply, so he knocked again. This time, a voice came,

"Enter." Albornoz followed the instruction but slowly, overawed by the honour.

"Come, my son." The interior of the study was lit only by two candles on either side of a large bible on a heavy oak desk. Behind it, shelves from floor to ceiling groaned under the weight of rolls of parchment and countless leather-bound volumes. It was identical to Brother Aldonso's room where he had sat earlier. He squinted to adjust his eyes to the dimness that surrounded him until his gaze fell on the tall, youthful, white-robed figure sitting at the desk, the abbot, silver crucifix on a chain around his neck. He cleared his throat and invited Albornoz to stand opposite him. Without further ado, he opened the bible and read several verses aloud, ending each with *Amen,* which Albornoz repeated. Crossing himself, Sabastian closed the bible and gestured for Albornoz to sit. This was the closest he had been to the abbot, who was usually viewed from a distance at services in the church. He observed the man's piercing dark eyes and furrowed brow, waiting respectfully for the monk to begin.

"I SUSPECT you do not know the purpose of our meeting?" Albornoz strained to make out the man's slightly stuttered question.

"I do not, Father Abbot," he replied with a slight tremor in his voice.

"You have been with us for one year, and as is normal for all novices, I have sought reports on your progress. It is gratifying to be able to say that your mentors have given you outstanding appraisals, for which you can be proud." He paused but still gazed directly at the young man.

"Regarding the scriptures, you have displayed an interest and maturity beyond your years. The military lay brother says that you understand the principles of combat, strategy and weaponry, even though you have never been near a battlefield. So, I would now know whether you intend to make a career in the Church?"

"I do not see — "

"The next logical step for a novice from this castle is to aspire to greater things, to become a priest, and...there are no limits to what you might achieve. Had you not considered such a path?"

The abbot's proposition regarding his future began to make perfect sense. He could feel the man's steely stare not straying from his countenance for a moment. Playing casually with the silver crucifix, he continued,

"Our vows of poverty, chastity and obedience are taken, with an absolute commitment, to better appreciate our Lord's Passion. We accept the rigours of the vows and embrace their daily challenge. Now, some students prove inadequate in this respect and part company with us, say, after one month or even one week." He raised his eyebrows as if to emphasise the contempt he felt for such weakness.

"However, I have witnessed few novices who demonstrate the incisive, intelligent, mature attitude that you do, and I congratulate you for your achievement."

"Thank you, Father Abbot, but what is your precise suggestion?"

Taken aback by the boy's forwardness, he breathed in sharply.

"You will be formally invited to accept our vows and adopt the title of *Brother,* remaining here at the castle for a lifetime's secluded devotion, but in all honesty, we have taught you to our limits. You require academic intensity of a higher order. So, there is Montpellier."

"Montpellier?" Albornoz asked.

"The university of Montpellier in the Kingdom of France. You will not be familiar with the place, but it is a pretty town with a climate similar to ours and only thirty leagues from Avignon, where the Pope and his Curia reside."

"You are correct, I am not familiar with it."

"It is a group of schools wherein the law, medicine, the arts and theology are studied to the highest level under the tutelage of the finest teachers in the land. The faculty of theology is directed by a number of our Cistercian brothers who take in our chosen novices from Calatrava. I propose to put forward your name for their consideration. What do you say to that?"

"I had not expected anything of the kind, but..."

"You hesitate, and that is natural. Should you agree, you will graduate at the end of your studies with a licence to teach in addition to your title of priest, and your progress in the Church will be assured."

"What aspects of theology?"

"In addition to a deep appreciation of the Scriptures, it is an understanding of Canon

Law — the ordinance and regulations of the Church as prescribed in Pope Nicolás's *Quia Sapienta* bull of 1289. Therein, the Supreme Pontiff dictated our universal doctrinal and moral Church laws, all encompassing the human condition." The abbot's address was interrupted by a bell sounding.

"We must attend vespers, Albornoz. Consider carefully what I have told you. I shall require your decision by tomorrow."

THE SERVICE PASSED ALBORNOZ BY; although present in body, his mind was preoccupied by the astonishing prospect of Montpellier. Sabastian read the valedictory prayer, and the church emptied for its assemblage to troop over to the refectory for supper. The novice stayed behind, alone and deep in thought, surrounded by the lengthening shadows cast by the oil lamps on the walls. The silence was so profound he believed he heard his heartbeat resonate. He needed to take stock of events, and a calm enveloped him.

'This is my calling, to be the Lord's servant and do His will. Yet, my life thus far has not been rich in experience, and I have much to learn.' He

searched the depths of his memory. *'Ramon gave me a beating down by the river, and that was wrong. Yet, when I had the chance to hold him down in the water, I spared him, and the bully had learned his lesson: I was right. Old Father Gelmiro and the bishop let the farmer off from eviction, although he hadn't paid his tithe. Then...I resisted my natural urge with Madelena, many years before taking the oath of chastity. The two priests in the sacristy were indulging in impure actions. Oh, it is so confusing! Or is it? I can recall the exact words I said to Brother Aldonso, shortly after I arrived here* —

"Right is the direct, unquestionable opposite of wrong, and there shall be no confusing or blurring the distinction between them. That is the way of God."

And, indeed it is!' Albornoz thought, struggling to avoid calling the words out loud. The longer he was immersed in religious considerations, the more his vision of how good Christians should behave became immovable in his psyche. His interpretation of the Scriptures would be unequivocal and, on occasions, create disharmony among the very people he sought to pacify through his beliefs.

'Since Father Gelmiro introduced me to the

cathedral of Cuenca, I have always felt a special, noble sensation whenever I am in the House of the Lord. Father Nicolás in the sacristy was a wrongdoer, sinner, offender of the Laws of the Church. If it had not been through my actions, reporting it to Gelmiro, he would have avoided punishment.' He rose from his bench and moved slowly down the nave towards the altar, where he knelt, piously, still alone. *'Dear Lord, I implore Your guidance. Should I accept the Abbot's invitation to study at Montpellier, a town in another kingdom, only if Thine in Heaven is the only true realm? I am much troubled by my own ignorance of the Canon Law...its precepts... especially with rich and powerful people who, it seems, do not have to follow Thy rules as do we. The wealthy are able to annul a marriage while the Church disallows divorce. Men of influence marry one woman but take, for mating purposes, as many as they choose and can afford. Again, such confusion, Lord! They cannot be both right and wrong!'*

At these words, the oil lamps flickered as if in response to his questions. Albornoz stood, bowed his head, and crossed himself. He turned, strode purposefully along the nave, and left the church. He waited for the brothers to finish supper — his own appetite had disappeared. Outside the abbot's study, he sat on a chair until the man came.

"Ah, Albornoz. I did not expect to see you before tomorrow, but…no matter, come."

Without prompting, Albornoz stood in front of the monk's desk as he had earlier.

"Sit, my son. Am I to take it that you have reached a decision concerning our proposition?"

"I have, Father Abbot."

The brother lowered his head to better focus his customary cutting gaze.

"Well?"

"I accept. I am honoured to be given such an opportunity, and I feel that the Lord had assisted my resolution."

"Excellent! I would have been greatly disappointed had your answer been any different. At your age, I, too, followed this course. You will not regret it for one moment." He opened a cupboard and took out a bottle and two glasses, ceremoniously filling each with red wine. He pushed one glass towards Albornoz.

"I only invite our brothers to imbibe at the Eucharist but, within the privacy of my chamber, I extend the invitation to guests on special occasions." He raised his glass in the boy's direction.

"Novice Albornoz, drink of His blood, as at Communion. I beseech thee, O Lord, to bless our son so that the next stage of his devotion will be watched over by Thee. May his journey prove rewarding, and may his dedication know no bounds. Amen."

Albornoz sipped the wine and answered *Amen.*

Sabastian smiled benignly and leaned back in his chair.

"I remember making the same promise that you have, and how I enjoyed my time at Montpellier. You have the advantage of speaking French. You must have had good teachers back in Cuenca."

"I did." He smiled back sheepishly.

"You will learn among Christian scholars, Jews, Muslims...all keen to discuss other religions in order to better understand their own. There are many squares all surrounded by cloisters, as here at Calatrava, and of course, it has its own church in which, as well as prayer, lively debates are held with people of opposing views sitting in opposite pews...

but enough! Finish your drink and visit the scriptorium, where you will compose a letter informing your esteemed parents of your move. Although it is evening and dark outside, our brother copyists work through the night, such is the volume of scriptures to be created for the greater benefit of our community."

"Thank you, Father Abbot. You will not be disappointed in me."

IN THE SCRIPTORIUM a long table extended its length, and candle upon candle lit the scribing and illuminating work of a dozen monks. Silence reigned, as was decreed by their vows, no speaking, the only sound a rhythmic scratching of quill on parchment. Albornoz stood in the doorway until one particular copyist, clearly the senior brother, rose and ushered him outside.

"Good evening, Albornoz. What is it you want of us?"

"Father Abbot has instructed me to write a very important letter."

"Quieter!" the brother urged, bringing his forefinger to his lips. "Take a sheet from the pile and sit down over there." He indicated a vacant space at the table. "You will find pen, inkwell, a rule and chalk for dusting. Catch my attention when you have finished, and I will take your...letter, you said?"

"Yes, a letter to be delivered to my father, whose residence is in Cuenca."

"Good. I will see that it is sealed and sent to its destination."

"Thank you, brother." He sat at the table and, without a fuss, placed the writing sheet square before him and laid the rule on top to ensure each line was perfectly level. Dipping the quill into the ink, he began to write:

'Dear father,

I trust that this letter finds you, mother and my brothers in rude health. There is much I could tell you after my year here in the castle of Calatrava, but I must restrict myself, for brevity's sake, to one momentous event that will determine my future life.'

He took a pinch of powdered chalk from a small dish, sprinkled it over the words, then gently blew it away to prevent the ink from running. He carried on,

'Our Father Abbot expresses his satisfaction with my progress and has offered me the chance of studying further at the

University of Montpellier in the Kingdom of France. I have accepted and will exchange towns and countries in the new year. May the Good Lord bless you, father, and all our household. With all respect, your son, Albornoz.'

He again dusted the sheet and raised his head to attract the brother's glance. The letter was, after a short time, received by Don Garcia Alvarez whose heart swelled with pride in his son's achievement.

THE UNIVERSITY OF MONTPELLIER, KINGDOM OF ARLES, 1321

ON A MORNING IN JANUARY 1321, the day dawned crisp and pleasant. As the bell for the prime service rang out around the castle of Calatrava, brothers in their white habits and novices in black shuffled silently into the monastery church. Among the congregation was Albornoz, now, upon completion of his internship and taking of vows, also smartly attired in Cistercian white, his scalp raw after its first tonsure. After breakfast everyone dispersed to prepare for the day ahead: for Albornoz, this would be in the form of a lengthy journey to Montpellier. Before departing he went up to the dormitory and bade farewell to his novice friends, then called in at Aldonso's room.

"Good morning, Brother Aldonso."

"Good morning to you, young man. So, you are leaving us today. God speed and my blessings to you for your path in the Lord."

"Thank you, brother, and goodbye."

OUTSIDE IN THE COURTYARD, the same cart with its steel-rimmed wheels, with the same postilion and horse that had brought him there the previous year, waited patiently. Again, the transport was provided courtesy of the benefactor Bishop of Cuenca.

The driver had already tied Albornoz's small wooden trunk securely on the cart. It contained his bible, a small pot of tooth powder, a brush and a few items of clothing; he was following his vow of poverty from the start.

"Climb up, sir," the boy invited cheerily. "We've a long trip ahead of us."

Under the clear, pale blue skies of a late winter in Calatrava, the wagon trundled through the ever-open portcullis gate and left the town for a new kingdom and chapter in Albornoz's life.

IN THE SCHOOL of theology at Montpellier university, Albornoz studied for some years. He read the Scriptures with a voracious appetite and related the parables about human behaviour in debate across the pews of the church, as Sabastian had told him would happen. His mind was inquisitive but allied to a gentle wit; he sought guidance on what we should and should not do in our lives; he earned the reputation of a cleric who did not suffer fools gladly and who always erred on the side of the righteous man. The qualities required of such a person had been carefully explained to him by Father Gelmiro many summers before, when he was a youngster in his hometown of Cuenca. His belief in the Church's capacity to dispense justice — in the form of penance or, in extremis, excommunication — polarised his evangelical pronouncements, and the more he studied and heard the wide range of views held by the cosmopolitan students at Montpellier, the more steadfast was his interpretation of right and wrong. He saw both judicial and religious punishment as an essential component of a civilised society.

He left Montpellier university as a *Fellow Magister*, a licence to teach and, of course, preach. His first clerical position was back in Cuenca, as priest to the bishop and his office, who subsequently claimed that he was too young to become their deacon. The real reason was that his father, it ensued, upon his passing had an unpaid debt that was not settled under the terms of his will. Once Albornoz had paid the 3660 maravedies, the bishop installed him with the title.

The new deacon of Cuenca could not have appreciated that a certain Marius Nerval, in Carpentras, had been obliged to pay an outstanding debt to the bishop of that town so he, too, could make progress with his life in Avignon.

· · ·

NO DOUBT through his novice association with Calatrava, he became its archdeacon, and thereafter bishop, where he was a prominent advocate of confession and believer in the deterrent power of magisterial punishment. He had little or no sympathy for anyone who contravened either the Lord's or the town's rules, and as the years slipped by, so his name spread abroad.

'I am now, through fate, the Bishop of Calatrava and in authority over the same abbot who taught me as a boy! And how my fame has spread: I am being sent on a diplomatic mission to the court of King Philippe of France! There is no reason to have any guilt through combining my success in both ecclesiastic and royal circles. I have worked hard, and it is surely the Lord's plan for me. Life has shown me that my uncompromising opinions enable those in power to feel comfortable in their dealings with me — I am of their kind.'

"THIS IS, for sure, a wonderful town. You are blessed to enjoy a God-fearing population with the Holy Father's seat secure within the Palais des Papes in fair Avignon," he remarked to a fellow delegate present for the consecration of Pope Bénédict.

"You are correct, er..."

"Albornoz, Bishop Albornoz of Calatrava in the Kingdom of Spain," he introduced himself, shaking the stranger's hand warmly.

"I am Bishop Joffroy of Orange. You have travelled many leagues to attend the ceremony."

"That is so, but I regard it as a duty and an honour."

"Quite. When do you return to Calatrava?"

"My carriage will collect me later today and —"

"Will you not be my guest for dinner this evening at the most agreeable tavern in the town? You could take a room and make the journey to your diocese in the morning."

There were many questions Albornoz had concerning the functions of the Papacy. Although his current career was blossoming, the ultimate jewel he desired was a place within the Pope's Curia in Avignon, and he immediately saw Joffroy's invitation as an opportunity to glean beneficial local information.

"That is most generous, Bishop. I accept."

. . .

LATER THAT YEAR, he assisted in raising funds for King Alfonso's Spanish campaign in Andalucia and was rewarded with a promotion to the monarch's Royal Council and the title of Primate of the Church of Spain. Accolade followed accolade, and he cast aside competition for the Archbishopric of Calatrava, then the coveted goal, Archbishop of Toledo, its designation conferred upon him in the same town where he had been dining so recently.

HIS YEARS in Toledo were very successful, and he was rightly proud of his achievements.

'I expect the highest standards of my clergy, and by and large, they behave accordingly. I have had the cloisters and bell tower of our cathedral rebuilt, to the envy of visiting dignitaries, and I have founded a priory near to our town,' he reflected, sipping a goblet of wine alone in his study.

'I have accompanied King Alfonso on our crusade to Sevilla to retake it from the marauding followers of Islam, advising him about tactics I learned as a novice. There fell an occasion, in a *skirmish, when the King was knocked from his horse and a Moor raised his sword to dispatch him. For Alfonso and his realm, it was opportune that I was by his side to stab the attacker with my dagger and save His Majesty's life.*

We again saw off Moorish invaders from Algeciras, but by now his coffers were all but empty, and he ordered me to Paris, where I raised 50,000 florins from the good and great. The King was most generous with his praise and permitted me often to share in the city's artistic and cultural programmes. I happened to pass most of the year 1348 there.'

ARCHBISHOP ALBORNOZ WAS fortunate to do so because a deadly epidemic raged through many parts of Spain and France. Whole villages were wiped away, and many thousands of people perished. For an inexplicable reason, Paris was hardly afflicted at the time when Albornoz had business there.

As the plague, for that was its common name, spread from the east into Mediterranean France and Spain and eventually affected the Kingdom of Britain, some towns and areas were spared the insidious, deadly bacillus. Not so for Avignon, which suffered cruelly and lost a greater part of its population. Had it not been for the actions of Marius Nerval and his squads of helpers, the disaster would have been even worse. This young man was elevated almost to the status of saviour within Avignon.

So, through fate and ambition, Marius Nerval and Alvarez Carillo Gil de Albornoz came to be together in the same French town.

The former, a man with wife and baby son, who had wished for a better life for his family but had been plunged into circumstances involving an evil, indiscriminate scourge, surviving and leading the poor people to triumph over adversity; the latter, a middle-aged cleric, promoted through the Church to Archbishop and ultimately member of the Papal Curia.

These two men shared humanitarian values but came from very different worlds. In promoting such noble ends, confrontation and despair would, all too soon, develop into a seemingly unbridgeable chasm between them.

CHAPTER SEVENTEEN
AVIGNON, KINGDOM OF ARLES,
JANUARY 1349

The traders had claimed their pitches on the Saint Bénézet bridge by daybreak, hoping for a good day's business after a disastrous year when the weekly market had been suspended, as had been so many of the town's normal activities. The opening of the bridge symbolised Avignon's surviving the plague: trade lay at the heart of its determination and spirit to move on with optimism and renewed zest for life. A few early risers were inspecting the wares for sale, searching for bargains, bartering to get this or that at a decent price. The cheesemonger displayed yellow-rind truckles and unctuous white cheeses he had made with the milk from his goat herd that was breeding once more. Peasant farmers from the fertile Rhône valley had been able to harvest winter vegetables, no longer fearful of hiring migrant labourers who, in the year of pestilence, had been shunned. Contamination by strangers, previously dreaded by the people of the town, was no longer a concern, and now they were welcome. Stalls groaned under the weight of onions, leeks, carrots, kale, and sacks of potatoes piled up on the ground. The wine merchant had no *Côtes du Rhône Nouveau* to sell — the best new vintage — because the grapes on the vine had been left to rot, lest they bore the evil bacillus. Instead of that new year's wine, he set out bottles and leather flagons of lesser quality but still saleable *vin de table.* The chandler arranged candles, soaps, and oils on his table with pride and artistry; the blacksmith was selling pots, pans, chains, and metal utensils now his supply of sheet iron had resumed, and he had good reason to fire up the hearth in his smithy. Bringing a splash of colour to the event, the draper put out rolls of cloths and silks, cut to length for the customer, their exotic patterns proclaiming their eastern origin.

Under the bridge's arches, hawkers without a licence to trade legitimately above peddled trinkets, bracelets, beaded necklaces, carved bone scrimshaw, and linctuses of dubious efficacy alongside cure-all balms and pardons — during the days of pain and desperation, the townsfolk lost confidence in promises of salvation and forgiveness. The opening of the gates on both sides of the river meant the lucrative business from the prosperous northern lands flowed once more into the town without checks or restrictions on who came or went: in short, everyday life in Avignon returned as swiftly as it had disappeared. The dwellers of Provence knew well that even the destructive, unrelenting Mistral wind that swept down the gorge of the Rhône was followed year after year by gentle respite, and their sunny demeanour could endure the worst tragedies that nature chose for them.

A gentleman leaned over the bridge's parapet, mesmerised by the swirling black eddies and whirlpools of the river below, amazed to see the only things swept along by the flow were green duckweed and broken branches. With the bad times, when the church graveyards were full, the Pope had issued a bull permitting corpses to be tied with weights and cast unceremoniously into the water. Many broke their chains and floated, ghoulish visages, upward to the surface — a stark reminder, if it were needed, that the epidemic was refusing to subside. However, this day, a better life had come.

As THE PALE winter sun rose, flooding comforting warm light into the old walled town, so it woke: shutters opened, voices could be heard, the streets began to fill. Greetings of *good morning* or *how are you today?* were exchanged, a smile on folks' faces, a spring in their step. Since the turn of the year, the evening curfew was lifted, as was the Avignon authority's prohibition on any gathering of more than two souls. Social activities resumed even if conversation, for the early days at least, focused more often than not on how terrible their ordeal had been and the friends and family they had lost.

By mid-morning, Marcel's tavern in the

Rue Vieux Sextier was crowded with market traders seeking refreshment, passers-by and regular patrons.

"Hey, Marcel! Ale, over here!" an old man called out, banging his empty tankard on the table to attract the landlord's attention.

"All in good time! You're not the only customer I've got to serve," Marcel retorted. As a citizen of the town who had been spared the infection, he was grateful, but a year without business had hit him hard. In this respect, he was not unique, and it was a season for rebuilding both commercial and human relationships.

"Angélique, my dear," he shouted to his wife, although she was but five paces away from him, "fetch more ale. There be gentlemen here who are faint from thirst." She did not reply but took a jug from the counter, opened the door leading to the cellar and disappeared into its dark depths. She soon reappeared, went to the table of the customer who had ordered the drink, and filled his vessel.

"My friends, too," the old man instructed her, gesturing to the two men in his company. "I'll settle my account later."

"Have no fear of that," Marcel chortled as Angélique moved off to attend to other drinkers in the hostelry.

"It's busy here today, isn't it? Market day, of course, and whether they're tradesmen or folk out buying, they're all making up for lost time," Baudri, the old man, observed.

"That's for sure. I don't like so many strange faces, though," Matelin interrupted his friend.

"Why is that? Ah, I see what you're thinking, but the plague is over now, and think about it, there's more chance the infection survives among our own, within the walls, if indeed it does…"

"Come, now, enough of that. Let's drink to the future." The third man, Franchot, raised his tankard in a toast, and the other men joined in, each taking a good draught of ale. A pause followed: nobody could swear that the death and suffering would not return; that was not within the remit of any inhabitant of Avignon.

"We would not survive, should it come again," Baudri resumed. "Half my street was wiped out, and you, Matelin, lost your wife and your wonderful daughters. We've all got tales to tell, but I'm relieved we had the old Magistrate working for us because without him — "

"You mean without young Marius, don't you?" Matelin cut in. "*He* was the reason we endured, so let's not forget that. It was one thing for the elders to order we wrapped the bodies, closed our houses, killed all the cats and dogs...all well and good, but it was Marius who organised the death carts to carry the corpses to the graveyards and have them buried quickly. *That* gave the rest of us a better chance of surviving."

"No denying that," Franchot reflected, usually the undecided one of the three.

"Who was it who made sure red crosses were painted on doors? Who closed the port so foreign bearers of the germ couldn't land and spread it around? Marius! Then don't forget that crazy band of maniacs...flagellants, marching up and down, whipping their bare bodies, crying and sending us to madness had they not been stopped," Matelin said, angry that the old Magistrate's assistant did not receive unquestioning acclaim.

"So...I guess he did much for us."

"*Much,* Franchot? You'd better believe it. And that zealot, on his box in the Place Pie, screaming *Repent! Repent! Blah! Blah!* — howling in tongues for all I know — did he do anything to encourage the rest of us? Not likely! But it was Marius who manhandled him through the Porte de la Ligne and threatened him with his life if he ever returned." Matelin stopped suddenly, aware that the whole tavern had fallen silent with everyone's gaze on him, hanging on his every word. He drained his tankard and rose from the table, facing his enchanted audience.

"To finish, let me remind you all of that deranged, raving freak, naked save for a loincloth, a dish of flaming oil tied on his head. He broke the curfew night after night, racing up and down the streets, banging on doors to terrify our neighbours. Remember that! I suspect some of you have short memories if you doubt the value of Marius's actions for us. He and the woman he has now married, Alice, apprehended the fiend when we were too afraid. So, he is our new Magistrate, and I, for one, will give him every assistance in his duties. We owe him a huge debt of gratitude."

The clientele muttered their agreement and resumed drinking. Matelin sat down for Franchot to clap his friend on the back with,

"That was well said."

"Ay, it certainly was," Baudri added, sipping his ale, his brow furrowed as he was evidently about to say something important.

"There's no contesting what Marius Nerval has done for us, but that's all in the past now. What of the future? As Magistrate, he will dispense justice on our behalves, rule on punishments, and if he's anything like the old man before him, he'll be too lenient. He's but a young man, so we can't expect him to understand the ways of the criminal, can we?"

"I suppose not," Franchot agreed.

"And I reckon he'll be kept busy once things settle down and the poachers, pickpockets, beggars, burglars and vandals get down to work. He was brave enough faced with the plague, but I just hope he doesn't turn out to be lily-livered with a felon in chains before him."

"We'll see soon enough," Matelin said, and making a decision for the first time that day, added,

"What we *will* need is a strong character who has a clear view of right and wrong."

The three men drank more tankards of ale, and Baudri, having settled the bill, left the tavern, uncertain about how effective a Magistrate Marius would prove to be.

THE MARKET HAD BEGUN at daybreak, as had Marius's duties. He was, as the three old men's discussions vouched, invested with the esteemed title of Magistrate only recently and unexpectedly. It was in the final days of the plague's malign presence that the aged justice did not answer Marius's knock at his office door on the quayside one morning. *'That's strange,'* the young man thought. *'It's market day, and there will be more boats than usual arriving shortly — especially as we are now allowing barges to unload freely once more.'* He knocked again, remembering the Magistrate was hard of hearing, but still nobody answered, despite a light showing inside. He turned the handle, pushed, and the door opened.

"Magistrate, it's time we were at work — "

and he stopped short, seeing the gentle grey-haired man's body slumped lifeless over an open ledger on his desk. Marius, greatly saddened by this discovery, summoned assistance, and the dead man was taken, ironically, on one of the very carts he had requisitioned for use by the death squads to his house in the town. An examination of the corpse revealed no indication of the scourge: the man had passed away from natural causes. The will, written in his neat hand, stated Marius to be his successor as Justice of Avignon.

As THE GOOD news spread that Avignon's port was trading again, barges laden with goods sent from the kingdom and beyond tied up at the quayside. Their crews, having registered their cargo with the Magistrate's office, piled up sacks of grain, bundles of cloth, barrels of wine, and merchandise of every description on the quay, and soon the warehouses filled: times of plenty. Marius continued his predecessor's tradition of meticulously recording every coming and going in the heavy leather-bound book and earned the reputation of an intelligent, fair-minded supervisor of the port. Importers and exporters, regardless of creed or colour, were welcome now the bad times were behind them. One business, however, did not enjoy such treatment.

Pagnol Fils, wool merchants, owned the largest warehouse in the port. The founding brothers, Jean and Thomas, had built their concern from humble beginnings. They had given Marius his first work the day he arrived from Carpentras, pushing trolleys of cloth. With their partner, Bruno, they had lived in an imposing house on the Rue Limas up near the Bénézet bridge. Now, they had to survive aboard their narrow barge moored at the far end of the quay.

Come the plague, they made a decision to flee the town to find safe haven in a place spared the disease. In this they failed and were refused entry by the citizens of Avignon when they had their change of heart. They were left with the barge as their only residence. Despite sending baskets of fruit and other gifts into the town to mollify their former neighbours, it came to nothing; the Avigonnais people did not easily forget, especially when *they* had remained to suffer, not having the wherewithal to escape.

They did not have the same cowardice running through their veins as the merchants.

One morning, Marius's calculating figures in the ledger was interrupted by a knock at his office door.

"Enter," he called.

"Good morning to you, Marius...umm... Magistrate." Jean Pagnol stood in the doorway.

"And to you, Jean. What can I do for you today? You cannot have a manifest for me, that's for sure." Marius's voice was tinged with sharpness. The wool merchant had been served notice that his warehouse was barred, pending consideration by the authorities. Pagnol continued but avoided eye contact with him, as if ashamed.

"Other boats are, at this very time, being unloaded and loaded; trade is going on as before. But Pagnol Fils are denied access to their living. When — "

"When," Marius cut in, "you, your brother, and the man Bruno sailed up the river to save your souls, whilst we did not have such a benefit. Surely you see why you are despised, why your name is reviled, and why your fellow townsmen do not want you back?"

"We understand all this, but too late now. It was, truly, a grave error, and we are living to regret it, but we were not the only ones — there were more who did the same. Are you holding us as an example?"

"Not at all, Jean. The fact is you three are the only ones foolhardy enough to try to return!" He looked steadily at the elderly bearded man, who walked with a severe limp, and felt sudden pity for him. "Pray, continue," he invited the wretched man.

"We seek forgiveness, Magistrate, then to resume the only trade we know. We want to live in our own house instead of that infernal barge. We will take the stocks, accept a flogging, time in the cells, whatever..." Tears ran down the man's sad face.

"Enough now, Jean. I have a degree of sympathy for you, but you must see that matters like this are decided by those above me. The Duke himself would have made the order and possibly the Holy Father's Curia."

"So, you are the Magistrate, don't you have their ear?"

"I am only in this post for a few months, and I do not know the answer to that question." He paused, then replied with words that gave Jean hope,

"I am due to meet with the Curia next week to review the state of our town from a magisterial consideration, you understand."

"I do," he blubbered, looking Marius in the face for the first time.

"I will see what I can do for your case. There are those who say you have now served your punishment, but others...anyway, I promise you nothing."

"I do not know how to thank you, Magistrate." He wiped his eyes on the sleeve of his tunic, gave an almost imperceptible smile, and left the office to pass on the good news to his brother and Bruno aboard their barge.

AFTER HIS MORNING'S work at the port, Marius made his way through the town to his house by the Magnanen gate. It was a fine residence boasting a garden, a well, and an orchard. As he approached the front door, he could hear laughter within — his wife Alice and young son Fabien playing games. His family situation was not as it might have seemed to the uninformed observer. During the final days of the plague, his first wife, Dominique, Fabien's mother, took ill, swiftly succumbed, and died. Prior to this, he had been conducting an illicit relationship with Alice, falling deeply in love with her and she with him. After Dominique's passing, there stood no obstacle to him marrying Alice, who adopted the young boy as if he were her own.

Marius often wondered at the way their paths had crossed, watching her intently as she sewed embroidery silently in her chair beside a roaring fire.

'Such beauty, such perfection,' he thought, 'yet how little the good folk of Avignon really know about her. She would always wear a black robe that enveloped her body and reached the ground. Long dark hair partly concealed her face. She was a mystery, an almost unseen lady who floated from one street to the next, head bowed, avoiding conversation. Some said she was a witch, a Sicani women from a tribe of pagans on the island of Sicily whose people danced round campfires and made sacrifices to their gods. They know nothing!' And he chuckled at the very idea. She had lived alone in a humble dwelling next to Marcel's tavern, but she was not poor; on the contrary, she was a niece of the Duke of Avignon, her family bloodline going back to Hugh of Arles: a wealthy woman whose fortune increased upon the death of her cruel husband when she inherited the grand house they presently shared. *'And how they would all scream if I told them she had been Pope Clément's mistress — but it was true! The irony was she worshiped every day in his cathedral! Because she didn't mix with the other women, she didn't give the slightest indication who she was or whence she came. Then she told me an even stranger story: she oversaw — her own word — Marguerite's House, a brothel, now our own abode! That was hard to believe, although it was easier when she assured me she did not entertain clients there. I believed her, and to her credit, she closed the place and showed the women who worked there that there is a better way, the way of the Lord. She repented and became my wife. Does that not prove that anyone can express regret and receive forgiveness?'*

So, that was how they found themselves — Marius, Alice, Jean, Marcel and the others — victims of fate, masters of their own destinies.

AVIGNON, SPRING 1349

ALBORNOZ, by virtue of his reputation and effectiveness in previous positions within the Church, now served as Cardinal adviser to Pope Clément VI in the Curia of Avignon. Since the new year, concerns about the state of the citizens' behaviour in the town had been brought to the Pontiff's attention. Having given Albornoz sufficient time to settle in at the Palace and assess the situation, the Cardinal was called to a meeting.

"Be seated, Albornoz, and may the Lord bless your good offices."

"Amen to that, Holy Father."

Their initial conversation covered administrative matters until Albornoz was invited to comment on law and order.

"My Holy Father will know better than I that when the epidemic reigned, all citizens were equal, for it had no favourites and it took no prisoners, that much is true. But now, I fear old differences rising. How shall I explain..." He paused. They were strangers, and each would have to weigh up the other. Then he continued, choosing his words with care.

"I observe a disparity between rich and

poor. Then, some of them are heathen, others religious, and it is our mission to bring them all to the bosom of the Church. We can never take issue with that. However, there are, from what I have seen during my short time in Avignon, undoubtedly honest and dishonest elements at large, and it is this latter type of person who does not respect the rule of law, who appreciates not the meaning of right and wrong. They have no excuse, because the Scriptures tell us — "

"Indeed, Albornoz!" Clément interrupted his Cardinal. "I believe the Pontiff needs no instruction in the messages of the Bible!" He was quite unaccustomed to such rudeness.

"My apologies, sire, I meant no offence. In short, I predict an increase in petty crime, leading only to graver transgressions. Our servant, the Magistrate, Marius Nerval, plays no small part in apprehending criminals and administering justice. So, in this respect, I intend to speak with him in the near future and ascertain his views on judicial issues."

"In that, you have my complete confidence. Nerval is a good man who is known to show mercy — "

"Say no more, Holy Father."

With the two men seemingly seeing eye to eye, their meeting concluded.

'Show mercy, does he? I wonder what the villains think about that...' Albornoz pondered as he left Clément's study.

CHAPTER EIGHTEEN
AVIGNON, KINGDOM OF ARLES,
SPRING 1349

Marius returned from his customary early morning walk to find his son at their dining table eating breakfast. Hanging his hat on the back of the door, he went over to the boy, ruffling his blond curly hair affectionately. Fabien was the apple of his eye, a handsome lad with a broad forehead, cheeky smile and inquisitive gaze.

"Good morning, my boy."

"Good morning, Father."

"Hey, Alice," he called through to the kitchen, where his wife was busy preparing vegetables at the stone sink. The poorer houses of the town had a single downstairs room — theirs boasted two.

"Did you have a pleasant walk?"

"I did. It's a fine, crisp day." He sat down beside Fabien to join him in their meal of milk and fresh bread the baker's helper had just delivered.

"It's just the weather to run through the wood, climb trees and play fight with your pals — I wish I was coming with you — "

"You're not allowed!" Fabien interrupted, sitting upright before seeing his father was teasing him. Alice collected their plates and cups, then reminded Fabien,

"Before you leave, don't forget to bring in the eggs." The property had a hen run, as well as a number of other outbuildings: a residence commensurate with the post of Magistrate.

"Alright," he replied politely. Eager to leave home and meet his friends for a morning's rough and tumble away from adults' prying eyes, he left the table, took a wicker basket, and went outside to the yard. He returned shortly.

"They've laid well today, Mother."

"Nine, ten, eleven, you're right. You can go now. Take care and be back before the nones service bell."

"I will, goodbye."

Marius watched the domestic scene unfold and smiled at Alice.

"I'm truly blessed to have such a beautiful wife and healthy young son, am I not?"

"Who am I to disagree?" she answered, returning a smile as impudent as Fabien's, although her own happiness for their relationship was tinged by Fabien not being her natural child, much as she loved him. She yearned secretly for a child by Marius.

"Tell me, what does today hold in store for you?"

"I will meet Luc at the port office presently."

"Yes, he's a good man to have gained your confidence."

During the plague, Luc and Marius had been fearless workers in the old Magistrates' team, putting themselves at considerable risk of infection when removing malodorous corpses from the houses and carting them away for burial. Alice's friendship had begun when Marius first arrived in Avignon and he was a labourer at the stonemason's yard where Luc was already working and had taken him under his wing while the newcomer settled in. Luc's and Marius's sons shared the same name,

Fabien. The former's son perished to the diabolic scourge. Marius continued,

"Now he's agreed to take over my duties at the port, it means I can concentrate my efforts on issues within the town. Later, I've arranged an appointment with Father Dizier, the priest of Eglise de l'Oratoire on the Rue Petite Fusterie. He's the longest serving minister in Avignon, and there are many matters concerning the Church and crime in the town about which I'm impatient to learn."

"Dizier has a decent name, and I'm sure he'll be of assistance," his wife observed, kissing him gently on the lips.

Marius walked along the Boulevard Saint-Michel, which followed the ramparts and entered the port through the south gate. He had to go the length of the quayside to reach his office at the far end. Barges had their holds open for derricks and winches to hoist out their deliveries. Piled up on the quay, barrow boys put them on their trolleys and pushed them to cavernous warehouses whose dark interiors were a mystery to all save the owners themselves. One trader guarded his stocks jealously, not wishing the other to gain any commercial advantage by knowing this or that commodity was the up and coming trend. He greeted and exchanged pleasantries with the stevedores and sailors. Luc awaited him outside the port office.

"Morning, Luc."

"Morning, Marius."

"It looks as if you'll have a busy day; there are quite a few boats moored up already. Now...where is it..." He fumbled in the pocket of his tunic then withdrew a key. "Ah, got it." Unlocking the door, he ushered Luc inside the dark cabin. Opening a tinderbox on the small windowsill, he dashed a flint to get a flame from a ball of hemp from which he lit two oil lamps. He withdrew the key from the lock and handed it to Luc.

"Keep it safe, my friend; it's an honour as old as the hills, you know."

"It is, indeed, Marius. I only hope I will repay your trust in me."

"Do not fear, I will explain everything to you."

The office, or rather shed, was scarcely wide enough to take a table that served as a desk. Two wooden stools and a cupboard in one corner comprised the furnishing.

"Sit, do. But first, a little refreshment." Luc

sat, as told, while the other man took a blue bottle and two glasses from the cupboard. Prising out the cork, he filled them.

"Here's to your success as the port supervisor." And they clinked the glasses together in a toast. Luc spluttered when the drink hit his throat.

"Not used to it so early in the day, I see! The old man told me to always keep a decent brandy ready for special visitors, and I guess you're one of them.'

'He was a good sort,' Luc said with a sigh in his voice.

On the table lay a heavy ledger with a flickering lamp on either side — a pile of plain parchment sheets, inkwell, blotter, and a bundle of quills completed the office trappings. Marius opened the ledger and moved one of the lamps closer to light the page.

"You see, each side is divided into columns. It will be your responsibility to ensure entries are made accurately, day after day. Should there be an occasion when you are indisposed, make sure I know, and I'll stand in for you. Is this clear, so far?"

"Perfectly."

"Good. Now…" He pointed to each column in turn. "There's date and berth number, that's straightforward. Next, the boat's owner and captain's name — it might or might not be the same person. Now, the goods they bring into the port, and finally anything being shipped out. Every forty days, you must copy the total number of boats with the dates and send it to the Palace, where there's an office dedicated to port business."

"And do I handle money?"

"No. There's an arrangement whereby port taxes are paid direct to the Palace. We do the work; they take the profit — that's just the way it is."

"Yes, Pope Clément has a reputation when it comes to the finer things in life," Luc said casually.

'If only he knew! The Holy Father is dependent on laudanum and pretty girls. I'm only too pleased that Alice no longer numbers among them.'

"So it's said, but it's none of our business." Marius emptied his glass. "I have to be elsewhere, so I'll leave you to your duties. Most of the sailors come here frequently and are used to the formalities. Remember, I vest my authority as Magistrate in you, and that means *you* say who comes and goes through our port." He paused and closed the ledger, then added, "One final thing: the Pagnol brothers are *personae non gratae*, by order of the Curia following the — "

" — the cowardice they showed last year," Luc completed Marius's sentence, "when they fled the town to save their skins, leaving us to cope alone, like rats deserting a sinking ship."

"Beyond doubt. The order I've received effectively prohibits their trading."

"And it serves them right! Their house was the only one on my street that did not have a red cross painted on the door, and we have long memories. Why should they return? My son died, yet they escaped the risk of dying."

"I understand what you're saying."

"Do you, Marius?" Then he realised the insensitivity of his question.

"Forgive me, of course you do. You lost your wife."

"Ay, but thank the Lord I'm happy once more with my darling Alice." Then he fell silent before revealing to his friend, "Jean Pagnol has approached me, and he is certainly remorseful. He sought my assistance, thinking that I might be able to get the prohibition removed. It's true to say the Pagnol brothers have performed kind deeds — they have distributed alms to the poor and attended confession..."

"Marius, you must do as you see fit. My own view is they should be held accountable for their actions."

"So, there is no place for forgiveness in our society?" came the answer in an impassioned tone. Luc did not reply. The Magistrate thought hard.

"I believe there is. Last year, a priest quoted me a biblical passage when I was consumed with the dilemma of seeing innocent children perish and others survive, blaming anyone, like an unbeliever, even accusing the Good Lord! When the plague was raging, I sat with the old Magistrate in this cabin, drinking his brandy, much as you and me today. We were desperate and felt we were losing the fight. I blamed this and that cause because, naïve as I was, I searched for answers where there none, and the old man knew it. In his wisdom, he explained to me that it is never the best way to demand convenient scapegoats or to harbour revenge. He took his bible from the cupboard, it's still there, and read me a passage:

'Get rid of all bitterness, rage and anger, brawling and slander, along with every form of malice. Be kind to one another, tender-hearted, forgiving as God in Christ forgave you. Love prospers when a fault is forgiven, but dwelling on it separates close friends.' I don't know whether it came from Matthew or John, or which chapter, but can you think of any better advice to guide me as the new Magistrate of Avignon?"

Luc answered, sheepishly, "Fine words, Marius, fine words, and you will act according to your conscience, but I'm convinced they did wrong. It's as simple as that."

Seeing there was no chance of them finding common ground, Marius placed a hand gently on his friend's shoulder and left for his meeting with Father Dizier.

From the already bustling port through the Saint-Roche gate, Marius took the narrow Rue Velouterin, which crossed a pretty, wooded corner of the town to the north. He felt confident about his decision to install Luc at the docks so he could now devote his energies to judicial matters. The street soon opened into a square, bordered by enormous terracotta pots overflowing with fragrant purple flowering lavender, shining white myrtle and bushy yellow broom. In between the greenery were stone benches, as yet vacant. As the day warmed, they would be occupied by residents of the square and strollers, chatting away and exchanging views. The modest Eglise de l'Oratoire stood in one corner. Its squat roof barely rose above a massive, arched main doorway, a flight of a dozen steps leading up to its heavy oak door. Constructed of yellow sandstone blocks, the building took Marius back to his early days when he had worked with Luc in the stonemason's yard. The sloping lower roofs on either side served as flying buttresses, indicating the arcades within. He knew little about church architecture but was at once enchanted by its spiritual simplicity. To one side of the church, set back, he saw Father Dizier's house, as similar in its plain design as any poor person's dwelling. He knocked on the door, the sound seeming to echo around the empty square. The priest greeted him,

"Marius. I'm expecting you. Come in, do."

"Good morning, Father, and thank you for seeing me."

"Seeing you? It's the reason I'm here."

Inside, Marius squinted, adjusting his gaze in a single dark room lit only by the sunlight of the early morning passing through one small window.

"Please, sit down," Dizier said. The priest was a short, fat man whose black cassock, too long for his body, dragged along the ground, and equally, its sleeves all but hid his hands. He cut a comical figure, but to those who knew him, he was the epitome of a sincere, dedicated cleric who had ministered to and supported countless families in his parish whenever they had needed him.

"Now, Marius — I will not call you 'Magistrate,' as titles mean nothing to me — how can I help you?" Then excusing himself, "Forgive my rudeness, may I offer you something to drink? I have fresh milk, delivered this very morning by a kindly member of my flock. I do not know how I would fare without their generous gifts...and I am sorry it is not anything stronger, but at this time of day — "

"Milk will be appreciated, Father." Then he

carried on, "As you know, I am a newcomer to both Avignon and the position of Magistrate, so my experience is limited to say the least, and I seek your advice. I have a vision for my duties that will include my wife, Alice, who has lived here all her life — maybe you know her?"

"Ah, Alice..." The priest spoke in a soft, knowing tone, "I know her, but I have not seen her for a long time. I knew her father and uncles better, a good family, we go back many years."

"Indeed, Father, and rest assured, I am aware of her involvement with women of easy virtue but also how she repented and converted them to more wholesome lives. She has had no dealings with her family lately, though."

"She will provide shrewd counsel, I am sure."

Marius sensed Dizier's remarks were prejudiced by her past, but continued,

"What was the state of criminal behaviour in Avignon before the plague, under the old Magistrate?"

Dizier sighed and became deep in thought. After a silence that to Marius felt like an age, the priest began,

"They say times are bad now, with ruffians and malefactors about to pounce around every corner, but that is idle gossip of the tavern. My memory goes back far to when times really *were* bad! When I was born, Pope Urban IV ruled our Church — and from Rome, before they came here through a most regretful division within the papal authorities, politics and the like. That was in the year 1261, last century. As a very young child I recall the excitement in the town when a hanging was imminent. Since you have lived here, Marius, have you witnessed an execution?"

"I have not, Father."

"And you are not likely to because it is now done in Marseilles or Lyon. Back in the day, the infernal gibbet stood on the edge of the woods up by the Rocher des Doms next to a wooden hut..." A shiver ran down Marius's spine.

'A wooden hut, did he really say that? That has to be where I used to meet Alice in secret.'

"...it is still there, but I dare say it is now overgrown and dilapidated, it has been so long since it was used. When a man — or woman, come to that — was found guilty of murder by the Magistrate and then confirmed by the ducal court, the whole street where the condemned lived was obliged to attend, by order of the Pope himself! Yes, they had to watch the entire grisly episode...the priest, too...they all packed into that hut if it rained... terrible." He breathed in sharply, realising he was daydreaming. "And why do you think that was, that they had to watch the penalty carried out? It was to force the citizens to observe the Lord's justice, or that is what the Palace said. However, the true reason was for the Church to exert power over the people through fear, so they would turn, cowed, meek as lambs to the Church for succour. As our Magistrate today, Marius, you will not have to worry unduly about what to do with murderers because capital punishment is decided by those far more important than you."

Marius nodded with relief.

"I have heard the confession of many a guilty assassin, and the cause of their crime was often not the popular concept of *badness*. No, a drunken tavern brawl could result in an unfortunate fellow being killed — but was it premeditated or the consequence of a simple argument? Boys, to impress the girls, perform playful sword fights, but let us say one succumbs to a strike to the head and dies. Is that murder? Whether or not, the boy is hanged. I have known of a man whose wounds from an accident were apparently not properly tended by his wife; the man dies, and she is convicted of murder. Can that be right? A similar case happened when a man who lived near to the Palace — an affluent area — one Le Barbier, hit his wife with a billiard stick so hard that she died, and the Duke's court found him guilty of murder. However, he appealed and claimed his wife deserved her suffering because she had nagged him so relentlessly in public, like a fishwife. He said he had not meant to kill her, only to scare her so she would be quiet. But the stick entered her thigh by chance a little above the knee. The man maintained she had died because she had not bathed her wound regularly rather than because he had mistreated her, and he was subsequently acquitted. Do you follow me, Marius?"

"Yes, Father. You believe there are various explanations for a violent death. Nothing is as it at first seems, and execution is not always just."

"Correct, my son. I was about fourteen

years of age, training for the priesthood in a seminary in Arles, and one day I took down a dusty parchment scroll from a shelf in the library. I began, idly, to read it. The account it contained had a profound and immediate effect on me. It is fair to say I am opposed to the gruesome process of capital punishment: there has to be an alternative practice in any civilised society."

"I agree. We should be thankful we are no longer obliged to watch such a scene."

"That account was part of a verse composed by a little-known poet who writes in the voice of a victim of the gallows moments after his execution. He addresses not only the spectators but also all the humble folk of the world, imploring their sympathy. To this day I can clearly remember his words. Would you care to hear them?"

"It must be a most powerful text."

"It is. Let me focus my mind a moment." He bowed his head, slightly moving it from side to side, concentrating, then,

'O Brother men who live, though we are gone, let not your heart be hardened at the view. For, if you pity us, God is more like to show you mercy too.

Pray to God that He forgives us all.

Rain has washed us, and the sun has dried and blackened us. Magpies and crows have carved out our eyes and torn off our beards and eyebrows.

The wind changes and tosses us around.

Do not then be of our brotherhood, but pray God that he wills to absolve us all. Prince Jesus, prevent Hell having lordship over us. With Him, we have nothing to perform nor trade.

Men, there is no mockery here. Pray God that He wills to absolve us all."

Marius felt tears welling up in his eyes, so moved was he by the poor man's demise. He waited a while until he was composed, then,

"It is a most harrowing petition, that I will say —

"But it does not at once relate to you, Marius. As I have explained, cases of murder, or even rape and treason, will be decided by the Ducal or Papal courts. *You* will hear charges of assault, petty theft, public drunkenness, land disputes, and other more minor offences. The townsfolk are entitled to attend your sessions, for it is they, most likely, who will have apprehended the felon and delivered him to you, if apprehension were necessary. I trust I make myself clear — legal matters tend to possess a language of their own."

"Perfectly, Father. Do continue."

"Witnesses can come forward to help you, as Magistrate, pronounce on their guilt or innocence and make a decision on their punishment as appropriate — time in the stocks, a flogging, a fine.

One of the old Magistrate's last hearings before his demise involved a lad — couldn't have been more than fifteen years old. A stallholder from the bridge had frogmarched the boy to the Magistrate's office, claiming a cheese had been stolen from his stall and he was presenting the thief before the Justice. At the hearing, the lad pleaded not guilty, and the Magistrate listened carefully to the stallholder's account of events. It seemed that the boy was, indeed, guilty, and sentence was about to be passed when a woman, there as a witness, stood up.

'Do you wish to speak, madam? If so, keep it brief and to the point, I have a busy day ahead.'

'If it pleases the Magistrate, I'd like to defend the young man. I've known him since he was a babe, and his mother, and — '

'Must I repeat myself? Get to the point!'

'My apologies, sire. I know there is a feud between yon trader and the boy's family — been going on as long as I can remember. The other day, I overheard an argument when the man threatened the boy's father with a good beating — I don't know why — unless... something or other. So, you see, any accusation is false.'

'Thank you for that, madam. Be seated.'

The old Magistrate asked the trader to stand.

'Is this true, is there bad blood between your two families?'

The trader bowed his head, embarrassed, and waited a time before answering,

'Ay, there is, that I can't deny.'

'Do you still sue the boy?'

'It's possible...yes, I think it's possible that the thief might be someone else...that...'

'It's called *mistaken identity.*'

'That's what I'm saying, Magistrate.'

So, you see, Marius, without that woman as a witness, the boy would have been convicted though he was innocent. With time, you will establish your own standards and a way of judging that is fair and will be seen by the

Avignonnais people to be so. Without the public on your side, your tenure will prove difficult, to put it mildly.

Most crimes, involving violence or not, are committed by folk enduring poverty, and perhaps we can do little to alleviate that. However, they are not inured to it — on the contrary, they care about it, worry about it, talk about it. You, Marius, are in an enviable position: a young, fresh face as the town's Justice, think of it as an opportunity to help people, as it were, rather than to simply chastise."

Marius said nothing. He knew he would not encounter any man as wise and astute as Father Dizier.

"To finish, let me warn you to be aware that some customs — or do I mean traditions — will strike you as bizarre and even discriminatory. A man can discipline his wife for disobedience.

There's the man Evrart, Rue Crémade, everybody knows he beats his wife, poor thing. But has she once complained to me? Never! She regards it as a normal aspect of her marriage. How might *you*, as Magistrate, distinguish between levels of acceptable domestic discipline and unacceptable domestic violence if a wife were to sue her husband? It is often claimed that it is permissible to beat your wife as long as the stick you use is thinner than your thumb! Have you seen well-off men around town with their walking sticks? Take a closer look and see how many of those sticks are thinner than a man's thumb!" Dizier paused, looked at Marius, and would continue, seeing he had the man's full attention.

"There exists a culture in which honour is paramount and violence is recognised as a means of communicating certain messages. If you hacked off a woman's nose, for example, most people would understand this as an indication of adultery. In the town, the punishment for forging money was to be boiled alive, as a spectacle to deter and awe observers. But, Marius, please forgive an old man for rambling on and, no doubt, boring you fit to fall asleep!"

"Father Dizier, may I thank you for your time this morning. What you have told me is not simply fascinating but essential for me to administer justice in an equable way. My first hearing is later this week. It concerns a fellow who is accused of stealing his neighbour's eggs from his yard in the middle of the night."

"Is that so? Then, a word of advice: there is a newly appointed cardinal in the Curia, goes by the name of Albornoz. Although I have yet to meet him, I hear he is on a mission to see that all crime is severely punished. He is of the opinion that Avignon is a present-day Nineveh!" He noticed the puzzled expression on Marius's face. "Nineveh was a great but lawless and ruined city in the Bible, and I do not recognise Avignon as such, but he is a hardliner who has Pope Clément's ear. He may well attend your first hearing."

"That is helpful, but my judgment will not be coloured by any cleric, regardless of his high standing. I wish you good day."

Marius wandered through the streets in the general direction of his house. His head was reeling with the many decisions he would have to make as the town's Magistrate. He was a man who would not be easily persuaded by men in cassocks.

CHAPTER NINETEEN
AVIGNON, KINGDOM OF ARLES,
SPRING 1349

The meeting with Albornoz concluded, Clément gave an instruction to the guard posted in the corridor outside his study door,

"See I am not disturbed."

The guard came to attention, his halberd drawn sharply, straight by his side.

"Of course, Holy Father."

Alone, the Pontiff took a bottle secreted in a small cupboard and filled a glass. He was partial to good wine, but fortified laudanum was his preferred tipple in private, even though its hallucinatory effect had frequently fuelled the paranoia of a troubled mind, wrestling with the requirements of papal standing and carnal desire. He hoped to have seen the error of his ways, returned to the Lord, and put the latter behind him when Alice had ended their affair. Equally, he had moderated his intake of the illicit drink. He took a sip of the reddish-brown liquid and breathed in deeply to consider his newly appointed acolyte.

Alvarez Carillo Gil de Albornoz, my cardinal adviser. Mmm...if his tenure here is half as long as his name, he will do well in my Curia. Another swallow of laudanum, then he ran his finger down the document that outlined the newcomer's career. *A novice at Calatrava monastery; student of theology at Montpellier university; Deacon then Archdeacon of Cuenca; Royal Almoner to King Alfonso in his Paris court. Archbishop of Calatrava then, latterly, the same post in Toledo. His is an impressive ascent in the Church, and I am confident he will serve me well.*

Clément's behaviour could be erratic, impulsive, and prone to angry outbursts, especially when he dwelt on his childhood or, more recently, his clandestine relationship with Alice. It was as if divine providence was tormenting him — she was now a Nerval. Three-quarters of a century ago, he had been beaten to within a hair's breadth of his life by his boyhood mate, Edmond. At that time, his name was Pierre Roger. The two boys' paths diverged, never to meet again. Whereas Edmond soon forgot about the attack, Pierre Roger endured a painful recovery, and try as may, he could not erase the event from his memory. Over the years, he had dispatched emissaries to find Edmond's whereabouts — even though he was unsure just what he might do if he was found. But Edmond proved elusive, and when he was at last located in Carpentras, any retribution was meaningless: Edmond had died.

The Pope returned to his reflections.

I am confronted by the players in this troublesome drama. Albornoz has gained his office on merit, and from what I hear, he will be the man to...to support the Magistrate's efforts in dealing with criminal behaviour in the town. Yet, with hand on heart, I blame Marius for Alice's decision to finish our relationship. An even greater anathema to me is that he bears his father's family name, Nerval! How I hate its sound! If Albornoz's observations demonstrate that the Magistrate's dispensing of justice is weak, I would be within my rights to seek his removal, would I not? It could kill two birds with one stone if crime were reduced and I could exact some revenge on old Edmond, even in his cold grave, through his son! It's sad to say that people are little different now than before the plague. They dance under the bridge, carefree and disrespectful of the past.

ALBORNOZ LEFT the Pontiff's study and entered the Grand Audience. A group of visiting nuns dressed in grey habits, faces concealed by veil and wimple, knelt on straw-filled hassocks in silent meditation in one of the many side chapels. The names of saints proliferated, whether lending their names to private chantries or through any of the numerous towers of the Palace.

The Cardinal bowed his head respectfully as he passed the nuns, although they were too absorbed in prayer to notice him. Feeling in need of spiritual contemplation, he entered his favourite chapel, dedicated to Saint Bénézet, after whom the bridge was named. He dipped a finger in the holy water of a small stone stoup, crossed himself, and knelt in front of the altar that bore a brass crucifix, single candle and two icons painted on wood, one depicting Jesus Christ, the other of a suppliant Bénézet. Rising and buoyed by prayer, Albornoz walked slowly through the Audience in the direction of the cloisters. He never ceased to be amazed by the grandiose beauty of the hall, even though the chancel and some of the side chapels were still under construction — their completed state would bear witness to the glory of God.

The cathedral of Toledo was certainly a treasure that he knew well, but this was its equal with the decorated panels in the vaulted wooden ceiling, as with the frescoed biblical scenes on fawn-coloured sandstone walls, one verge thick — the esteemed Italian artist Matteo Giovannetti had certainly been inspired when he had worked there, the Cardinal thought, drinking in the colourful scenes. Quite a contrast to the chancel where a rood screen, one third the height of the building, constructed of gilt wrought-iron work, separated it from the nave. The smooth, square granite slabs of the floor afforded a sensation of strength and permanence, while tall, narrow stained-glass windows created a gloomy interior.

Soon after his elevation to Cardinal

Adviser, Albornoz began to collect a notable range of benefices — incomes requested and granted by Clément. He became titular Archdeacon of Ledesma and Evora and had become familiar with the luxurious lifestyle of the royal French circle. Since his arrival in Avignon, he had integrated into the comfortable ambience of the cardinal and papal courts, all of which suited his quest for self-aggrandisement. Increasing his wealth, prestige, and power all came naturally to him; consequently, his perspective on life in general and religion in particular were seen through rose-tinted spectacles. He wanted for nothing.

Upon promotion, they allocated Albornoz a three-storey *livrée* — a grace and favour house in the Rue Banasterie, close to the Palace. Such were his personal finances that he chose to purchase the property outright, commissioning lavish murals and decorative wall hangings in the manner of his superior, Clément's, accommodation. His education, his diplomatic activities as a royal chancellor to Alfonso XI, and his role as Archbishop of Toledo provided him with an exceptionally rounded knowledge of both lay and ecclesiastical politics and affairs. But with this valuable insight came an intransigency, an adherence to moral dogma, and a disdain of anyone who did not share his own unequivocal view of the world.

He came out of the Grand Audience and crossed the cloistered square, the only part of the Palace where silence was strictly observed. He entered his house and lit two candles on his desk. Opening his beloved bible, he began to read the chosen verse, but softly. He spoke to his invisible companion, the Lord Jesus Christ. His prayers over, he closed the bible and returned to matters temporal.

'To properly assess the state of crime in this town, I must talk with the Magistrate but not before I have seen how he conducts his hearings. There is an interesting one later this week that I will attend.'

Albornoz anticipated that he would see what punishment was administered to the guilty fellow — the possibility of an innocent verdict did not cross the Cardinal's mind.

"HEY, MARIUS! ARE YOU READY?" Rostand called out, reining his horse and cart to a standstill outside the Magistrate's house. The two men were going to collect benches and other items from the stonemason's yard. Soon after taking on the mantle of the Justice, Marius decided the town was worthy of a proper courtroom, and a disused barn a few streets away from his own house was the ideal building, but it was an empty shell that required furnishing. Marius came out and climbed up to the seat next to Rostand.

Carel Rostand was now the Deputy Magistrate. During the time of the plague, he had been the old man's right-hand assistant, collecting corpses and transporting them on his cart for burial. Marius intended to use him, alongside Alice, to advise him and share his thoughts on whatever case before he himself made the final decision.

Alice could not resist suggesting,

"Do you realise we comprise the triumvirate in ancient Rome — Pompey, Crassus, and Julius Caesar? They were more than satisfied to throw a condemned man to the lions — "

"Alice!" Marius interrupted. "How on earth do you know such history? You will be the only person in Avignon who is aware of that fact!"

"You're right, husband, but although we

may not have wild beasts or gladiators at our disposal, we wield considerable power in considering a man's fate."

"Of course, Alice, and we must ensure that we act wisely."

ROSTAND'S RISE to his present position had surprised many people. For years, he was known as a beggar at the town gates, dressed in shabby, well-worn clothes yet sporting an incongruous velour hat. He accepted coins from passers-by he deemed to have the wherewithal. With the poor, he merely exchanged a 'Good morning.' At the start, Marius mistrusted him, perturbed by his begging one day on the occasion of a funeral wake in a tavern. He was a tall, thin man with dark, twinkling eyes. His nose and chin were slender, pinched lips revealing even white teeth. This man was no fool, nor did he beg out of poverty: his family came from a line of the Counts of Provence. So, although wealthy, he kept it a secret. During the heinous epidemic, the sights he saw tormented him, but he knew there were rays of light and hope, acts of kindness and unselfish behaviour that fuelled his optimism. He knocked on doors to bring out corpses but also — and this earned him recognition and admiration — to donate money to any poor mourning family he encountered.

He had explained himself to Marius at the time,

"I possess more money than I will ever need, and these impoverished folk have little or nothing. Will I continue to beg once the scourge is over? My answer is yes! There is no justification for the rich leading an easy debt-free life while other sorry souls struggle to provide basic commodities for their families. All my wealth will not be spent in a lifetime!" With his appointment as Deputy Magistrate, he ceased begging.

Rostand tugged on the reins, and the cart trundled away up the street towards the stonemason's yard, through its gates and to Bruno's workshop, which stood in a far corner. Marius jumped down and called,

"Bruno! Anyone there?" A short, rotund man in a leather apron came out.

"Master Marius, good morning to you — and to you, Rostand."

"Good morning, Bruno. Is everything ready?"

Marius had sent a note to Clément stating his requirements to set up the new courtroom, and the Pontiff had readily agreed to fund *'le tout nécessaire'* — whatever was needed — eager to facilitate his new Magistrate.

Bruno answered, "Ay, I finished the last seat just yesterday." He was responsible for all day-to-day joinery work in and around the Palace, but his first love was decorative woodcarving. His consummate skill could be seen in the Pope's screens, pews, altars, and lecterns.

"You've done a fine job, Bruno. We'll load the cart, but I think it will need two trips." They piled on the benches and threw over a rope to fasten them down securely. After an hour or so, the empty old barn had taken a new lease on life. Twelve benches, as long as church pews, arranged in rows; a dock with a railing around three sides; a podium supporting the Magistrate's lectern. He now had a real courtroom. To either side of the lectern were two low stools — one to the right for Rostand in his capacity as Deputy Magistrate — the other to the left for Alice as his wife.

Pleased with their labours, Marius slapped Rostand on the back and, with evident satisfaction, pronounced,

"Bruno's done us proud, don't you think?"

"He certainly has. I reckon Avignon's got the best courtroom this side of Paris!"

Adjoining the barn was a building that originally served as a stable and that they now used as a gaol. Each of the four partitions had an iron ring set into the wall to take a chain should a prisoner need restraining. The next hearing was due in two days' time, and Marius had decided to make known the oncoming sessions with a notice nailed to the courthouse door:

"EVRART – BEGGING – this Friday morning"

ALICE HELD Fabien's hand to help the toddler walk beside her down the street to the house of an elderly spinster who, on occasions, cared for the boy if his mother had to attend to some business or other.

"Be a good lad, Fabien, and I'll come for you later this morning."

"I will, mother," he answered. He thoroughly enjoyed visiting the lady who spoiled him with her special blancmange and sweet baked pears.

Inside the courtroom, the stage was set for a people's drama. All twelve benches were occupied by townsfolk with either a vested interest in the hearing or simply a ghoulish preoccupation with this, their first experience of the new judiciary procedure. When there was no more sitting room, they lined up three-deep at the back. In one corner stood a tall, thin man dressed like the others in a coarse thigh-length tunic and boots, but his hood was pulled down to conceal his identity. It was Cardinal Albornoz, present to observe and assess the conduct of the trial.

The air was malodorous from sweaty people packed tightly together, and the atmosphere in the dark room was expectant. Alice sat on the stool to the right of her husband. Marius stood behind the lectern, waiting for the accused, and viewing the assemblage, he mused,

'Alice suggested I would oversee the affair much

like the Roman Caesar, but I feel more like Pontius Pilate adjudicating on the trial and crucifixion of Jesus! The man's fate is in my hands.'

After what seemed like an eternity, the door opened, and Carel frog-marched the prisoner to his position in the dock to thereafter take up the other stool. An audible hum, as if from bees in a hive, began to rise, the people nudging each other, whispering and pointing at the wretched old man. Seeing everything was in place, Marius struck his gavel on the lectern three times.

"Order! Quiet!" he called out in a confident, authoritative tone, and the courtroom obeyed, an eager silence reigning, church-like, although in a secular setting. The Magistrate continued,

"As we begin this hearing, I would warn all speakers that to give false evidence will be punished most severely." He turned towards the dock.

"Your name?"

"Aleron, sire."

"Now, your family name is?"

"Aleron, sire," he answered, plainly confused. The room erupted, mocking the man's mistake, and Marius brought his gavel down again.

"Quiet! This is my courtroom, and I will have respectful behaviour! Otherwise, you will be ejected."

The man in the dock cut a sorry figure in a threadbare tunic. He had a hunched back and long, grey, straggly hair. An almost silver beard framed a toothless mouth. His knuckles turned white as he gripped the front rail of the dock, as if to maintain his balance. Marius continued in a soft voice that contrasted with his commanding instructions to the general court.

"The name friends use to speak with you is Aleron, so what is your *other name*, that of your father and mother?"

"Ah, I see. It's Evrart, sire."

"Good. So, you are Aleron Evrart?"

"That is correct, God be my witness — "

"*Blasphemy! Blasphemy!*" someone cried out, but Marius ignored it.

"Who sues this man?"

"I do, Magistrate. My name is Richeut."

"Tell the court the offence committed by Evrart."

Mouths opened, gawping in anticipation of Richeut's account.

"Sire, I do not know the man, but many

times, whenever he sees me in the street, he follows me, making strange faces and noises you might hear from a cornered wild boar, or even the Devil himself! At first, I pressed a coin into his hand that he took and then left me alone, but that was the only way to get rid of him. He scares me...yes, puts fear in me... and for all I know, he's a murderer possessed by Satan! *That's* how he makes me feel, and I want the powers that be to do something about him!"

The courtroom gasped in horror and began muttering to one another. Once again, Marius brought the room to order.

"Does any person bear witness to this felony, if so it be?"

A man sitting next to Richeut stood.

"Yes, I do, Justice. Richeut speaks true, I can vouch for that, and I've seen the vexation it causes him — it's begging, if you ask me."

"Ay! Something should be done!" shouted one woman. But Marius waited for the clamour to subside, turned to the dock, and asked Evrart,

"Are you guilty of aggravated begging, for that is the allegation?"

"Magistrate, I do not understand your

words…I am only Aleron. I admit I have tried to talk with Richeut because he seems a friendly soul and I like to talk with friendly souls, and I think to know the man and — "

"But do you admit to begging from him?"

"I do not, sire! My mother always warned me that bad men go a-begging, and I am not — "

"That is enough, Aleron. You need say no more."

"Thank'ee kindly, sire."

Marius gestured to Alice and Carel to join him in a huddle behind the lectern, where they would not be overheard.

"He is feeble-minded, that's for sure, but harmless, and I didn't recognise the felon in him," Alice whispered.

"He is a lonely old man seeking company, and he does not belong to the begging fraternity, believe me; I would know him from my former life if he did," Carel said.

"I agree with you both: he has no case to answer."

Alice and Carel resumed their places while Marius stepped up onto the lectern, a single strike with the gavel sufficient to regain silence.

"Good people of Avignon, let it be known around our town that begging is strictly forbidden. However, I find the man in the dock guilty of nothing more serious than desiring a cordial word. If you, Richeut, have coin to spare for the poor and needy and can overcome your fear of an occasional funny face, I urge you to continue your charitable donations." At this, the place burst into laughter at Richeut's reprimand — he was not a popular man in Avignon. Then, Marius turned to the dock.

"Aleron Evrart, you are free to go, but heed my advice and do not follow people in the street in future, for it can land you in trouble."

"Aleron thanks you, Magistrate," the acquitted man replied with tears in his eyes.

Cardinal Albornoz left the building with the rest, his disguise maintained, and went directly to the Palace to give his report to Pope Clément.

"Holy Father, the accused man has been freed. In spite of the strong testament of witnesses, the Magistrate has ruled that following a man until coin is obtained does not constitute the requirement for begging. I find that most strange and lenient, to put it mildly."

"I tend to agree, Albornoz, and it does not give an appropriate message to the citizens of Avignon. Minor, seemingly trivial offences can lead to far more serious ones if not nipped in the bud. The Magistrate's performance of his duties calls for our close attention."

"In me, Holy Father, you have the right man to carry out your wishes."

CHAPTER TWENTY
AVIGNON, KINGDOM OF ARLES,
AUTUMN 1349

The Palace refectory was crowded with priests and other members of staff taking their evening meal on either side of the long oak dining tables. The atmosphere was jovial, the conversation animated with the day's news and gossip — supper was rarely an occasion for theological considerations. While the room could not compare with a raucous tavern, it was a time for the clerics to relax, savour their food, and enjoy good company.

"Have you met the new Cardinal yet?" one priest asked his colleague across the table.

"Albornoz? Yes, but briefly. He introduced himself then left in a hurry, having duties to see to in the town. What about you?"

"Me? No, I'm of no consequence, but no doubt our paths will cross eventually."

"He's often seen entering and leaving the Holy Father's study, but as he is his Adviser, that's what you'd expect."

"Indeed, it is."

A third priest, overhearing their talk, joined in.

"He's not endearing himself to those who've had dealings with him."

"How so?"

"I've heard he's a cold, distant man. When he speaks to you, his eyes are elsewhere, and he doesn't take a real interest in you. His abrupt manner has offended quite a few to my knowledge." A pause followed, as if the three priests were considering what to say next. Then one continued,

"His rise in the Church has been, to put it mildly, notable. He hails from a small back-of-beyond town in Spain, and after passing through Montpellier university — with flying colours — he picked up deaconries and positions in the priesthood before becoming Archdeacon of Calatrava."

"Ah, I know that Calatrava is an important seat within Alfonso's Kingdom of Castile, and that explains how he was noticed in royal circles — "

"But I'm sure he was promoted on merit; I'm not suggesting anything else, and you don't receive the honour of Archbishop of Toledo unless you're worthy and able."

"So, he arrived here after his association with the Spanish then the French courts — "

"Listen," one priest interrupted, "it's what Albornoz does *here* that matters. His past is of little significance. He's now the Cardinal Adviser with particular interest in law and order in and around our town. Give the man a chance, he's only been here for two minutes!"

With that definitive address, the topic of conversation changed, and the priests carried on eating supper.

SUMMER TURNED into autumn and the days got shorter and cooler, but this did not dissipate the warmth that the people of Avignon felt for their Magistrate and his dispensing of justice: he was regarded as a fair-minded and sympathetic man, hearing cases with a calm, implacable attitude towards anyone unfortunate enough to find themselves in the dock.

As usual, Alice had taken young Fabien to the old lady while she sat by her husband in the courtroom. Her experience of associating with the underclass of Avignon, who lacked any stake in the prosperity and well-being of the town, proved invaluable in advising Marius on appropriate sentences.

"What case are we hearing this morning?" she asked her husband, who was straightening the rows of benches before letting in the public.

"A young man, married with three young children, accused of stealing from a farmer. We'll find out about it in greater detail when they give their accounts to the court." Surveying his courtroom and ensuring everything was in order, he went to open the doors, on which he had nailed his announcement of the day's business:

"WIBALD – STEALING – this Friday
morning"

OUTSIDE, a good number of people were waiting — not as many as for the earlier trials when proceedings had a novelty attraction but enough to take up all the benches. There was impatient muttering and shuffling until Rostand escorted the accused into the courtroom and led him to the dock with no need of any form of restraint for a shy, nervous young man. Marius stood behind the lectern to begin the affair, and the public fell silent.

"Good morning, ladies and gentlemen. Would the accuser make himself known?"

A burly ruddy-cheeked man rose from the front bench. He was a local farmer, a man with a certain notoriety for avarice towards his family and the workers he employed. Marius, although aware of the character of the man, was determined to listen to the statements without prejudice. Turning to the farmer he began,

"Your name?"

"Ymbert, Magistrate."

"And you, in the dock?"

"Wibald, sire."

"Ymbert, tell us what charge you bring against Wibald."

"He has stolen wheat from my fields, and at night, too. Growing is my living, and I can ill afford to lose wheat that's my main crop."

"I'm sure you can't, but have you caught the accused in the act of stealing? If it's at night as you say, you'd be hard pressed to see him."

The room laughed at Marius's question, and the farmer became visibly flustered, his ruddy face turning a darker shade of its already crimson hue.

"I've not exactly seen him, but I know he's been taking my wheat off my land!" His voice rose. "Me and my men toil long and hard to scythe then put the sheaves into stooks ready for threshing."

"To be clear, Ymbert, you charge this man with stealing wheat stocks from your land, is that so?"

"Magistrate, I have witnesses." Facing the fellow sat next to him, the farmer ordered sharply,

"On your feet!"

The witness was at once recognised as a man of suspect character about Avignon, and sneering guffaws resounded around the courtroom.

"Quiet now! Hear him speak!" Marius called out. "Tell us what you know."

"Sire, it was dusk, and me and my son were wending our way back home across the farmer's field — it's a shortcut, you see — when my dog started to bark, and I knew there was a stranger near. True enough, we saw Wibald at the far end of said field with a sack over his shoulders, sneaking off, like a thief does — "

"Next morning, I found a stook that was fallen over, damaged," the farmer butted in.

"That will be sufficient, thank you." Marius paused, taking in the witness's testimony, then he addressed Wibald,

"How do you defend this charge?"

Watching the hearing from the back of the room sat the hooded figure whose presence was, by now, regular, although ignored. Cardinal Albornoz had observed a good number of cases.

"Sire, I do not contest what the witness says."

The stupor was general as the public sensed a guilty verdict was a given. Marius's policy of inviting the townsfolk to the courtroom, while welcomed, encouraged a voyeuristic element:

one woman brought her needles and wool, knitting to pass the time; a man unwrapped bread and cheese for his lunch, determined he would not miss anything. Wibald waited for the hubbub to subside.

"It is correct I was in the field, and I did carry a sack, but I did not touch any stook, I swear. I collected up husks and grains of wheat that are left on the ground after scything, stuff that will just rot but what I use as pig feed. I soak it in water, and my pigs cannot eat enough of it! I need a good fattened animal to fetch a decent price at market — that is my only income. My family would not survive without it. So, I did not think to be committing a crime, nor did I ask permission of farmer Ymbert — perhaps I should have. I use the remnants of the crop that he does not need."

The farmer could hardly contain himself.

"What I need or do not need on my land is for *me* to decide. Stealing is stealing!"

Applause rang out, and Marius conferred with Alice and Rostand in whispers behind the lectern. The wait seemed interminable to Wibald, whose wife, hair brushed to a sheen and wearing her best shawl, sobbed quietly, dreading the imminent pronouncement. The Magistrate's assistants regained their stools as he spoke his judgement.

"Wibald, I cannot ignore that the fact — as you have admitted — stands: you have removed property unlawfully, and the common man would understand that those words mean you *stole,* contrary to civic or Church values. I appreciate you will bear this cross, a burden that will be your penance, for ever. The label of a thief will take many years to be forgotten, and having made that side of my verdict, I am obliged to mete out a punishment."

'You most certainly are,' Albornoz thought to *himself, 'and it had better be a good one — no more pandering to thieves, brawlers, and the like.'*

All eyes were fixed on the Magistrate, anticipating the penalty.

"Taking into consideration your impoverished family circumstances and the minimal value of the chaff you pilfered, I order that you will work for two weeks, unpaid, on farmer Ymbert's land, at his discretion. Additionally, you will make an apology to him this day. That concludes the business; you are free to go." Albornoz's lips tightened, fists clenched in anger at such a soft result. The guilty man's wife threw her arms around her husband: this outcome could have been far worse. As they made to leave the courtroom, they both nodded towards Marius, grateful and respectful.

IN THE TAVERN, the three old men — Baudri, Matelin and Franchot — who had shared their views on Marius just as he had taken up the position met to drink ale and generally put the world to rights. They had, this day, joined the public benches in the courtroom and had followed a number of hearings, now feeling able to pass opinions based on fact rather than supposition.

"I think Marius is doing a good job for us," Matelin said. "He's patient and courteous, and I, for one, approve of the sentences he's passed. What's the expression...*to crack a nut with a hammer*? Yes, that's it, don't have to send a man to the gallows for absconding with a loaf of bread. In the old days, the Magistrate was too heavy-handed, whereas Marius has a more thoughtful approach, especially for one so young."

Baudris took a draught of ale, then, speaking in a disdainful tone, said,

"What you describe is a man who's too lenient. I've watched criminals he's let off too lightly smirk on hearing their sentence, then wink at their mates. What sort of example does that set? People will think they can get away with any wrongdoing and behave with impunity."

"He's right," Franchot piped up, "and we know what's happened regarding the Pagnol brothers. They're living comfortably once more in their fancy house. Don't tell me the Magistrate hasn't been party to that. He'll have colluded with the Pope and probably the Duke to lift the ban on them residing within the town walls."

A patron sitting at an adjacent table leaned across, interrupting the men's conversation.

"Franchot is not mistaken. I've heard it from a friend of mine who works at the Palace — waiting on tables in the refectory. He's told me that the Magistrate and Clément were overheard talking in the Grand Audience. They definitely mentioned *Pagnol*, then *their house*, and even *Yes, they may return*. It wouldn't happen to the likes of you and me, though, would it? The Magistrate's used his influence, that's what I say."

Marius and Luc were discussing port affairs in the quayside office when they were interrupted by a knock at the door. Jean Pagnol entered.

"Good day, Magistrate and Luc. I won't detain you long from your work." Then, looking directly at the Justice, he said, "But I owe you a debt of gratitude. I've received notice from the Pope's officials to the effect that I, my brother, and partner, Bruno, may open our warehouses and, after many long months barely surviving on our boat, have permission to return to our dwelling within the walls. Without your intervention, all this would not have been possible."

"I spoke up in your favour, quite simply, Jean, because you made a mistake but saw the error of your ways. Anyone deserves a second chance."

"I'm a man of few words, so I say thank you and will disturb you no longer. Call in at my warehouse whenever you're passing. As you know, I keep a stock of fine wines."

"Indeed, Jean." The wool merchant left the

office, grateful that his problem had been solved by the Magistrate.

"Aн, my trusted Adviser, Albornoz — come in."

"Thank you, Holy Father."

Clément indicated one of two chairs with comfortable upholstered seats either side of the fireplace in which logs burned, their bright flames affording a pleasant warmth to the Pontiff's study.

"I've had them make me a fire; it gets chilly this time of year."

'The old man's been drinking — he's slurring his speech. I'd heard he likes a tipple but wasn't sure if it was just idle gossip. Drink affects folk differently: some get angry, others open their hearts. We'll see what it does to Clément.'

He filled two glasses with a dark liquid and offered one to his Cardinal, who knew from its appearance that it was no simple wine. He raised the glass, sniffed the contents and immediately put it down. He rarely partook of alcohol.

Clément coughed gently then continued,

"So, you have been my Adviser here in

Avignon now for some time. About what would you advise me?" He hiccoughed then.

"You were appointed at my behest principally to examine the state of law and order in the town, so what is your assessment thus far?" he asked casually, his face showing a vague faraway expression, holding his glass up to the fire as if inspecting its contents.

"There are matters of great import for your Curia to address, but in that we are no different from administrations past and yet to come. The Lord sends challenges to test our faith and resolve."

"Do get on, Albornoz," Clément said in a sharp tone.

The Cardinal sipped his drink, realising he had the spiritual and intellectual upper hand over the tired, aged, mellow Pontiff before him, and with a steely gaze and deliberate voice, he continued,

"Since my arrival in this fair town, I find the administrative offices and other agencies of the Curia effectively and extensively organised. Missionary and evangelical enterprises reach across the known world, and our recently established university in Arles attracts students of theology who, we expect, will minister in this kingdom upon completion of their studies. The plague exacted a high death rate on the clergy, leaving us with inexperienced and often corrupt priests — ”

“And we will, of course, deal with such malpractice. There is no place for unscrupulous behaviour in the Church. Only the highest standards will be accepted.”

“The College of Cardinals have strengthened their role in the government of Church affairs — the bulls lately issued are excellent measures to settle secular conflicts that diminish our authority.”

Clément leaned back in the chair, his chin touching his chest, deep in thought. *'I trust he's not nodding off! My report can't be that sleep-inducing, can it?'*

“Should I carry on, sire?” The cleric jerked his head to again follow Albornoz.

“No…er…yes, of course.”

“We receive entreaties, daily it seems, from our states in Italy under domination of heathen dukes and counts that we restore our rightful place in Rome, but they are helpless without our military intervention — a pressing issue for certain, Holy Father.” He could not have known it would be he who would lead such an armed force.

"Your observations are noted, Cardinal. Are you sure you will not join me, for purely medicinal reasons?"

"Thank you, no," was the reply.

Undeterred, the Pontiff poured out more laudanum for himself, his hand shaking slightly.

'*I've seen such trembling in men who drink to excess. Next, I know, he will ask about crime.*'

"To conclude this audience, what do you have to say on the subject of crime in the town?"

"I anticipated your enquiry and to that end have spent much time recently investigating the matter of punishment." Clément spoke first,

"There are many who are displeased with our new Magistrate, Marius. Is that so?"

"On the contrary, I find them in great numbers who approve of his conduct of judicial duties but do not see the wider picture. By that, I mean they do not know what is best for themselves."

"Explain yourself, Albornoz."

"The Magistrate's sentences, as I have seen

at first hand, are all too often unreproachful and in no way can be considered punishment for those who merit it. The ultimate moral power rests with the Church; it is *our duty* and God's will to exact retribution on whoever is deemed guilty of committing criminal acts. *We* must ensure that Marius applies *our* rules, *our* laws, the Lord's Commandments!" Albornoz spoke with rising excitement, beads of sweat forming on his forehead. The Pontiff sat bolt upright, taken aback by the man's passion, and for a moment was lost for words. Then, feeling a sudden affinity with his Cardinal's words, he spoke,

"Naturally, I have been informed of your ecclesiastical positions prior to Avignon..."

"Naturally."

"I contend I am an astute judge of character, so may I suggest some event in your past has, over and above the power of the Scriptures, imbued in you such a strong sense of right and wrong?"

"The Holy Father is, I agree, astute: I have not since revealed that happening to man or beast." He took another drink, the strong liquor making him feel relaxed.

"Then perhaps you should." A silence followed.

"I was only eight or nine years old and an altar boy in a church in Cuenca, my place of birth, in the Kingdom of Spain. I loved my duties, lighting candles, filling the chalice with wine, setting the bible open at the chapter for that day. It was there that I experienced my calling in life, and they were good times, thank the Lord. However, and quite by chance, I happened to see two priests in the vestry performing ungodly acts, the likes of which are proscribed throughout our reading of the Holy Book.

In Leviticus we find: *If a man lies with a male as with a woman, both of them have committed an abomination.* In Genesis: *The Bible condemns sexual activity that is not between a husband and wife.* In Romans: *The men, leaving the natural use of the woman, burned in their lust one toward another.*

An old priest, my mentor and friend, persuaded me to tell him what I had seen, what troubled me, and so I did. He assured me he would investigate the two men, but as far as I know, they were never reprimanded, even though their behaviour was undeniably wrong.

Since that moment, I have believed in the power of praise rewarding good but chastisement falling on the bad."

Both men sat gazing into the fire, absorbed in the important matters Albornoz had raised. Clément resumed the conversation, his tongue loosened by the beverage.

"It is sometimes healthy to open one's soul and eliminate the tensions a secret can engender. After all, as clerics we hear confession and encourage, nay, insist, that the truth is spoken. Is that not so, Albornoz?"

"It is so, sire."

"I, too, harbour a miserable sentiment that has haunted me since I was a young boy — "

"Not — "

"No!" Clément interjected. "Nothing of a sexual nature. I was born in a small town, many leagues from here. I had a best friend, and we were inseparable. One day, and the details are unimportant, that boy beat me and left me for dead. He escaped any punishment, and that injustice remains with me to this day. The boy who attacked me was named Nerval, Edmond Nerval."

At this name, Albornoz's jaw dropped as he took in the revelation.

"Our Magistrate is Marius Nerval," the Cardinal established out loud. "Are the two related?" he asked.

"They are. Marius is Edmond's son, and I am confessing to you that the quest for revenge burns inside me still — no greater despicable propensity, and in the leader of the Church!" *I dread to think what he would say if he knew I'd had carnal relations with Alice, she, the Magistrate's wife! I suppose there's a satisfaction, having used her, then through Marius and finally to old Edmond. But is it sweet revenge?*

Albornoz hesitated a while before replying,

"That is a concern for you, and I, of low standing, would never presume to comment on what is, to use your words, a confession."

"You are right. That is a most commensurate answer."

The two men discussed a range of Church matters, stopping only when the bell for nones rang out.

"We have lost track of time, and I am sure you have responsibilities elsewhere."

"I think I will take to my bed as my head is spinning — with the bible by my side, though."

Clément grinned, then rose and placed a hand on his Cardinal's shoulder.

"One further thing."

Albornoz looked up.

"My Cardinal Treasurer has approached me on several occasions, going back to last year when the old Magistrate was with us. The Curia receives its revenue from diverse sources — tithes, taxes, donations, bequests, and so on, and the fines imposed by our judiciary are an invaluable contribution. However, the money from these fines has decreased to a seriously low amount, and the reason is incontestable: fewer fines equals less income. The Curia hopes sincerely that this situation will be reversed. Do I make myself clear?"

"Perfectly, Holy Father. Even if it is contrary to Marius's sentencing policy, the inalienable distinction between right and wrong must be established, and should it unfold that the Magistrate is incompetent, failing in his duty, the Curia — through its authority bestowed by our mighty College of Cardinals — will be quite justified in removing him from his post."

"You have grasped the problem with great insight, one of the reasons I moved for your appointment."

"My thanks are in order, sire, and I have an idea that may well satisfy the Curia and my own thirst to see the Magistrate's feeble running of his courtroom redressed."

"I sense it will be diplomatic if you do not implicate me in your...idea. Discretion, Albornoz; I have a pontifical reputation to consider."

"I understand and wish you good day."

CHAPTER TWENTY-ONE
AVIGNON, KINGDOM OF ARLES,
AUTUMN 1349

The water in the quay was still and shimmery with barely an eddy lapping against the wooden hulls of the barges moored securely to iron bollards that ran the length of the wharf. Some ten boats could dock, end to end, and this morning every berth was taken, such was the increase in river trading after the long months of plague. The river Rhône was not always as placid, for seasonal storms could stir it up into torrents of foaming white-capped waves without warning, making sailing a hazardous occupation. The bargees who transported merchandise from Marseille in the south to Lyon and beyond in the north were a hardy, singular breed, often braving treacherous waters to deliver and collect goods. Unfamiliar tongues that indicated faraway origins afforded a cosmopolitan, diverse air to the port and town of old Avignon.

Marius strolled along the quayside, and his progress was frequently halted by the many greetings that saluted him from sailors he knew from before the scourge; entering or leaving the port had been strictly prohibited, but they were now at liberty to come and go again. Walking past one particular boat, he heard a voice drifting out of the open hold in a foreign accent that he recognised.

"Mahi! Is that you?" he called, then again,

"Mahi! Show yourself, you lousy dog!" He was right — a broad-shouldered, bald, muscular figure, bare to the waist, emerged and answered,

"Hello, Marius, of course it's me! The small inconvenience of a pestilence can't finish me off, you should know that." A giant of a man with the leathery brown skin of an African climbed out of the hold and stepped onto the quayside, a wide grin on his weather-beaten face. The men embraced, as old friends do.

"After we buried your two crew members,

you sailed away from Avignon, and I feared the worst for you — you'd been with them aboard the boat, cooped up like chickens, and I didn't think you stood a chance of surviving...of it not smiting you, too. But here you are! Alive and, as far as I can see, well."

"It's a miracle, I know, because even my poor old cat succumbed."

Marius recalled the day they had dragged two corpses out of Mahi's boat and how the stout bargee, a man well-known to hardship and deprivation, had passed up his black ship's cat to him, stiff as a board, to be interred alongside his men. He had brushed away a tear, embarrassed by his own emotion, hoping no one would notice.

"All's well that ends well, as they say, and it's good to see you. What have you got for us?"

"Pitchers of fine wine from the best vineyards of Provence. I'm told they're for your master, the Pope, but I don't care who it's for, none of my concern. Then, I've got crocks filled with spices — they're for one of your stallholders — and rolls of silk for a seamstress. So, you see, all sorts, and business is booming."

"I'm pleased to hear it. Anyway, I'll let you get on with your work."

"Thanks, Marius, and I'm glad you're still going strong! With luck, I can unload this stuff and catch the northerly wind that's forecast for later today."

Further along the quayside, at the open door to a cavernous warehouse, stood a man Marius knew well — Jean Pagnol, the wool merchant.

"Ah, Magistrate, a very good morning to you."

"And you, Jean. I'm most gratified to see you're trading again and, as I understand it, living in your family home."

"For that, we owe you a debt, and our lessons have been learned."

"I'm sure they have. Where's your brother, Thomas?"

"He's away with the horse and cart delivering bales of wool to the weavers' cottages outside the walls. They've been cruelly affected by the plague: no wool, no spinning, no money. Simple."

"It is," Marius agreed.

"Will you join me in a glass to celebrate the...well, you know what it celebrates."

"It's early for drinking, but I give in to your powers of persuasion!"

Inside the dark warehouse, they entered the merchant's office, where Jean uncorked a bottle and poured red wine into two glasses.

"Your health, Marius." They touched glasses in a toast.

"Where do you want this, Jean?" A young boy, thirteen or fourteen years old, stood beside a trolley loaded with three bales of wool.

"Over there, Philippot, with the decent stuff."

"Right away." The boy lifted the handles of the heavy trolley and wheeled it in the direction of bales piled high in one corner.

"Who's that?" Marius asked, taking a drink of wine.

"A fine lad, Philippot, he's my barrow boy."

"Barrow boy?"

"Yes, let me explain. Thomas and me are getting on — long in the tooth, you know — and Bruno, although he's a third partner in the company, he spends less and less time working down here. I think he's quite satisfied making sails in his workshop, and his services are in demand now traffic on the river is picking up.

So, partly because we can use the boy's brawn but partly for another reason..."

"What's that?"

"We're fortunate to have been given a second chance to continue Pagnol Fils, we realise that, and it's not easy for youngsters like Philippot to find work. We heard of his family, from a poor part of town, where the mother did her best to raise four children alone — the husband had taken off ages ago, so she relied on charity to feed them. Philippot is the eldest. I went to their house to introduce myself to the woman, who had no idea of the reason for my visit. Their poverty was there for all to see, but to the mother's credit, the children were well-scrubbed and polite. I explained that I had need of a willing worker for my warehouse and that, if she and the boy were agreeable, I was offering honest employment. Their joy knew no bounds, and here he is today."

"Jean, I'm truly moved by this story. You are, without doubt, a generous man and have repaid a debt, as it were, to the town you once turned your back on. My entreaty to the Holy Father on your behalf has been completely justified."

"The good Lord decides who's done right or wrong...he's the final arbiter," Jean murmured thoughtfully.

"That's true in Heaven, Jean, but here in Avignon, it's *me!*" Marius spoke with an authority that belied his tender years.

"I must be off, my friend." At the doors to the warehouse, he turned round and, for a moment, watched Philippot hump a bale off the trolley and with the strength of youth pile it onto the others.

HAVING EXCHANGED pleasantries with bargees and stevedores he knew, Marius reached the port office. It was not so long ago he would have found the old Magistrate there, hunched over the leather-bound ledger by candlelight, diligently filling in the columns he swore by to record goods in and out, dates and boats. The system worked well, so Marius, and now Luc, continued to enter figures in between the Magistrate's beloved hand-ruled lines.

"Good morning, Luc. Is everything fine today?"

"Hello, Marius, and yes, we've had twelve boats unload already, and fifteen more are due later. They sail in here fully laden, pay the port tax at the Palace, load up, and off they go — everyone has a smile on his face."

"That's how it should be, Luc."

The Justice left the port near to the Porte Saint-Roch and remained outside the town ramparts, walking towards the banks of the Rhône. There, he paused, gazing out over the dark swirling waters that only one year previously had, on their surface, swept along corpses wrapped in their shrouds but whose weights had become detached. The authorities had, by decree, ordered that the bodies should be weighted down to rot on the riverbed.

'It's hard to believe the beauty of our almighty river was a forlorn, watery grave for so many innocent souls, but it was thus. Thanks be that those sad times are behind us.'

Making his way northward, he cast an eye through the Porte Dominique, Porte de l'Oulle, Porte du Rhône, and other sundry passageways in the walls and was struck by an observation,

'I can't see beggars at any of the gates. That's strange. Last year and for always, as I know it, the town entrances and exits are the favourite haunts of beggars and thieves. Ah, of course, Carel will

have cleared them away, even though he's not
mentioned it to me. That's just the sort of man he is,
modest and kind. He's lived with beggars and their
kind in the past to amuse himself, he told me. I
think he wanted to understand their minds, and by
threatening them to never return unless to search
for law-abiding employment, he's done them and
the town a great service. Scared 'em off!'

Shortly, he reached his intended
destination, the Saint Bénézet bridge. That
yellow stone structure comprised twenty-two
arches, connecting the town of Avignon to
Villeneuve-lès-Avignon on the west side.
Anyone wishing to take goods across was
obliged to pay a tax at the gatehouse on either
end — a useful addition to the Papal coffers.
From Lyon to Marseille, this was the only
crossing point over the Rhône, so its
importance in economic and social terms for
the town was considerable.

The Magistrate visited the weekly market
held on the bridge as regularly as his duties
permitted to ensure everything was as it
should be.

On the first span, he entered the small
chapel of Saint Nicholas, erected for travellers
to offer a prayer for their journey to pass

safely. He knelt on the footstool — the only item of furniture — in front of a painted icon of the saint, crossed himself, and spent a few moments in silent reflection.

Then, he passed from one holder to the next, greeting them, enquiring about business, their families, the weather, whatever civil exchange came to mind. His encounters, though, were not purely social: he wanted to check the traders had paid the licences that allowed them to erect their stalls on the bridge.

"Show me your token, Guillaume. I'll have to run you off if you don't have it!" Guillaume fumbled around in his money pouch and retrieved a small metal disc onto which was stamped a number corresponding to the particular arch that was his pitch.

"Here it is, Magistrate." He handed Marius his disc.

"Number two. That's correct, and don't forget to renew it at the Palace office come the end of the year."

"I won't, and I'd like to thank you for all you do for the town. I'll wager folk don't often thank you."

"Now you mention it, Guillaume, they do not. But that's not what a Magistrate expects."

Further across the bridge, a man, his woman, and three young children approached Marius. He recognised the man: it was Wibald, who he had heard in the courtroom some weeks back. As the family came closer, the little ones huddled shyly behind their mother. The man doffed his cap and held out a hand to Marius. An awkward silence followed. Then, the Justice spoke.

"Good day, Wibald. I have the right name, do I not?"

"You do, sire."

"And how are you and your family?" He thought, *'I'm embarrassed asking him that, after I pronounced him guilty and a thief. It's a ridiculous question!'*

"I'm well, thank you. This is my wife and, of course, my children." She blushed, and the children smiled then giggled, peeking at Marius like impudent urchins.

"Forgive me, Wibald, but I am obliged to ask whether the sentence I passed has been carried out — the unpaid work?"

"I went to Ymbert's farmhouse and told him I was sorry for what I'd done. Reluctantly, or so it seemed, he forgave me. From what I know of his meanness, he never readily gives anything away, if I make myself clear?"

"I understand you, Wibald. That man would not have sued you for taking chaff and husks from his land if he was a kind sort. But I had to perform my duty as the Justice. What about the two weeks' work you have to do for him?"

A smile lit up the man's face.

"From your courtroom I went straight to see the farmer, as I've said, and offered my services to him. He'd already compiled a list of jobs — the pigs and the pigsty, splitting logs ready for the hearth, cutting back ivy creepers that had all but covered the front of his house, mending broken fences, and...well, in short, that was more than enough to keep me busy for two weeks. I began the very next day."

"I'm satisfied you have completed your sentence."

"That's not all, though."

"Not all?"

"No. Farmer Ymbert visited our cottage one night unannounced. Why would he do that, I asked myself? Anyway, he said he was *just passing* and had decided to call on us to bid a *friendly good evening*. I asked him to sit at the table and offered him a cup of weak ale — that's all I can afford. He accepted and stayed until he'd emptied his cup without saying very much at all. His eyes moved around the room, and from my wife he gazed at my children cuddled close and fast asleep on the bed they shared. Then he left."

"There's no fathoming some folk," Marius concluded, his brow furrowed. "I know him as a surly man and not the nicest of characters."

Wibald continued,

"When my two weeks were completed, he sent for me and said, in the strongest of terms, that he was most impressed by my work.

'Wibald, my lad, I've seen for myself that you and your family live a poor life, in a material sense, but your love for your wife and children makes you rich beyond words. You deserve better. I'm in dire need of a reliable hand here on the farm, so if you accept, I'm prepared to give you regular paid employment. Furthermore, we can put the past behind us. What say you, Wibald?'

I could have snapped his hand off — except I didn't! You know what I mean, though. I will be able to buy food again at the market; my wife will have a decent tunic and my children new shoes."

Marius smiled at Wiblad and shook his hand.

"I am, indeed, pleased for you and wish you good luck."

To END his tour of the market, he came back through the gatehouse and went down the flight of stone steps leading to the riverbank and the bridge's arches, under which unlicensed men were known to trade shoddy goods, offering pardons to purge the soul, and even utensils or other objects made of brass but highly polished to pass as gold — fool's gold — to dupe the gullible, and there were plenty of them about. Marius saw it as his duty to protect his people, but to his surprise, today there were only bona fide traders there, each with a statutory metal disc, properly stamped. He approached one man selling spices and dried herbs to be mixed with oil for an unctuous balm, as well as enhancing the flavour of stews, and asked,

"Where are the rogues? I'd expected to seize their bootleg goods."

"Gone, Magistrate," came the reply. "The deputy Justice, Monsieur Rostand, saw them away. He threatened them with a good stay in gaol, or worse, if they ever came back. They got the message and moved on to some other unsuspecting town, but not Avignon! Now, we honest citizens can make a living again."

En route to his house, Marius stopped at a tavern to quench his thirst after a morning well spent. Although he knew many of the drinkers there — market day encouraged them to congregate and do business over a tankard of ale — he chose a table in the corner where he could drink undisturbed and ponder over the town's progress in recovering after the plague that had brought such horror and social destruction.

'Life is returning to normal at the port, and just one sign of our regeneration and moral improvement, Jean Pagnol has given a young boy hope for his future. The beggars at our gates seem to have been banished. The market is thriving, and I see smiling faces — smiles that have replaced tears that once flowed as fast as the turbulent Rhône. As with Pagnol's new barrow boy, taken on to absolve his guilt, farmer Ymbert is a reformed man. He announces to the world that forgiveness can triumph where previously there was only revenge. And, to conclude the best morning I've known since *becoming Magistrate, fraudulent, deceitful pedlars appear to no longer take advantage of our genuine men and women: my office serves them well, it seems, and I'm confident the sentences I pass are compassionate and encourage wrongdoers to reflect on their offences. It is to be hoped that the people of Avignon have learned lessons from the past. Last year, there were tell-tale signs that a calamitous scourge was growing in our very bosom, yet we paid no heed. We were too complacent, too smug to recognise there is always one bad apple in the barrel.'*

CHAPTER TWENTY-TWO
AVIGNON, KINGDOM OF ARLES,
SPRING 1350

The new year of 1350 dawned on the town of Avignon, and with it came optimism borne out of adversity. The plague was now well and truly in the past for the townsfolk — all nightmares end eventually, as should be the case. They looked forward to a healthy and prosperous future. The spring sunshine was pleasantly moderate, ideal for sitting out on the benches on either side of the streets, squares, and stream. The intense heat of the Provençale summer, when they would be forced to seek cover behind shutters and closed doors, was still months away.

Alice strolled through the streets with her robe, made from fine beige linen, dragging along the ground, as was the fashion for women of standing. The Magistrate's wife had taken to her role with a distinguished, even regal air. While coming from a wealthy family, she had mixed with the low life of Avignon, sneaking along the side streets and alleyways in the dead of night as she visited the Holy Father to satisfy his carnal needs. Why had she done that? It was a question she had asked herself a hundred times. Was it the thrill she felt as she slid between the sheets of the Pontiff's bed? As far as she knew, no one had ever slept with Pope Clément except her. She did not enjoy the physical liaison — he was an old man who drank too much — but she went through the motions: she was an ordinary girl from Avignon in his eyes, but she controlled the most powerful figure in Christendom.

She wandered across the vast concourse in front of the Palace, lined with huge barrels cut into two. Spring crocuses were pushing their tips through the soil; lavender and rosemary cascaded over the edges, their aromatic fragrance wafting on the air. Then in the direction of the Bénézet bridge to a household she knew could benefit from her influence and determination to afford women — the likes of which she had been — who sold their bodies and souls to earn a few coins to prevent their families from starvation.

She knocked on the door and waited, children's squeals and laughter coming from within. Finally, a voice,

"If you want to see Madame Alaire, come back later, she's busy!"

Alice knocked again, this time harder, and the door opened. There stood a young woman whose appearance suggested she was in her forties, whereas she was, in fact, twenty-three years old. Her tunic was grubby, her hair unkempt, and when she opened her mouth to speak, she had a gap where her two front teeth should have been. One eye was practically shut with angry purple bruising around the socket.

"What do you want, and who are you?" The girl spoke in a brusque, stuttering tone. She held the door half-open as if she would slam it closed at any moment. It was hard to not arrive at the conclusion that she had been recently mistreated. Alice smiled and said, gently,

"Are you Alaire?"

"Maybe I am, maybe I'm not. Who wants to know?"

"Don't be alarmed, pray, my name is Alice Nerval, and if you could spare the time, I may be able to help you — "

"Help me? Nobody helps me! I've got three toddlers, and once the rent's been paid, there's nothing left for food. If kind folk don't offer a few coins and leave a sack of potatoes or carrots, whatever, on the doorstep, we'd starve. So, how do you think you can help me?"

Alice was moved by Alaire's frank words.

"Can I come inside?"

"Suppose so."

The children, scruffy and under-nourished, rolled around noisily on a straw mattress in one corner — the only bed in the room — pinching and slapping each other. Their cries were peevish and petulant. They obviously had no concept of co-operation, one with the other, because they lacked interaction with other children. At least, that was Alice's assessment.

A fire blazed in an iron range over which hung a line with tattered items of clothing, drying.

Alaire made no attempt to hush the children, choosing to talk above them.

"You say you're Alice Nerval? The Magistrate's called Nerval, isn't he?"

"Yes, he's my husband."

"I've done nothing wrong, and the loaf of bread at the market...well, you can't prove anything!"

"No, my visit has nothing to do with the Magistrate. I know that the way you earn money, *Madame Alaire*, gives you no satisfaction, but nonetheless, you're a prostitute, and I guess you're not too proud to admit it. I understand this."

Alaire stared hard at this woman who had arrived with her fine robe and shiny hair, then said calmly,

"We used to do...do our business in Marguerite's house and...hey, I recognise you now! You'd charge us for the privilege of a room, but you threw us all out so you could have the place to yourself with your new husband. It's all right for you, that's what forced us to do it in our own homes, in full view of the children — unless they sleep through. Not right! But we have no choice." There was palpable anger in her words.

"I understand what you say, but people can change."

"Is that so? What do you suggest for me, then? I have to feed my little ones, and even if they don't know the luxury of meat or fish, they eat whatever frugal broth I put in front of them. They're still with us, so I must be doing something right." Alice smiled at the woman's dry sense of humour.

"Would you prefer you were doing something else to earn money?

"Of course, I would — anyone would say the same." Alice paused, waiting for the question about what she had in mind. Alaire asked, suspiciously,

"Please tell me what work you're thinking of, madam."

"Across the Bénézet bridge is Count Mabile's chateau, and I vouch he's a good man. Behind his house are stables where he breeds thoroughbred horses. I hear he is in need of a stable boy or girl — "

"I know nothing of horses! What use would *I* be?"

"You could do this work, believe me. You'd have to comb their manes and tails, wipe them down after a gallop, keep fresh hay in their feeders, and muck them out."

Alaire pursed her lips in quizzical thought.

"I suppose it's work I could turn my hand to, and it would get me out of this sordid whoring that shames me in the eyes of all decent women of the town."

"That's decided, then. You must pay the Count a visit and tell him — most important — that you come on the recommendation of Alice Nerval."

"I will, and thank you."

Alice became increasingly convinced with each woman she helped that by sympathy, understanding, and realistic suggestions, they could be persuaded to leave a pernicious way of life and enter the world of another that was better.

CAREL ROSTAND, like Alice, came from a well-to-do family and received a monthly provision from his father. One would not have guessed this same Rostand ate and slept on the streets with vagabonds and beggars, but this he did and was now in an informed position to know how and why they had chosen such an existence.

One day, he approached a beggar he knew

who had been at the Porte Thiers, close to the barracks, for a week or more. Soldiers and residents alike who used this gate had complained about his begging to the Magistrate's office. Marius had sent Rostand to investigate the situation. He had every confidence in his deputy.

"A coin, spare a coin, monsieur… my wife is ill, and my children go without shoes…spare a coin…"

The beggar sat cross-legged, a wooden bowl in front of him to collect donations. Rostand kicked it, sending a couple of coins clinking on the stone slabs. The man looked up.

"What the — " Then he saw Rostand standing over him.

"Ah, it's you!"

"Were you expecting me?"

"No, not many folk about today."

"Because they all know you're here and avoid you."

"Is that so?"

"It is, and it's common knowledge that you don't have a wife or children."

"I do not, and I admit it, Rostand."

"So, I'm minded to arrest you and put you

in front of the Magistrate. But, and out of the kindness of my heart, I have a suggestion."

"What's that then, and I know if it's left to the Justice, I'll be locked up. I've been caught begging so many times that I think he'll run out of patience — he told me last time, '*My man, it is against my sincere philosophy to give people the chance of reform, but if you end up here once more...*'"

"Listen, there are three coins here on the ground. Is that all the money you have?"

"It is, truthfully."

"I'm prepared to make it up to ten."

"Ten?"

"That's what I said, and here's my plan. I know an old-timer who has a warehouse on the quay. He's decided to retire, and he's selling off its contents — furniture, scales, everything. There's a well-built handcart, and I've told him to reserve it for me at the heavily discounted price of ten coins."

"How does this keep me out of gaol, Rostand?"

"With the money you now have, you can buy that cart. Trade is flourishing, and I guarantee you'll make an honest living wheeling goods to and fro between boats and merchants. What do you say, is it not a perfect opportunity for you to reverse your fortunes?"

The beggar picked up the three coins and rose to his feet.

"It's a dream...to have my own business!"

"Here are ten coins — seven to make up the cost of the cart and three for you to go and have a decent dinner in the tavern."

"I won't let you down, Rostand, I promise you."

MARIUS INVITED Rostand to his house for supper. Alice had laid the table with cheese, cooked meats, and freshly baked bread. Young Fabien slept soundly upstairs.

"Pass your glass," Marius said, "this is a fine red wine from a vineyard of Bordeaux."

Rostand took a sip and licked his lips in appreciation, and Alice did the same.

"It's not often for the Avignon triumvirate to meet.'

Rostand smiled, knowingly familiar with the history of Roman governance. Marius continued,

"I think that we can be satisfied with the Magistracy. Our Friday sittings hear any man who sues another, and we deal with many less serious offences informally, as it were. I consider the sentences I have passed to be fair and proportionate."

Alice and Rostand nodded their agreement.

"We see far fewer beggars in our town, and that's due to your work, modest Carel, and I have met many women who tell me their lives have changed for the better, wife."

Alice blushed.

"Therefore, raise your glasses. To the Magistracy."

"To the Magistracy!" they toasted in unison.

AVIGNON, LATE SPRING 1350

'MISTRAU,' in the Provençale variant of the Occitan dialect, means 'masterly' and is the perfect word to describe the character-determining Mistral wind. This violent, cold northwest gale passes down the valley of the Rhône to the Mediterranean coast. From days to weeks, it is accompanied by clear, fresh weather as it blows away dust and dries stagnant water — it gives the skies over Avignon their still blue clarity.

Marius had not lived long in the town before the name Mistral was heard in conversation, and drinking ale with some senior patrons of his favourite inn one evening, he wanted to learn more.

"Tell me about the Mistral," he said to one old man.

"Where you come from, Magistrate, you may well have been spared it."

"Spared?"

"Ay, but it's insistent, never seems to stop once it's started. It gives folk headaches, makes them anxious and prone to hand-wringing. Children behave badly — or, at least, more badly than usual, believe me."

"What he says is true," another man chipped in. "We're protected by the town walls, but take a look at the old cottages outside. What do you notice? Their front doors face south, you see, so it can't blow into them. Another thing, why do you suppose so many of the bell towers on the churches are open ironwork? To allow the wind to blow through without causing damage...doesn't always work, of course..."

All the men at Marius's table had a contribution to make; everyone had some time been affected by the infernal wind.

"You see those tall cypress and poplar trees planted in straight rows? Why do you think it is so? To protect crops from blowing down — they're trees that bend but don't break, see?"

"I do," Marius answered, fascinated.

The oldest man in the group, silent thus far, spoke softly,

"Around these parts, the Mistral sends men and horses insane, running berserk." Marius looked at him, incredulous — *'Amusing, I suppose, but it's the stuff of myth and legend.'*

A few weeks later, the most serious case of his Magistracy was to be heard: no individual sued the person in the dock, it was *'The town versus Rainfroy.'* The man had been involved in a drunken brawl in the street after a day's heavy drinking. What could have remained a minor fracas escalated violently, and Rainfroy had landed strikes that felled his opponent. The latter died from his wounds the following day, so the charge was that of *murder.*

The courtroom was packed to overflowing with a populace that was accustomed to hearing pilfering and gossip, but *murder*, that was quite another incident.

Marius tapped his gavel on the lectern, and the room was enveloped by an unnerving, expectant silence. Then, the Magistrate spoke up, clearly and steadily.

"People of Avignon and all places not present, this case is grave, indeed. Should Rainfroy be found guilty of the charge, the penalty will be the gallows." At this, sharp intakes of breath could be heard around the room. "I have already been presented with versions of the affray from the landlord of the inn and also passers-by who saw it in the street. I intend to inform the Duke of Provence of these accounts, for it is his court that will conduct a final trial, given the grievous nature of the charge." One could have heard a pin drop; no one dared even cough.

"Rainfroy will be escorted to the Duke by my deputy, Rostand, but is there any person who wishes to speak before I close proceedings?"

"Yes, I would," came a meek voice from the front bench.

"Please stand," Marius instructed. "Who are you, pray?"

"I am Rainfroy's wife." This was a signal for applause to burst forth because he was a popular man, and the deceased was not mourned by many.

"Quiet!" Marius ordered the public. "What do you have to say, woman?"

"Magistrate, my husband is not guilty because the fight took place when the Mistral blew for its third day. Anyone around these parts knows a man is excused as crazy for *anything* he does on that infernal wind's third day. He's not guilty because he wasn't responsible for his actions — I don't talk any foreign talk, but I *do know* he's said to have been not *compos mentis.*" At this, the courtroom cheered with raucous cries to raise the roof. Marius looked at Alice, who shrugged her shoulders, then at Rostand, who indicated that there was something he could say, but in private.

"I am suspending the court for ten minutes while I, with my deputy and wife, discuss the statement the woman has made."

The three members of the triumvirate left the room for the street, where they would not be overheard.

"What's this about madness on the third day of the wind? I've not met this before."

"Nor me," Alice said. Then Rostand spoke,

"What the woman says is correct, at least according to legend. People around here fear the Mistral and give it an almost religious importance. Now, they know it was a crime, but on the special third day, he cannot be convicted of murder. Brawling, yes; affray, certainly — but not murder. So, be careful, Marius; we do our best to keep the citizens on our side, to achieve a better, more civilised town, and we cannot afford to lose their approval."

"You're right, Carel. Let's go back inside."

Again, the room fell quiet.

"I have conferred with both my deputy and adviser, and I recognise the validity of the third day of the Mistral when Rainfroy was not in control of his faculties. I shall inform the Duke accordingly and feel sure he will reduce the sentence."

Rostand led Rainfroy towards the gaol, and everyone clapped at Marius's decision.

His recommendation to the Duke would be that leniency be exercised, given the fact that

brawling outside inns was by no means
uncommon. More often than not, fisticuffs left
both malcontents with only cuts and bruises; a
handshake and a parting of the ways saw it
finished. A death, he concluded, was usually
unpremeditated — a prerequisite for the charge
of murder. He also entreated His Grace, the
Duke, to be mindful of the belief held by the
people of Provence that any man committing a
crime on the Mistral's third day should be found
not guilty. The Magistrate's and, by extension,
the Duke's reputations as Justices who dispensed
fair and impartial sentences was at stake.

ON THE DAY of Rainfroy's appearance, the
Duke, dressed in a long, plain black robe, a
white ermine-fur stole, and a gold link chain
of office, sat majestically in a heavily carved
ceremonial oak chair. In the wood-panelled
room, a large desk stood between him and a
lower simple seat for the accused.

Pope Clément had appointed Albornoz as
his *ex officio* Judge Delegate to thus vest his
papal judicial authority in his Cardinal. But on
the cleric's arrival at the chateau, he had been
advised, unmistakably, by the Duke,

"You are welcome, Cardinal Albornoz, and we acknowledge the esteem in which you are held by the Holy Father. However, be it known that as Duke of Provence, my decision, by virtue of my ducal standing, is final."

Albornoz said nothing.

"Guard! Bring in the accused!" the Duke ordered. A soldier pushed Rainfroy, his hands shackled, roughly into the room.

"No need for that. Take off his irons."

Rainfroy rubbed his raw wrists and began to tremble uncontrolledly in fear, dreading what might become of him.

"You may sit, Rainfroy. I see you are in no fit state to stand."

"Thank you, sire." He sat, and the trembling lessened somewhat.

"We have examined the full details of your case and have taken into account the undeniably powerful effect of the Mistral blowing in its third day — that is, what it can force a man to do. Accordingly, we find you not guilty of murder but guilty of serious affray. You will be incarcerated in our gaol of Arles for a period of one year. Guard, remove the prisoner. Cardinal Albornoz, we thank you for your attendance."

Albornoz's jaw dropped in dismay and rage, but diplomatically, he bowed, turned, and left the Duke's office.

Driving his horse-drawn carriage on the journey back to Avignon, the Cardinal vented his anger on the poor beast, lashing it with his whip but unnecessarily hard. He could not accept that Rainfroy was not facing the gallows as he should, in his eyes. His mind raced, a myriad of emotions but dominated by that of bloodlust, his quest to see punishment inflicted whenever any man transgressed: he sought it to satisfy his proclivity for justice and, consequently, *pour encourager les autres.* He thought,

'Marius's and the Duke's world is far apart from that which I inhabit, and I'm afraid the very moral heart of Avignon risks destruction through the Magistrate's weakness. It's my duty, nay, my calling, to remedy the situation before it's too late! After all, that's the reason Clément brought me here.'

SOME DAYS LATER, a knock came at the Magistrate's door. A boy from the Palace handed him a rolled parchment sheet.

Marius unrolled and read it, looked up, and read it a second time.

"What does it say?" Alice asked her husband.

"Pope Clément wants to speak with me, you, and Carel. He says it is a matter of immediate concern. We have to report to him tomorrow."

CHAPTER TWENTY-THREE
AVIGNON, KINGDOM OF ARLES,
LATE SUMMER 1350

"The Holy Father will see you now. Please enter," the Pontiff's assistant announced at the study door. Alice, followed by Marius and Carel Rostand, filed in, each bowing respectfully as they approached the desk.

"Sit, if you will." They obeyed, sitting on three hard chairs — Clément did not like his visitors to feel too comfortable.

Wearing his house dress of a white cassock, its symbolic plainness broken by a pectoral cross suspended from a gold cord, he gave them a forcibly affable, unsettling smile when, to his left, as if from nowhere, appeared Cardinal Albornoz, his face indicating not the slightest emotion.

'I don't like Clément's countenance; it's too friendly, and I wasn't expecting this fellow, Albornoz. What's this all about, I wonder?' Marius thought.

The supreme cleric, as he was known informally, broke the silence.

"May I offer you wine? It's a fine vintage that I reserve for special occasions, or is it too early in the day?"

Alice nudged Marius in the ribs as if to wake him up.

"Ah, that would be most agreeable," he answered sharply.

"Excellent." On the desk, the only items other than a huge bible were glasses and a dark green bottle, its cork loosely fitting the neck, ready for pouring. Then he looked at Albornoz, who rose and proceeded to fill the glasses with rich red wine. He handed one to each of the three increasingly curious members of Avignon's judiciary. Before they had time to take a sip, Clément stood up, his hands clasped religiously together just below his cross.

"Hoc vinum benedicte Domino. Amen."

'Bless this wine, Lord,' Marius translated the Latin to himself.

"Amen," everyone repeated.

"We thank you for your attendance. This is my Cardinal Adviser, Albornoz."

The Cardinal remained impassive. Alice stared severely at the Pope, musing,

'The last time I was in this room was to tell him our relationship had to end. He wasn't best pleased, either, if I remember correctly. Mind, he could barely stand after a morning on laudanum. I rushed directly from here to meet Marius at the hut in the Rocher des Doms woods. I'm sure — she thought, whimsically *— I have made the right decision.'*

Clément resumed,

"Since the new year, upon my instructions, Albornoz has observed forty or more hearings in the courtroom. You will not have been aware of this since he has been wearing ordinary clothing, not his religious robes, sitting among the people, anonymously, so the conduct of business would in no way be compromised by the presence of my representative." He paused to drink some wine. "My Curia informs me that revenues, in the form of fines imposed by your good self, Marius, are significantly down on the previous year when the old man was Magistrate. The only logical reason for this decrease is fewer men being found guilty of their charge and, therefore, not paying anything in fines. This said, I invite Cardinal Albornoz to report on his observations."

"Thank you, Holy Father. I will begin by referring to the recent case of a man who killed a fellow in a brawl. His wife contested the Magistrate's initial verdict of guilty, citing an ancient myth whereby the Mistral wind blew, a weather condition capable of sending a man insane, rendering him unable to make proper decisions. I never heard such stuff and nonsense! He deserved capital punishment for his crime, if anyone ever did, but the Duke — upon an entreaty from the Magistrate — passed a sentence of just one year in gaol."

"Albornoz," the Pope started, "we must respect His Grace's supremacy in legal matters. May I suggest you are an old-world type where retribution is concerned, and this sets you apart from our present Magistrate."

"You might say that, Holy Father, but my upbringing and many years of serving the Church in diverse capacities have convinced me that with right and wrong ne'er the twain shall meet. Some things do not change."

"Quite," Clément said thoughtfully, "but do continue."

The gazes of Marius, Alice, and Carel fixed on the Cardinal, waiting expectantly and, as yet, unaware of the man's agenda.

"As has been said, over several months I have watched ruffians, vagabonds, pilferers, burglars, dishonest pedlars — all nature of criminal — come before the Magistrate. The sentences passed were, without exception, excessively lenient and could not possibly serve as a deterrent to potential felons. That, Holy Father, is the reason, above all else, why offences against the law in our fair Avignon are not far fewer than they are. The new courtroom is fit for purpose: seating for the public is properly arranged; from his lectern, the Justice has a good view of the place; the accused are always treated with consideration, as it should be; the Magistrate is ably assisted by his wife, Alice, and Monsieur Carel Rostand, both present today. This is all well and good, but it counts for nothing if it not upheld by appropriate punishments."

Alice and Carel exchanged glances, taken aback by Albornoz's criticism. She glared knowingly at Clément as if saying, *'You and your Cardinal should be careful. Remember what I could reveal about us.'* But she bit her tongue and remained silent. Clément rose.

"Your comments, Albornoz, are noted." He then looked directly at Marius.

"The Church, through its ministry, prayer, and confession, shares the Justice's mission to enforce the laws of Avignon. To this end, we take a keen interest in the penalties you dispense, but we are concerned by inappropriate tolerance, as referenced by our Cardinal. We trust you will give this matter serious address. The meeting is concluded."

'Confound Clément! He sides with Albornoz, if I'm a good judge of character, and doesn't give a fig for my opinions,' Marius thought.

The three visitors bowed and left the Pontiff's study, crestfallen and perplexed. Back home, they reflected on their audience with the Pope and his Adviser. Marius spoke in a soft tone.

"I think that Albornoz, and by extension Clément, inhabits a world that is punitive and vengeful. He quotes this and that verse from the Scriptures to support his belief in flogging and hanging, but in my experience, *we* will arrive at a society that's more compassionate,

one that understands there's a better way of
living than crime. We won't always succeed, of
course, but that should not discourage our
magistracy. We perform our duties in the real
world, not the cloistered existence in the
Palace fortress. I see the value of a man
pleading his victim's forgiveness, apologising,
and serving a community penance. If we find
him guilty of this or that transgression, is it
not more worthwhile to toil in his field, sweep
his yard, or assist an elderly woman to carry
her purchases home from the market than
spend a day in the stocks or a week in gaol?'

"You're right, husband, but I sense there are
those who disagree, and they frequent the
higher echelons of the town."

"Albornoz didn't exactly hide his meaning,"
Carel added.

"That's as may be, but I refuse to bend the
knee to their likes just because they carry a
fancy title. The victim of a crime will not
always find it in him to forgive the offender,
but nonetheless, what I'll call *restorative justice,*
for want of a better description, can be such a
valuable tool. I might well see this *in addition* to
a statutory penalty, not *instead* of one, so I can't
be thought of as timid, can I? We've known,

the three of us, a victim who wanted to explain to the perpetrator the effect the misdeed had had on him and his family, in the Christian hope that the man will not reoffend. Such a positive reaction is due, in part at least, to the climate of fairness we are creating for the Avignonnais people. Clément's and Albornoz's world is not ours, but that's no reason to succumb."

The other two expressed their agreement. She had seen fallen women change their lives; he had known a man's gratitude on finding honest employment. The triumvirate believed, sincerely and passionately, in the path they were taking.

ALONE IN HIS HOUSE, Albornoz suddenly felt totally isolated. He contemplated the day's events, but the more he thought, the more his mood deepened from annoyance to anger and rage. He could not, nor did he want, to diminish his profoundly entrenched views on how a good Christian life should be conducted, and this certainly did not correspond with Marius's. He struggled to control a troubled state of mind.

'I cannot conceive of what my journey will be after Avignon, except it will be in the service of the Good Lord, so I have no fear of what I am doing while the Church, in its wisdom and benevolence, sees fit to perpetuate my position.'

He lit a candle, sat at his desk, and opened his bible.

'The Magistrate believes that showing mercy whenever possible is preferable to a punishment that will better teach the criminal a lesson.'

A knock came at the door.

"Sire, the Holy Father would like to talk with you on Church business."

"What?" was the reply. "Tell him I am occupied!"

"Are you sure?"

"Of course, I am sure! Be away!"

Such was the Cardinal's anguish that he failed to appreciate the disrespect his message would convey. He ran a finger down the verses of Samuel.

'Ah!' and he read,

"David said to Gad, 'I am in deep distress. Let us fall into the hands of the Lord, for his mercy is great, but do not let me fall into human hands.'"

He had chosen the verse quite at random,

and stuttered,

"Even David, the great King of the Jews, shied away from mortal mercy that is only for God to grant!" Then he came across Psalms, where he found,

"Righteousness and justice are the foundation of Your throne; mercy and truth go before your face."

'Again! Mercy is not in man's gift. Do you hear me, Marius!"

There was another particular text that he sought, and eventually, he had it in the prophet Zechariah.

"...show mercy and compassion, but execute true justice first."

For a third time, the holy book vindicated his philosophy.

'Look at the Scriptures, Magistrate! They tell you to pass a genuinely chastising sentence before you get to your clemency predilection! But how can I persuade you to rule more people guilty? If I, the lowly Albornoz, can solve that riddle, my reward will be assured in Heaven.'

That night, his sleep was broken as his thoughts grappled with the dilemma facing him, and he woke early, still mightily troubled and without an answer. Then, like a revelation from the Kingdom of the Lord, came a stratagem, a way ahead. Sitting bolt upright in his bed, he spoke, the four walls his only audience.

"All the hearings I have attended have resulted in the accused being either acquitted or handed down a token sentence. This is by virtue of the Magistrate's belief in rehabilitation and restorative justice. But it is also due to the absence of witnesses who vouch the man's guilt and, thus, make for a strong indictment. If there were such attestants, Marius would be obliged to pronounce a different verdict that reflects the wrongdoer's transgression. So, I will buy men to discredit the defendant's plea of innocent: everyone has his price! I can arrange it so the court will suspect no ploy. Now, where will I find suitable candidates? Ah, I have it! Our parish priests know the common people and will give me the names of members of their flock who, how shall I put it to them...are in need of spiritual enlightenment and will be counselled by my cardinal colleagues. No one will question such an evangelical mission, and to my advantage, these men will be poor and disposed to accept payment — some might call it a bribe; I see it as the Lord moving in ever more mysterious ways — to carry out my instructions."

The Cardinal had no difficulty in obtaining names of fallen souls from his parish priests. Next, he would meet them face to face. The priests had also told him the taverns they frequented.

The first case Albornoz chose concerned a pickpocket, and he soon found his *witness*. Disguised in a well-worn tunic and boots that would let in rain from the lightest shower, he executed his plan.

"Allow me to refill your tankard. Landlord! Over here!"

"Who are you? I don't know you, do I?"

"You do not, but that matters not. I have a proposition that will interest you. Would you pass the chance to earn some easy money?"

The man immediately sat up, staring hard at Albornoz.

"I would not. But it depends — "

"It depends on the coins I have here." The Cardinal pulled out a pouch from his tunic and shook it, the rattling of money causing the man's eyes to open wide, his attention held like iron to a magnet.

"There's enough here to keep you in ale for a year!"

"What do I have to do?"

"That's more like it. Come close, we must not be overheard."

He explained in a whisper that he would sit with the public in the courtroom that coming Friday. He would wait until the Magistrate invited comments from any witnesses.

"At that moment, you will stand up and announce: 'I want to speak. I have seen that man in the dock stealing. He comes up quiet behind somebody, puts his hand in the pocket, and off he goes with whatever he finds. Seen him just last week in the market...he's always at it.' Can you do that?"

"Yeah, course I can."

"Good. So, this Friday morning at the courtroom. I'll give you half the money now and the rest when you've done it. Be aware, my friend, I'll be watching, and it will be more than your life's worth if you let me down. Understand?"

"I understand. Now, give me the money."

Albornoz emptied half of the pouch's contents into the man's pocket, rose from the table and left. He was exhilarated by the meeting, confident that when challenged with the testament, Marius would be compelled to pass a severe verdict: justice would be achieved, finally.

THE DAY of the pickpocket's hearing, Albornoz sat, his identity disguised, at the back of the courtroom. Proceedings ran their normal course, and Marius asked,

"Is there any person present who wishes to speak either for or against the accused?"

After a silence during which the Cardinal feared his plan would fail, the man he had bribed stood and began to speak as instructed and condemned the pickpocket unequivocally. Startled, Marius conferred with Alice and Carel, then, facing the room, he pronounced the man guilty. This came as no surprise to the assembled onlookers, but he then continued and ruled that the man would spend three days in the town stocks from sunrise to dusk, whereby Avignon's citizens were permitted to pelt him with soft rotten fruit as they chose. This was met with audible gasps — nobody had known their Magistrate to mete out such punishment.

Albornoz left unnoticed with the rest of the public.

He could scarcely contain his pleasure at how well his deception had worked, although he could not share it with a living soul. The following week, the owner of a hostelry in a poor quarter of the town was charged with selling watered-down ale to increase his profits at the expense of his customers. The Cardinal paid a second man — as dishonest as the one in the dock — to speak out, again, and swear he had seen the landlord pouring water into a barrel in his yard and even bragging about his fraud to his friends.

Marius, faced with such evidence, had no alternative but to impose a heavy fine and have a notice nailed to the tavern door proclaiming his shameful duplicity. He might have let the man off with a severe warning as for his future behaviour but could not now do so, given the statement made to the court. Albornoz bribed one false witness after another, week after week, causing Marius to issue verdicts that flew in the face of the enlightened, compassionate *modus operandi* he hoped would epitomise his tenure of office as justice of the capital of Provence.

. . .

"SIT, ALBORNOZ," Pope Clément bid his Cardinal. "I will not unduly detain you from your duties. It has come to my attention that the Magistrate has been dealing properly, as it were, with the miscreant element in our midst. His change of heart is, shall we say, welcome. The Curia will soon see their coffers augmented, and an appropriate message is sent to the populace. You and I have deliberated and, at times, agonised over the previous inadequacy of the legislature."

"That is so, Holy Father."

"Yes. So…umm…well, I have no idea why he has aligned his sentencing more to your and my preference. May it be noted that the Pontiff approves." He looked searchingly at Albornoz, whose expression betrayed no emotion.

Albornoz considered, *'The fewer men know of my false witnesses, the better will be the outcome for the enforcement of true justice. I dare not think what would become of me should I be discovered.'*

CHAPTER TWENTY-FOUR
AVIGNON, KINGDOM OF ARLES,
AUTUMN 1350

T he summer of the year 1350 rolled inexorably into autumn. The fierce Provençale sunshine eased to become a soft, more mellow warmth, bathing old Avignon in a gentle light that reflected off the yellow sandstone so characteristic of the town's buildings. Dawn arrived later, dusk sooner than the previous sultry months; residual daytime heat dissipated into chilly evenings. It was the season to replenish the family's log store in anticipation of a fire in the hearth, with the hours after supper spent around its cheering, comforting blaze. But not every family had the wherewithal for a decent supper or logs, for which they had to journey outside the town and cart them back. The only woods within the walls were at the Rocher des Domes, but the removal of timber was strictly regulated by the Palace, who granted felling licences to the likes of the woodcarver's workshop by the cathedral or boatyard at the docks — those who could afford the privilege. Any man caught stealing wood from the Rocher could receive a penalty from the Magistrate and, equally, from the Curia.

Unlike the season, some things in Avignon did not change. The Mistral might roar at any moment, blowing over haystacks or lifting tiles from the roofs. Despite the Magistrate's good offices, pickpockets continued to steal, and men would find reason to brawl. Imposing residences of well-to-do merchants sat incongruously next to run-down cottages inhabited by families who struggled to make a living. And just as a physical difference in wealth could be seen, it could also be heard in the gossip of the market or tavern. Upon Marius's investiture as Justice, the people were enthusiastic and supportive of his work, and the pickpockets and brawlers — and even the timber thieves — felt a certain confidence by virtue of the Magistrate's lenient sentences:

they recognised that he was fair and on their side. But now, come the autumn, the mood in the town had altered. Marius Nerval wielded a double-edged sword: damned if he let the accused off too lightly, and damned if he punished him too severely. He turned to Alice and Carel, the other two of his time-served triumvirate, for their advice.

"These are hard times for you as Magistrate," Rostand said to him around the table after an evening meal eaten with young Fabien tucked up in his bed.

"That, I can't deny," he replied, "but since my first case, I've invited witnesses to come forward. That done, I'm under a moral and legal obligation to have their voice heard by the people. I have to then pay attention to that voice and arrive at my verdict accordingly."

"You do, and this is to your credit, Marius," his friend and colleague concluded, "though so many passers-by and earwitnesses submit their testimony and force your hand. We could be returning the old days of the *hang 'em and flog 'em* brigade who seek public hangings and whippings in the squares if things continue thus. I've lived here many more years than you, Marius, and I've seen it with my own eyes."

"But I'm not passing sentences like those."

"Maybe not, but you're having your compassion and mentality almost wrenched from you, and who knows where it will end?"

"Carel is right," Alice spoke, "it seems so many witnesses have stood up since Cardinal Albornoz arrived in Avignon. However, he just reports what he observes to Clément."

"I know that!" Marius retorted, his tone rising. "And our estimation, by a populace who calls the tune, determines whether we succeed or fail. We depend on their support, which is, I fear, at a low point. So, should I ignore the witnesses?"

"Certainly not!" Alice replied. "We have to persevere as honestly, as sincerely, and with the greatest integrity as possible. We can only judge the accused on the evidence before us. Yet, of late, women I know have passed me in the street saying, and not quietly, 'Your husband's showing them ruffians he's not one to be messed with,' and 'They're not getting away with nothin' when Marius is in charge.'"

ALBORNOZ CONTINUED to bribe witnesses without anyone suspecting him; his serious challenge to justice grew apace. Finding yet another suitable candidate, once more in a tavern, he confirmed that the man, one Criou, would act as instructed for a pouch of coins.

"You're clear what you've got to say?"

"People think otherwise, but I'm no bonehead, believe me."

"I do," Albornoz said softly with a smile intended to cajole his man. He handed over the pouch, shrugging the smallest nagging doubt about the man's dullness aside, and Criou shook it, immediately turning up his nose.

"That's only half the money. You get the rest afterwards, see?"

Criou pursed his lips as if he was going to argue, but he refrained.

COME FRIDAY MORNING, the courtroom was crowded. The people who had braved the autumnal chill to be first in the queue outside were rewarded by taking up the front benches closest to the dock for a good view. Over the previous months, the hearings had become a grim form of entertainment: any milk of human kindness had gone sour, with an increasing number of men presumed guilty, receiving harsh sentences. It was now a sport, a distraction, a lark to watch the poor wretch grimace, every bead of sweat on his forehead noticed. He would wring his hands, holding them together, twisting and turning them through worry and despair, waiting to hear his fate. Even before the Magistrate had spoken, he exuded sorrow with every slight movement of his body, regretting his lot, one he could not determine.

Until the proceedings unfolded, details about the crime were scarce — only the man's name and *Theft of animal* written on notices posted around the town. That was sufficient for tongues to wag and rumours to abound. The *animal* cited could have been any creature from a cockerel to a suckling pig; the man was assumed to be a serial implacable criminal, and his family might be ostracised even before the verdict. It was precisely this bigoted condemnation that Marius, Alice, and Carel Rostand sought to diminish, hoping that enlightenment borne out of equity would prevail to create a better society for the men, women, and children of Avignon.

. . .

MARIUS STOOD at the lectern and brought down his gavel to silence the room. Alice sat to one side, Carel to the other: the triumvirate. A second strike was needed before the Magistrate could begin.

"Tell us your name."

"Martin," came the response.

"Is that your family's or your given name?"

The nervous man, his bewildered brow furrowed, answered,

"Sire? They call me Martin."

"That will suffice, then," Marius decided, writing it down on a parchment sheet on his stand.

"So, Martin, the farmer sitting to my left sues you and maintains you stole an animal from his land."

"Then, I plead guilty, sire. I know my action is unforgivable under the gaze of the Lord and in the eyes of the Justice."

"Your confession, Martin, would be penance in itself. Do you agree to return the animal to its owner?"

"I do, sire, and I've learned my lesson. I won't never thieve again. I crave the court's pardon and the farmer's forgiveness."

"I am sure you do. Now, before I pass

sentence, are there any witnesses who would speak?"

Albornoz's man stood and confidently announced,

"Me, if it pleases the court to endure my story that concerns..."

"No need for all that fancy language. Speak clearly, man."

"I know that one day, Martin has no animals, but the next there are two sheep in his field. I saw them, honestly."

Martin gripped the edge of the dock, his knuckles white, his body trembling.

"Magistrate! What is he saying? I have admitted my guilt, my wrongdoing in taking a cow. I hoped the farmer would not notice one missing from his herd."

"Did you say...you saw...two...*two...sheep?*" Marius asked the corrupt man, pausing after each word.

"That's correct."

Marius gave him a long questioning stare. Nudging, whispering, then sniggering developed; chuckling built into laughter, faces smiling, applause ringing out.

"Enough! Quiet in the court!" the Magistrate cried, and after an embarrassing wait, the din subsided. Marius again looked at the witness.

"Tell us, what is your name?"

"Criou, sire."

"Criou, you have given us your testament — a declaration that, within the four walls of this courtroom, must be truthful, as sacrosanct as a confession of sin before a church altar. Do you understand?"

"I understand."

Guffaws filled the air once more, and as before, applause echoed. Albornoz could not believe his ears. His *witnesses*, time after time, had spoken out and compelled the Magistrate to revise his initial lenient punishment into a hard rigorous one, then this man, Criou, could not follow a simple bidding. *What now?'* He asked himself. *'I should have listened to my doubts. This dullard will ruin all my plans!'*

Marius waited, saying nothing, until the clamour abated, then,

"Criou, I trust you would not intentionally hold this court in contempt!"

"I don't know what that means, but I swear I wouldn't do it." The room laughed.

"Do you accept that cows and sheep are different animals?"

"Of course, I do."

"So, how do you explain a *cow* in Monsieur Martin's field — I repeat, *a cow?* This is a fact. I asked my assistant Justice, Rostand, to investigate before today's hearing, and he has reported to me that there is, don't you know, a *cow* in Martin's possession. How do you account for this beast metamorphosing from *two sheep?*"

"What? Ah, I see what you mean." His face reddened with beads of sweat forming on his brow that he wiped away with his sleeve.

"I meant to say a *cow,* sire, don't know what I was thinking..."

"Neither do I!" Marius interrupted, then an expectant hush engulfed the room: the people realised that the amusing scene they had just ridiculed was anything but humorous — it was ludicrous, bizarre, and remarkable.

"The Magistrate's set his store by giving offenders a second chance, so what will he do now?" one man said in a muffled tone to his neighbour.

"That's anyone's guess," was the phlegmatic reply.

Marius stared hard at Criou. His eyes bored into the man so deep as to melt his inner soul. He beckoned Alice and Carel to join him in a huddle to arrive at a considered outcome. After a brief deliberation, he turned back to the court.

"Your testimony, we have decided, is, for whatever reason, false. You claim to have seen a completely different animal to the one clearly abducted from the farmer's land. In short, you are a liar!" Gasps rose, the public enthralled with the drama transpiring before them. Marius continued,

"Martin, considering the inconsistent evidence presented to us, we intend to dismiss the charge against you." The accused looked at the Magistrate, his eyes wide open in disbelief.

"You are free to go, but one condition: should there be, by any chance, a *cow* on your property, it will somehow find its way back to the farmer's field, so nobody ends up worse for the story."

The man simply nodded his agreement, too emotional to speak.

"Criou, I hope you never cross our path again. You will be sorry if you do."

. . .

THESE EXTRAORDINARY PROCEEDINGS COMPLETE, the courtroom emptied. Two streets away, Albornoz caught up with Criou, grabbing his arm and hauling him into an alley where they would not be seen. He pushed the startled man against the wall with one hand, his other going for the jugular, squeezing the throat hard, sinking his nails into the flesh. Criou spluttered, trying to take a breath but unable to do so. The Cardinal held him in this position until his face changed colour to red, then to a purple hue. When he released his grip, Criou gulped in air, his eyes running, saliva dripping from his mouth.

"You didn't keep your side of our agreement, did you?" Albornoz said through clenched teeth, thrusting his knee sharply between the man's thighs, causing him to bend double.

"Get up! I shouldn't have trusted you from the start, and needless to say, you won't be getting the rest of the money." With this valedictory message, Albornoz delivered two hard blows to Criou's solar plexus and walked away leaving the *witness* collapsed in a heap on the ground. After several minutes, the man regained composure and hauled himself to his feet.

"You bastard! I'll get my own back," he promised, struggling to breathe.

MARIUS, Alice, and young Fabien were at their table eating breakfast when there was a single knock at the front door. Alice opened it expecting a caller, but there was nobody to the right or left, only a piece of parchment on the ground that she picked up and took inside.

"What's that?" Marius asked.

"It's a note."

"That's strange, pass it here." The sheet was torn off one of the Papal or Magistrate's notices displayed around the town. Scrawled on the back in a broken hand was written, 'Man paid Criou — witness.'

Marius read it aloud, 'Man paid Criou — witness.'

"What on earth does it mean?"

Alice was equally bemused and said,

"Criou was the man who lied in our courtroom, was he not?"

"How could I forget," Marius murmured. "Man? Paid? It doesn't make sense. The affair was disturbing, to put it mildly, so I'll send Carel to find Criou and enquire further."

Two days later, Carel met Marius.

"Were you successful?"

"Yes. I asked in a few taverns then tracked him down in a poor cabin near the quay — more a shack than a house, so I can see why he was drawn into the deception by the lure of money."

"Did he explain the note?"

"It appears that someone persuaded him to attend the hearing, to stand up as a witness, and that's what he did, except he got the animal wrong — as we know, he's of limited intelligence. The man beat him, so he seeks revenge."

"Did he know this stranger?"

"No, but he described him, and at once, I recognised who it was — tall, thin, long nose."

"Albornoz!"

"It has to be!" Marius concluded. "And if Criou has been paid to give false witness, are there others?"

The two men realised at once that they had discovered an unpleasant, immoral, illegal situation — but one they could not ignore. Here was a problem that had frustrated them over many months. So, they revisited the hearings since Marius had become Magistrate with such a number of witnesses giving *evidence* that forced his hand to dispense harsher penalties than his heart desired. The late Justice, upon his first dealings with Marius, had emphasised the essential function that maintaining accurate records served. He recalled the old man saying,

'Now, young man, if you're going to make a success out of running the port office, make sure you've got your columns ruled in the ledger. See, first column is the date, second the name of the boat, third the goods brought in, and so on. You'll not regret it.'

Nor did he regret it. He had recorded the name of every witness since he had held his post.

"I think we know what we must now do," said Carel with a determination in his voice.

"We do. Make a list of the witnesses we suspect were bribed by Albornoz. Find them and ask them if that occurred, and — I think it will help us — tell them their anonymity will be respected and there will be no charges brought. That should loosen their tongues. We just need them to confirm it was Albornoz."

"I'll start right away," Carel said, taking the court ledger from the shelf, and he added, "It will need some time, mind you; we have their names but no addresses."

"I have every confidence in you, my friend."

THE DEPUTY MAGISTRATE diligently located the whereabouts of fifteen out of the twenty named *witnesses*. He asked after them in the taverns and inns, at the market, in the stonemason's yard, and even among the now diminished company of beggars. His hard work produced the result he and the Magistrate expected: thirteen men and women confirmed they had received money from a mysterious, tall, thin man with a long, slender nose.

"Do you think the Holy Father was involved in this — " Carel paused, "crime?"

"We can't say, but we're obliged to inform him that a senior member of his Curia is, for want of a better word, a felon."

"I agree completely." Marius was experiencing a torrent of emotions: surprise, disbelief, anger, and disappointment. He felt downhearted that his sincere approach to governing Avignon was threatened by Albornoz and, by extension, the Church itself. Even before he could arrange an audience with the Pontiff, rumours were inevitably rife given the number of people implicated. Women washing their clothing on the stone boulders that lined the stream speculated — gossiped, more precisely — about quarrels within the courtroom. Drinkers in the hostelries discussed a hue and cry rising in the Palace; workers in the stone-yard raised a local disagreement between the Magistrate and his good lady wife to the level of an altercation that was heading to bitter divorce.

THE TRIUMVIRATE of the Justice was made to wait outside Pope Clément's study — a common ploy that he used to unsettle his visitors, giving him an upper hand in meetings. It had the desired effect on Alice and Carel but not so on Marius.

"Be calm," he whispered to them, "he always does this. When we're inside, let me do the talking unless he asks you a specific question or I invite you to speak. Is that all right?" They nodded. After nearly a quarter of an hour, the door opened, and a scrawny black-draped assistant beckoned them to enter. Their chairs were arranged, as for their previous audience, in front of the large oak desk.

"Good morning, and God bless you. Please sit. On the occasion of your last visit, I, in company with my Cardinal Adviser, expressed our concern about a climate of excessively lenient sentences in your court. It is, therefore, pleasing that the situation seems to have reverted to a regime more commensurate with our expectations. However, the request for an audience comes from you, Magistrate, so would you kindly appraise us of its nature?" The Pontiff played nervously with the cross hanging around his neck. Marius mused,

He knows why we're here! His body language says so. His hands don't shake, so maybe he hasn't had a drink yet. What's this man like, inside? Day in, day out, he wears a false face, abides behind a countenance given him by the Church that he speaks for. Is his soul at peace when he sleeps, or do nightmares about what he really wants to be haunt him?

"We are waiting, Magistrate," Clément said sharply.

"Holy Father, it is with heavy heart that I

423

am required to report a violation, a contravention of the law."

"A violation? You are appointed Magistrate to deal with violations, so for what reason do you involve me in a secular affair?"

Marius took a deep breath, glanced at Alice and Carel sitting either side of him, and explained,

"We have exercised due diligence following a worrying incident in our courtroom, and we have discovered that your Cardinal Albornoz has, over several months, perverted justice."

"Albornoz? My trusted Adviser and member of the Curia? How dare you! Do you appreciate the gravity of your allegation?"

"Of course, sire, but we have incontrovertible proof." He turned to Carel. "Monsieur Rostand, please stand and address the Holy Father." The deputy Justice began,

"Sire, our suspicions were raised when a certain witness cited an incorrect animal in a theft. Then, we received a written note saying, simply, that Albornoz had paid him. We pursued thirteen more witnesses, all of whom admitted the Cardinal had, indeed, induced them with coins to give a particular testament that would condemn the accused. We are convinced that your cleric has corrupted our magistracy. Here, I have a list of those thirteen men and women."

Clément rocked to and fro in his chair, fidgeting even more frantically with his pendent cross. He rose and took a bottle from the cupboard behind him.

"Will you join me?"

The triumvirate shook their heads. Clément poured a full glass of the liquid and drank.

"Any misdeed by any member of my administration is reprehensible. Should the probity of a close and trusted priest be called into question, that is a matter of great importance." He drank and continued,

"Therefore, I will put all you have said to Cardinal Albornoz and convey my thoughts to you without delay. You may leave."

CHAPTER TWENTY-FIVE
AVIGNON, KINGDOM OF ARLES,
WINTER 1350

"Sit," Pope Clément barked at his Cardinal, the acrimony in his voice unmistakable, so Albornoz sat as told, needing no further encouragement. He felt like a naughty schoolboy in front of his master, waiting for a punishment.

"Do you have any idea why I've summoned you?"

"None, Holy Father."

"None! None, he says! Who's the fool in this room, I ask you? It's not *me,* so it leaves only *you,* Albornoz."

He picked up the parchment sheet Marius had given to him and waved it around like the sails of a windmill, first this way, then the other. He approached his cleric, arms still flailing, his face red with anger. Holding the sheet so it touched the Cardinal's nose, he tried to speak, but his opening words were lost in a garbled outpouring of noises, a stammering that he could not control when he became excessively emotional.

Returning to the chair behind his desk, he waited, and for several long moments, a heavy, charged atmosphere filled the room. Then, having regained sufficient composure to speak without his cursed stammer, he began, now softer than before,

"This is a document presented to me this morning by our Magistrate. Here, read it, and tell me what its meaning is."

"Meaning, Holy Father? It's but a list."

"Yes, imbecile! Do you recognise any names written down? Because you should!"

Albornoz froze, suddenly petrified on realising who they were. His jaw brushed his chest and his eyes fixed on the floor.

"Your silence would indicate that these men are known to you. While you gather your thoughts, allow me to recount my audience with Marius, his deputy, Rostand, and wife, Alice."

He filled his glass with a familiar dark liquid, not even asking whether the cleric would care to join him. He took a long draught, then resumed, calm and speaking precisely,

"The Magistrate informed me that the thirteen names on the list have stood as witnesses in his courtroom. Nothing amiss with that except he alleges they have each received financial inducement to present false testimony. In short, Cardinal, to lie. In itself, that is dishonourable in a court of law, but yet more heinous still is his belief that it was *you* who paid them. Now, we could discredit, say, two or three names, but *thirteen*!" He drank again and waited.

'Heaven help me! My game's up, and it has to be that moron Criou who's blabbed. There's no denying it, so I'll have to tell him the truth.'

"What do you say, Albornoz? Are you responsible for this perversion of justice?"

"I am, Holy Father. It was my plan to restore a Magistracy for Avignon that properly reflects what is right, so felons do not escape without a just penalty. I told you, many months ago, that I would address the problem."

"You did! And I recall warning you that I must not be implicated in any way."

"Sire, you were never mentioned — "

"Of course, I was, you oaf! Anything you do as my Cardinal, you do in God's name, and *I* am the Church's representative, so I *am* implicated! Colossians 3:17,

'Whatever you do in word or deed, do all in the name of the Lord Jesus, giving thanks through him to God the Father.'"

"Holy Father, I acted in good faith. The Lord desires what is right in us." A certain defiance entered Albornoz's words. "My actions were for the greater good." Clément recognised his sincerity and relented his tirade by a degree.

"That's all as may be, but I find myself in an invidious position because you have admitted your guilt, and as such, that is a crime that could be prosecuted in the Magistrate's civil court. However, as my Cardinal, you are answerable to the Apostolic Penitentiary. I see by your expression that you have not heard of that body — not a surprise, few people have because it is a special court, convened very rarely to adjudicate on transgressions committed by ordained members of my entourage: felonies, as it were, against my authority. I have no choice with so many witnesses involved; it is not a matter we can conceal."

Albornoz was overwhelmed — he had not envisaged such a turn in his fortunes.

"Therefore, Cardinal Albornoz, I am placing you under house arrest until the Apostolic Penitentiary can consider the affair. You may not leave your residence. You have a fresh water well in your courtyard, and food will be delivered daily. I regret having to put you through this most unpleasant procedure, but as I have said, I have no alternative. You may leave."

ALBORNOZ LEFT Clément's study with his mind in turmoil. He thought his efforts since arriving in Avignon to improve the moral tone of the citizens through ensuring appropriate sentences were passed would be met with approbation from his master, the Pope. He could not have anticipated the opposite. Walking from the Grand Audience, the cloisters seemed more resoundingly silent than usual, if that were possible, and he felt alone in an angry world that significantly failed to understand his intentions.

The deserted refectory added to his sense of isolation. *What's to become of me? Is my time in this town nearing its end, after all I've done for it?'* Then, his reflection was interrupted.

"May I join you?" Albornoz looked up to see the kindly avuncular face of old Cardinal Baudet, a priest who had befriended him in his early days at the Palace.

"Why, of course." Baudet sat on the bench next to him. A layman came to fill two beakers with wine, and another placed a platter with bread and cheese on the table. The two Cardinals exchanged pleasantries, and whereas Albornoz had no intention of revealing the impending confinement to his house, through shame, he decided to ask his colleague about the court that would soon be passing judgment on him.

"Baudet, what do you know about the Apostolic Penitentiary?" The old man raised his eyebrows, although the academics around the Palace were, by now, accustomed to the Cardinal Adviser's proclivity for knowledge, like a magpie collecting adornments for the family nest, like the boy at eight years of age demanding that Father Gelmiro, in his home town of Cuenca, told him the meaning of *righteous.*

"That's an uncommon question, for sure. In my twenty-five years here, I can remember it being summoned only twice."

"Please, tell me exactly what it is — out of a purely scholarly interest."

The elderly grey-haired man drank some wine, then began,

"It is sometimes called the Tribunal of Mercy because it can forgive sins. As you are well aware, sins adopt many different forms: those that damage the public and social good — that might be examined by the Magistrate — then, those that subvert the morals and discipline of the Clergy. This court has the right to impose corporal punishment or even excommunication, *in extremis.* It consists of twelve Cardinals, led by the Cardinal Elector, who is, despite his title, an Archbishop. The accused will write a petition of defence, but under a pseudonym to ensure secrecy and impartiality. Finally, the Holy Father has a final legislative veto and, also, executive and judicial capability for the reversal of a verdict. That said, it would fly in the face of reason were he to disagree with them. That, then, is the Apostolic Penitentiary. Why do you ask?"

Albornoz avoided the man's questioning eyes, emotionless, chilled by the appreciation of this court's might. He tore off a hunk of bread and bit into it, casually commenting,

"I consider it incumbent on a Cardinal to be familiar with the workings of the Papacy — you never know, one day I might become the Pope!" But he saw the irony of making light of the institution that would soon determine his future. Baudet smiled.

SEVEN DAYS LATER

ALBORNOZ STOOD in front of Clément's desk as he had a week earlier. The Pontiff's head was bowed, his countenance dark, lips clenched tightly together, eyes half-closed. The Cardinal did not need telling that the news was not positive.

"Be seated," came the curt instruction that was anything but gentle. Albornoz obeyed and waited for what seemed like an age until the Pope looked up, breathed in deeply, and spoke.

"The Apostolic Penitentiary has met and considered your transgressions. It has concluded that your part in making pecuniary inducements to men to deliver false testimony is incontestable. In so doing, you have brought the honour and probity of the Church into gross disrepute. We have found you guilty of the charges. The Penitentiary has remitted to impose a range of punishments but has voted against a corporal or custodial sentence. Do you have any comment, thus far?"

"No, Holy Father." He dreaded what might come next. Clément resumed,

"We will inform the Magistrate of this confidential conclusion. You will be dispossessed, forthwith, of the most prestigious title of Cardinal. A few people will be aware of the sitting of this court and the events responsible for its convocation, but most will be unknowing, so you will not suffer widespread ignominy."

Albornoz's ashen-grey features lightened somewhat at this assurance.

"However — " The conditional adverb boded ill. "The titular confiscation is but one part of your penance. The court has noted your military training as a novice in the monastery of Calatrava and also, since then, your involvement with the King's soldiers, their deployment and best manner in which to benefit His Majesty. Additionally, you are privileged to have received a legal education and have represented us in numerous embassies to the French court. Your eloquent negotiation skills are well respected. All this is correct, is it not?"

"It is, sire." His mind raced as he tried to guess where this was leading.

"It is now fact that we have experienced serious instability within the Church of Rome, caused by politics and insurrection that have plagued us over the years but, and to a greater degree, also by bands of local lords and despots: Pepoli in Bologna, Ordelaffi in Romagna, Manfredi in Emilia, Malatesta in Rimini, to name but a few. Today, in Rome itself, the dukes Orsini and Colonna strive for supremacy. It is my Curia's avowed intention that this unrest is quelled for good so that order may be restored. All this in the hope that the Papacy will return to its natural home. It is for the record of history that my predecessor, Clément V, moved the Papal residency to Avignon in the year 1309. He spent much time and money in vain attempts to reclaim the Lands of Saint Peter so we could once again dwell in the Church's rightful sanctuary, the Vatican City. The Holy Father Benedict XII sent legations to Italy but failed to obtain the desired outcome; control of our subject territories was rapidly dissolving. Shortly before your appointment, I dispatched a French bishop, Bertrand de Déaux, with unprecedented powers, but to my chagrin, he was assassinated. Do you follow this, Albornoz?"

"I am doing my best."

"It is crucial that you understand the background to what I will next say, so I make no apology for a lesson in history."

The Cardinal's hands shook, his teeth chattered, and his whole body trembled in a frenzy of fear and excitement as intense as anything he had known.

"The Curia of the Catholic Church invests you, Albornoz, as its Papal Vicar General. Under this authority you have the right to raise and deploy armed forces as you deem necessary, all with the goal of recovering the lost domains."

The cleric was completely unsuspecting of this development, but he at once grasped the opportunity rather than the penance of such a mission.

'I will be a general commanding my army, tasked with reinstating the Church's former possessions through what I know is right — defeating whoever or whatever I see as wrong. God moves in mysterious ways: fortune has prevented me from achieving this by reforming the Magistrate's liberal modus operandi, but the Good Lord has given me the means to succeed elsewhere. I will lead a crusade against the enemy! To the rebel overlords I will offer a chance to talk with me, but if after threats of excommunication or interdict they do not yield to my demands, I shall resort to an armed response.'

Clément had expected a reaction from the Cardinal, while all he saw was the slightest of smiles.

"For your violation, the Almighty is bestowing on you a way to attain redemption and, equally, to serve the Mother Church at a time of great need. Vicar General, do you accept this challenge?"

"I do, Holy Father."

Clément now filled his glass with the obligatory dark liquid. His Cardinal declined an invitation to partake. The old man was bewildered that his proposition had been so readily accepted, although he knew it required acceptance or a different harsh penalty from the Curia with its ensuing humiliation and likely exclusion from public service.

"I will send for you at a later date with precise towns and cities in our Italian territories, along with the dukes and clerics who aspire to the restoration of the Papacy. The focus of your engagement will be on crushing the resistance of the rebels and despots who lend their support to this and that anti-pope to advance their own secular ambitions. You have but a short time to place your affairs in order, as you will leave for Italy early in the new year. The one hundred soldiers billeted here at the garrison will comprise your initial army."

Albornoz gave no reply. He simply bowed, turned, and left the study.

Avignon 1351

The January morning of the Vicar General's departure dawned with pleasant pale-yellow sunlight bathing the garrison's sturdy walls in a warmth that belied the cold nature of the army's assignment. On the barrack square, row after row of wagons laden with provisions, swords, shields, and the countless accoutrements necessary to sustain a fighting body of men were having the ropes to the tarpaulin covers tightened. Stable boys gave the strong, sinewy horses, hitched and anxious to move off, their final drink and feed. The burly soldiers climbed onto the carts and sat on their long facing benches, chins set firm, one slapping another's shoulder for encouragement and out of comradeship.

Clément, flanked by two guards, had come to the garrison to wish his emissary God speed and stood close to him, intoning a muffled prayer. Making a sign of the cross level with Albornoz's face and touching his arm, he then turned and returned to his Palace.

· · ·

Soon after Albornoz's leaving for Italy, Clément had summoned Marius.

"As you may have heard, I have commissioned my Cardinal Adviser for a hazardous expedition to reclaim Saint Peter's Lands, and I have no doubt there will be a wonderful outcome for our Holy Church. We will receive news of his victories in due course, though his absence will extend to several months, even years. I trust this satisfies whatever punishment you had in mind for Albornoz, our Vicar General?"

"Holy Father, you have regarded his misdemeanour as a matter for the Church. I have no further comment. In a similar vein, I do not expect the Church to interfere with decisions reached in my own court."

The Vicar General led his army first towards Milan, then Marche and Umbria, steadily taking control of the rebellious towns that, for the greater part, surrendered. He was a practical man in a foreign, hostile land, with limited resources, and his decisions were perhaps too easily judged from the comfort of the Palais des Papes. But this man of resolve followed his political instincts and, at times, disregarded Papal opinion. The local populations commonly rejected the authority of the Church and expressed their resentment at being governed by outsiders. Albornoz was sensitive to their feelings of mistrust. He would, cleverly and almost exclusively, appoint Italian vicars or deputies, accommodating regional government practice.

Clément announced the nomination of the Cardinal and his retinue to the citizens and priesthood of the relevant crucial districts of Northern and Central Italy who, thus, were obliged to contribute financially to maintain the Vicar General, as were the Avignon Papacy and Spanish grandees sympathetic to the Catholic faith — mainly to hire the services of mercenary fighters.

His relentless work ushered in a decade of warfare and atrocity, even if he would deny it, and he showed himself to be an effective adversary and tactician, as well as an astute manager of men. He employed intrigue and brute force to reinstate the Pope's authority in Rome with remarkable success. The final victory, prior to achieving his ultimate goal, was his defeat of Velletri, an independent and, ironically, walled town like Avignon.

This Vicar General, Cardinal Adviser, Albornoz, died in 1367 in the Italian city of Viterbo, at peace for serving God and procuring the rights of the Church — an insatiable quest that had lived with him since his days as a novice in Calatrava.

THREE MONTHS AFTER ALBORNOZ'S DEPARTURE

ONE EVENING, Marius, Alice, and Carel strolled along the Rhône riverbank, taking the gentle spring air. Passers-by nodded and smiled: the triumvirate was by now well-established, familiar and respected in Avignon.

"It's time I visited Luc again in the port office," Marius said casually.

"From what I've heard, he's making the job his own. Nothing gets past him that shouldn't," Alice observed.

"I suppose the old man, watching us from

above, will be happy then," her husband said thoughtfully.

"Through your dutiful offices," Carel contributed, "the port's success and the court's honest, honourable execution of its responsibilities are owing to you, my friend, the Magistrate of fair Avignon."

Marius blushed. He was a modest man, not one accustomed to such compliments.

From the turn of the year, cases were heard whenever necessary, and an increasingly confident and trusting populace would speak up as witnesses: the significant characteristic of these declarations during Albornoz's time away was that as many people spoke *for* the accused as did *against* him. Marius's constant motivation evolved to establish a Magistracy that recognised the best in the folk of the town, but also the worst, when necessary — he treated them with even-handed justice.

EPILOGUE

Pope Clément VI died in his sleep in the Palais des Papes one fine morning in the year 1352 but not before he had sent for Marius to attend his deathbed.

The Magistrate knelt and placed an ear to the Pontiff's face to better hear his fading voice.

"Marius, my Magistrate and, I hope, my friend." He held the Justice's hand. "My time is at an end, but I am not afraid to meet my Maker. There is one last confession… I have held an enduring rancour…vengeance for a deed your father perpetrated when we were mere children. Any need for retribution, I wish you to know, is satisfied forever. Please forgive me, Marius…you are a credit to his memory…"

With that, Clément breathed his last. His soul was finally at rest.

The End

**John Bentley
Heckington, November 2019**

Dear reader,

We hope you enjoyed reading *Fist of the Faith*. Please take a moment to leave a review, even if it's a short one. Your opinion is important to us.

Discover more books by John Bentley at

https://www.nextchapter.pub/authors/john-bentley

Want to know when one of our books is free or discounted? Join the newsletter at

http://eepurl.com/bqqB3H

Best regards,

John Bentley and the Next Chapter Team

You might also like:
And They Danced Under the Bridge by John
Bentley

To read the first chapter for free go to:
https://www.nextchapter.pub/books/and-
they-danced-under-the-bridge-historical-
fiction

CPSIA information can be obtained
at www.ICGtesting.com
Printed in the USA
BVHW071653280121
599005BV00002B/144